WORTHLESS REMAINS

WORTHLESS REMAINS

A Chris Honeysett Mystery

Peter Helton

Severn House Large Print
London & New York

This first large print edition published 2017
in Great Britain and the USA by
SEVERN HOUSE PUBLISHERS LTD of
Eardley House, 4 Uxbridge Street, London W8 7SY.
First world regular print edition published 2013 by
Crème de la Crime Ltd, an imprint of
Severn House Publishers Ltd.

British Library Cataloguing in Publication Data
A CIP catalogue record for this title is available from the British Library.

ISBN-13: 9780727893024

Severn House Publishers support the Forest Stewardship Council™
[FSC™], the leading international forest certification organisation. All
our titles that are printed on FSC certified paper carry the FSC logo.

MIX
Paper from
responsible sources
FSC® C013056

Typeset by Palimpsest Book Production Ltd.,
Falkirk, Stirlingshire, Scotland.
Printed and bound in Great Britain by
T J International, Padstow, Cornwall.

Author's Note

Thanks to Juliet Burton, to everyone at Severn House and to Clare Yates for making this book possible. Thanks also for fourteen series of *Time Team* and special thanks to Phil Harding for talking to me about the excavation in Bath. Naturally all mistakes are my own. No thanks to Asbo the cat for abducting my wireless mouse and waging cyber war from behind the sofa.

He digs for all manner of things which are no manner of good to anybody.

John Wyndham, *The Secret People*

One need not be a chamber to be haunted,
One need not be a house.

Emily Dickenson, *Time and Eternity*

One

'He's not going to like it; you should have warned him,' said Annis.

She was scraping paint from her palette straight on to the floor. We use the draughty old barn at the top of the meadow as a studio and half the floor is made up of dried paint, bottle tops and mouse droppings. The old sash windows we botched into the side of the barn are just big enough to keep the place in perpetual gloom. It's hot in the summer, the patchwork roof leaks when it rains and in winter the pot-bellied stove keeps it just above freezing. Ah, the romance of being a painter.

'If I had told him he'd have rejected it straight away. But presented with a *fait accompli* he'll come around to it,' I said. Though I was by no means sure. The private investigation side of my life had earlier in the year taken me to Greece where I had been seduced into abandoning abstract painting for figurative work. The ghost village in the mountains of Corfu where I had stayed had cried out to be painted. When I got back to Mill House in our valley just outside Bath I found that everything I looked at suddenly wanted to be painted – Mill House for a start; the overgrown three acres surrounding it; the dilapidated outbuildings; the willows by the mill pond.

Simon Paris, our gallerist in Bath and London, was on his way up to select paintings for a two-week autumn show of my work. I hadn't told him of my change of direction, which is why I was nervously tinkering in the studio this morning, staring at my new post-Corfu canvases, looking for flaws. Annis, safe in the knowledge that her painting got better year on year, was just clearing her palette before starting on a new canvas. Annis and I lived together, painted together and from time to time worked on private-eye business together, though Annis was much happier in the studio than sitting in cars watching lights go on and off in bedroom windows. Weren't we all? But rambling old Mill House devoured money. My father had left it to me. Not out of kindness, as he made perfectly clear in the will he made before committing suicide in his favourite armchair, but in the hope that the exertion necessary to hang on to it would succeed in turning his feckless vagabond of a son into a responsible citizen. Here I was, ten years down the road, against expectations still hanging on to the albatross of Mill House, though I'm not sure there is general consensus on the responsible-citizen bit.

I hadn't heard Simon arrive; it's a long way down to the yard and the purr of his five-litre Merc was lost on the breeze. The first thing I knew about his arrival was when he darkened the barn door behind me. His eyes blinked for a moment over his delicate gold-rimmed spectacles to adjust from glittering summer sun to Rembrantish gloom. Then he frowned. His frown

2

deepened as he advanced towards me. Simon Paris stopped halfway across the barn, whipped his glasses off and lifted his face in supplication towards the rafters. 'Please let my eyes be deceiving me. *Please* let this be some kind of mirage. Honeysett, have you gone completely mad?'

Annis wiped her hands, freed her strawberry curls and shook them loose. 'Morning, Simon. I'll leave you both to your discussion,' she said and made for the door. Deserter.

'There won't be much of a discussion,' Simon said ominously. 'But yes, sorry, good morning, Annis,' he added softly. Then he turned his schoolmasterly eyes on me. 'Figurative painting. You've gone figurative. What happened to your beautiful, lyrical, atmospheric abstract canvases?'

'I needed a change. These are my beautiful, atmospheric, what was the other thing . . .?'

'Lyrical.'

'Lyrical landscapes.'

Reluctantly Simon bent his face closer to the painting on my easel and put his glasses back on his nose. 'This one's got a sheep in it!' he said with the same voice he might use if he found a slug in his salad.

'It's a black-faced sheep. I borrowed a couple from the farm up the road to keep the grass down.'

'What next, cat paintings? My clients are expecting abstract paintings from Chris Honeysett. You'll have collectors coming to see a certain type of work.'

'They'll see something different.'

'I'm not sure you'll take them with you,' Simon

3

said seriously. 'I mean, this isn't a bad painting, it's just so . . . totally different.'

'There you are then, just different.'

'Yes, but quite apart from the change . . . you're not ready.'

'What do you mean?' I had very nearly spent every penny I had earned from my supermarket-sponsored Greek adventure and my bank account was very ready for this show. 'I'm ready.'

'It's not coherent enough.' He stepped back so he could take in four of the canvases that I had lined up against the wall opposite the windows. 'They don't look like they were painted by the same artist. You're still feeling your way. That one over there is, well, it's a good enough painting but in the canvas next to it you've moved on already. This doesn't make a show, Chris. Not this autumn. Next spring, perhaps, if you keep hard at it.'

I argued, but in my heart of hearts I knew he was right. 'I'm broke though; I really need the money,' I whined.

We were standing outside the barn at the top of the meadow, looking down on the house, the cobbled yard and the dilapidated outbuildings. 'You'll have to do some PI work then, won't you?'

'Business is slow.'

'Because you never pick up the phone. You do realize, of course, that you could sell this place and retire on the proceeds? It's falling down but it's still a massive property.'

'Not a chance.'

'I wasn't seriously suggesting it.' He took a

deep breath, sniffing at the country air he liked to pretend he loathed. 'You and Annis. Everything all right there?'

'Yes, I think so.' Did I think so? 'Yes, definitely. We're getting on like a hearse on fire. Why?'

'Well . . .' He hesitated for a moment. 'It's none of my business but . . . that Tim character, the computer chap who works for you sometimes?'

Tim Bigwood is the third leg of the shaky tripod that keeps Aqua Investigations, my shambolic private-eye business, from collapsing. Tim also works as an IT consultant for Bath University. An ex-safe-breaker made good – or so he says, though how he affords the new Audi A4 on his uni pay is beyond me – he helps out with all things electronic, door-opening and closing and, of course, computing. 'What about Tim?'

'Well, it's none of my business, but the other day I did see him and Annis together in town. And they seemed, you know . . . more than just friendly.'

'Really?'

'I mean they were kissing.'

'Were they? How long have you been representing me and Annis now, Simon?'

'Let me think, Annis about five years. You a bit longer than that.'

'Five years, Simon, and you've only just noticed that Annis is going out with both me and Tim.'

'You and Tim both? Five years? Seriously?'

Actually it was about six years ago that Tim and I found out that we were sharing Annis's favours. It was an indication of her persuasiveness that this odd triangle survived intact. Or perhaps a token of our lack of total commitment, depending on how uncharitable you are feeling.

'Seriously,' I said aloud.

'And you three . . .?'

'Nah, we're not in a *ménage* together. You look shocked. Didn't you tell me you'd led quite a bohemian life in your youth?'

'I did, too,' Simon said and walked towards his car. 'But even in those days I could always afford a whole girl, Chris.'

And there I was, standing in the yard with half a girl, waving Simon Paris and my autumn show goodbye just as the postman came down the potholed track to hand me a fresh fistful of bills and demands. I'm only telling you all this to explain how I got myself into the mess that was waiting for me around the corner.

Since I couldn't pay the bills there was little point in opening the envelopes. I left them on the hall table and went to find Annis, which was easy – I followed the smell of coffee into the kitchen.

'You were right, of course.'

'Sorry, hon. Have some coffee.' She shoved the cafetière across the table. Strong coffee is Annis's usual remedy in a crisis. I tend more towards the Pilsener Urquell myself. 'Does that mean you're looking for a new gallery?'

I poured myself a mug. 'Not quite. He said "perhaps in spring".'

'That's not so bad then; he hasn't completely rejected it.'

'No, he just thought it *commercially unwise* and he said I needed more coherence.'

'In other words, do more painting. I think you're lucky; you have until the spring and with no pressure. I promised the Salthouse Gallery four canvases *and* I'm showing in Bath in November.'

'And what are we going to do for money until spring? Remember last winter? We were burning the furniture to keep warm.' A slight exaggeration; we burnt broken junk from the outbuildings, but still.

'Something will turn up. Something always turns up.' Far away in my attic office the phone rang. 'There you go, right on cue. I bet it's business.'

I sprinted up the stairs in record time and snatched up the receiver on the seventh ring.

On the other end was a familiar, pedantic voice. 'Mr Honeysett, Giles Haarbottle of Griffins.' The insurers. I had done work for them before. Griffins often come to me with the kind of things they can't ask their own staff to handle or don't want to become public knowledge. But most of the time it's just our old friend insurance fraud.

'What can I do for you?'

'A little matter we would like you to look into for us. Could we meet in town today?'

I checked my watch; it said half past ten. 'How about the Pump Rooms in one hour?'

Haarbottle was delighted. 'How civilized. The Pump Rooms it is.'

Two

Naturally, as a private eye I'm supposed to walk around in moody black & white, drink cheap whisky and live off junk food, but this isn't south London, it's the city of Bath, and the chandeliered Pump Rooms of the Roman Baths with their aproned waiters and the fragrance of freshly brewed coffee are much more my style. I admit I spoiled it a little by arriving in clumpy boots, leather jacket and motorbike helmet. I hadn't found a replacement yet for my beloved Citroën and was still running around on Annis's ancient Norton. The lanky figure of Giles Haarbottle waved at me from a table near the stage; behind him the famous Pump Room Trio, which for some reason was comprised of four musicians, played Mozart. Some people like to do business via email, I'm not sure why.

I ordered smoked salmon and poached egg on toasted soda bread with a pot of Earl Grey while Haarbottle made do with a Bath bun, cinnamon butter and a cafetière of coffee. Civilization having thus been reaffirmed on this sunny morning the sad business of business took over. Haarbottle fiddled with the combination lock on his faux leather briefcase and extracted a yellow file adorned with the Griffins logo. He pushed it across. I flicked it open. On top lay an A4 colour photograph of a man in his late thirties with a walrus moustache, wearing full motorcycle leathers and standing next to a red Ducati motorcycle. He carried his helmet under his arm like an astronaut and the whole thing was posed in front of a garage door.

'Right down your street, that, I thought,' Haarbottle said.

'Not really. For a start I'm trying to get back on to four wheels. And a 1950s Norton can't keep up with a shiny Italian job like that one.'

'Doesn't need to; he's no longer riding it since someone knocked him off that very motorcycle. He's also on four wheels now. Turn to the next picture.'

I did. Same chap, shorter hair, but no longer smiling proudly below his big moustache. In a wheelchair. The picture was taken somewhere in Bath, probably the Circus. He was on his own, propelling himself along the uneven pavement. 'Bad accident then.'

'It was. Three years ago. Head injury, broken this, broken that. His name is Michael Dealey. He claims to be unable to walk as a result of his head injury. No sense of balance, no control over his leg movements.'

'Hang on, he *claims* to? You don't just claim these things, there must be doctors involved. What's the medical report say?'

'It's all in there. They're saying much the same. But we've taken independent advice and he could still be faking it. It isn't that his spine's broken or anything.'

'Right, and because he had the temerity not to break his spine you suspect him of faking it?'

'No, because of an anonymous tip-off. Received by the police. Turn to the next photograph please.'

The next picture was smaller, incredibly grainy and showed a man getting ready to cross a street. Somewhere. The bloke was wearing some kind of jacket, some kind of trousers and some kind of baseball cap. Judging by the quality of the picture it was taken on a twenty-quid mobile from outer space. 'Is that supposed to be him?' Haarbottle nodded. 'That could be absolutely anybody with a big tash. It looks like one of those UFO or Loch Ness pictures; they're always like this too. His own mother wouldn't recognize him from that. Oh, I get it, and that's what the police told you, too, wasn't it?'

'Pretty much,' Haarbottle admitted. 'But why would someone make it up? Turn the picture over.'

On the other side, written in ink and capital letters, it said: MIKE DEALEY. IS HE NOT SUPPOSED TO BE IN A WHEELCHAIR?

'"Supposed to be" sounds a bit harsh.' I turned the photograph over again. 'This is the original then,' I said. 'If they let you have it that means the police are definitely not interested.'

'You're right, they're not. It could be malicious or a hoax. But if this is a hoax it's a strange kind of hoax, isn't it? It's enough for us to investigate, anyway, even if the police can't be bothered. To them it's just work, but to us it's money. A lot of money. I can offer you one per cent.'

'What was the payout?'

'Three-quarters of a million.'

'Plus expenses.'

10

'Naturally, but *reasonable* expenses – no need to check into the Queensberry.'

'Only if Mr Dealey does. Where does he live?'

'We've no current address.'

'In that case I'll work on my standard rate until I find him, and on percentage after that.'

I preferred working for a daily rate but a percentage deal could sometimes work out very well, especially if it only took you a couple of days to get a result. Of course if you came up empty-handed then you had worked for nothing. Over the years I'd become a reluctant expert in that.

'I thought you might say that. And that's all I'm authorized to offer you. All the details of the case are there. Find him quickly and nail him. Of course if it was me I'd just tip him out of that chair and see what happens,' Haarbottle said sweetly.

I looked up from the photograph. Haarbottle was a tall thin man in a pale blue M&S suit and looked totally harmless, but he was an insurance man through and through – suspicious, vicious and stingy. 'He'll claim a sudden improvement brought on by the shock,' I told him. 'That's not the way to get your money back.'

Haarbottle grunted contemptuously and jabbed a moistened index finger at the crumbs on his plate. 'Just make sure he's not booking himself on a flight to Lourdes so he can come back miraculously cured. I tell you, these people stop at nothing.'

'Steady on.'

'Anyway, onwards and upwards. Call me

personally; my numbers are on the file.' He grabbed his briefcase and strode out of the Pump Rooms without paying for his bun. No matter, I was now on expenses, so I ordered a fresh pot of tea and some crumpets. While I piled black-currant jam on to those I went through the file. It made depressing reading.

Mike Dealey had been minding his own business one sunny day, riding his Ducati along the A4 towards Bristol when a builder's van pulled out in front of him. It was a classic T-bone sorry-didn't-see-you-mate accident. Dealey was lucky to survive. He spent three months at the Royal United and left it in a wheelchair. According to the file he was a broken man in more ways than one. He had been a heating engineer yet the head injury had left him unable to walk, with painful spasms in his legs and a host of other ailments, like a fear of loud noises and bouts of depression. His fiancée left him while he was still in hospital, which might not have helped.

Three-quarters of a million pounds didn't seem much money, considering, and I was beginning to hope, for his sake as much as mine, that he *was* only faking it. But how did you fake a girlfriend dumping you?

It did occur to me as I left the Pump Rooms that we didn't exactly have a sworn statement to that effect – it was only hearsay, things the Griffins people had perhaps picked up at the hospital. Who was to say that she was the dumper? Mike Dealey could easily have decided to make a fresh start by himself with the aid of all that money. Not that these days three-quarters of a million set you up for life but it did give you a certain head start.

I had parked the bike opposite the Pig & Fiddle and while I walked there the sun disappeared behind dark rain clouds. I didn't see it as an omen since at that moment I still felt at one with the world, something that new expense accounts and fresh assignments often do to me. My first task was to find Dealey and that was a job for Tim. Not that I was incapable of finding people without him, but Tim was so much better (and quicker) at it that I had come to rely on him a lot. And since he often worked for no more than a few beers and food I called him at work, told him what I wanted and invited him up for a barbecue after work. Then I popped into the nearest super-market and bought stuff Tim could incinerate and then drown in barbecue sauce.

A few hours later the barbecue was sizzling with lamb kebabs. Ever since our return from Corfu we had been eating *à la Greque*. The earlier rain clouds hadn't come to much and late evening sunshine gilded the valley. Tim eased his broad shoulders into a wicker chair on the Mill House verandah and shook his woolly head. 'Drew a blank. Couldn't find him on the register or anywhere else. He's keeping a low profile. We'll find him though.' Tim had been gesturing with his closed bottle of Pilsner and when he opened it he sprayed himself and surroundings with beer froth.

'Cheers, Tim.' Annis mopped at her jeans with a napkin.

Tim's chrome, leather and hardwood flat in

13

Northampton Street was stuffed with computer gear and he kept it to laboratory standards of cleanliness by eating out and drinking in the pub next door. He liked to leave his mess elsewhere, like at my place.

'So how are we going to go about it? If I don't know where he lives then the job's a non-starter and at the moment I need all the work I can get.'

Annis gave the kebabs a last quarter turn on the barbecue. 'What else do you know about him?'

'Hang on, the file's still in the kitchen.' I fetched it and flipped it open. 'He used to live in a third-floor flat behind the Circus somewhere, which he can't now because of his legs, but where he eventually moved to it doesn't say.'

'How come Griffins don't know?' Tim asked.

'Because he doesn't want them to know?'

Annis doused the kebabs with lemon juice and handed them around. 'It does look a bit suspicious. On the other hand he could simply have moved away.'

'The anonymous tip-off came in a letter that was posted in Bath. If they had seen him in Majorca they probably would have said so.'

'Is that him there?' Tim pointed with the end of his kebab and dribbled meat juice over the photograph.

I held the pics up in turn. 'Yup, that's him in a wheelchair; that's him supposedly walking on his own two feet; and that's him taking possession of his car, a Honda modified for wheelchair use.'

'Can you read the number plate on it?'

14

I squinted. 'I can, just. Oh good, we're sorted, then.'

'We'll ask PC Whatsisname to find out for us.'

'That means wine labels,' I reminded Tim.

'No probs. I'll print some out on your computer later, if you've got the bottles.'

We call him PC Whatsisname because Watt's his name, Police Constable Nick Watt. Doubts about the precise wattage of Nick's brain have long been dogging his career. We got quite friendly a few years back and he can sometimes be bribed to find out things for us. It saves Tim trying to hack into police computers and risk a lengthy jail term, but then bribing a police officer isn't popular with the courts either. Five years earlier Nick had won a competition in the Police Gazette. His prize: a week in France. The *happiest* time of his life. While there he fell in love with an unapproachable waitress and discovered French wine; he had even brought an empty bottle of his favourite tipple back as a souvenir but had been unable to lay his hands on any more of the plonk, for the simple reason that it was rubbish and didn't travel. It was simply called JM Blanchard, probably after the chap who made it in his garage. We scanned the label, stuck them on a half-decent Merlot and Nick, suffering badly from nostalgia for his untouchable French waitress, swore it was the very vintage he had been drinking on holiday while adoring her from afar. Naturally these bottles were *fiendishly diffi-cult* to get hold of and Nick appreciated all my efforts on his behalf.

'The DVLA will have a record of the registered

15

keeper,' Tim said, spraying feta crumbs over his jeans. 'They'll even have the name of his last MOT garage. By this time tomorrow we'll have Mr Dealey pinned down.'

It was to this end that at noon the next day I was sitting in the Café Retro drinking cappuccino opposite Constable Watt. Unlike most of his colleagues he shunned the current fashion for extreme crew cuts and looked uncommonly cuddly for an officer of the law. He was out of uniform, on his way to clock on at Manvers Street nick around the corner, but looked shiftily around him as though fearful of spies. Nick loved a bit of conspiracy. I saw he had brought an optimistically large bag with him to carry off the plonk.

'I could only get hold of four bottles this time,' I told him. 'It's getting very hard to find.' I simply didn't have any more of the Merlot at the house and while he had convinced himself that it tasted exactly how he remembered the original, he might well notice if I changed over to yet another substitute.

'That's OK. I'll make them last. What are you after? Nothing too dodgy, I did warn you.'

'Not at all.' I simply relayed the whole story.

'Three-quarters of a million? That's a nice nest egg. OK, if he's on the database I'll find him. Soon as I get a chance.'

We were interrupted by the chime of my mobile. It was Jake, calling from his car restoration workshop.

'Honeysett . . .' There was a sound as though

16

someone was grinding a cat in half. 'Get yourself up here.'

'Look, if it's about the van . . .' Opposite me Watt pulled a knowing face. He imagined my life to be a series of crises and wasn't far wrong.

'Forget the van,' Jake shouted over the background of workshop noises. 'I never expected to see much of it again. Wouldn't have lent it to you otherwise.'

'What, then?'

'It's a surprise. You'll like it. Some of it, anyways.' He hung up.

Watt widened his eyes expectantly. 'Trouble?'

'Apparently not. Which is most mysterious. I'd better go and see what it's about.'

Watt checked his watch. 'I'm due to clock on anyway. Got to hide these in my locker first.' He lifted the bag and the bottles clinked their nostalgic promise.

I watched him walk guiltily towards Manvers Street while I started up the Norton. The noise of the thing always turned a few heads, which was another reason why it was pretty useless for a private detective. So Jake had a surprise for me. I didn't dare hope.

Jake lived up near Ford, on the way to Chippenham, on a rambling smallholding. Originally the plan had been to breed ponies there and when that venture failed he had turned his hobby, restoring vintage cars, into a thriving business. Jake looked after Annis's 1960s Land Rover and had for many years – and under protest – kept my equally ancient Citroën DS 21 alive. Jake specialized in British classics and professed to hate French motors.

My last DS had literally rusted away beneath me and Jake had towed it to the scrapheap with many a told-you-so.

It was another fine day and once I had left the tortuous traffic of Bath behind I opened the Norton's throttle to an ear-splitting fifty miles per hour. The vibrations numbed my wrists, tickled the soles of my feet in their boots and it all helped to remind me that fifty years is a long time in motoring. Still fun, though. I turned into Jake's yard and found a space to leave the hot, ticking machine. The fawn and rust of the Norton blended in well with the rest of the scenery up here. The workshop and the outbuildings surrounding it looked nearly as dilapidated as my own place, only with the addition of automotive junk of every description; whole engines, part engines, wheels and axles, car doors and bonnets. Neatly parked were a few whole cars inside lockups and under tarpaulin. There was a brown Rover in mint condition, just arrived or ready to be collected. Not far away stood the – to my eyes at least – unpromising remains of a pale blue Wolseley. You didn't see many of those on the road.

I found Jake in his workshop underneath a black 1940s Riley in the company of one of his mechanics, a factotum with white, electrified hair. They were making an awful racket and were swearing a lot. There were tools and oil rags on the ground around them. The air smelled of hot metal and burnt rubber. Give me detective work any time.

'You'll have to wait until we've got this bastard sorted,' Jake said to my legs.

'It's probably the floggle-toggle,' I said helpfully.

The banging stopped long enough for Jake to growl, 'Shut up, Chris, and put the kettle on.'

While the clanging and grinding and swearing resumed I filled the kettle. Barely audible, my phone chimed again. This time it was Annis. Something about another job. Something about digging something up? I was desperate for more work so didn't quibble. 'I can hardly hear you!' I shouted down the phone. 'Tell them I'll definitely do it!'

Anyone can make a mistake.

I made tea and had time to drink it in the sunshine outside. Thirty yards or so away, behind the farmhouse proper, Jake's wife Sally gave me a wave, then returned to taking colourful washing off the line; Jake's two mongrel dogs ran senselessly to and fro across the yard for the heck of it; a collared dove landed on a fencepost and took off again; bees buzzed. At last the workshop noise stopped and soon after that Jake emerged. His overalls looked like he had been in a fight and there was a new tear on his knee. The knuckles on his right hand were freshly grazed and his face was a mask of oil and sweat but he seemed happy enough.

'Got the bugger sorted,' he said, wiping his hands on an oily rag, which made them dirtier.

Since I probably wouldn't understand the answer I didn't even pretend to be interested in his fight with the Riley. 'So where's the surprise?' I asked instead, feeling like a kid.

'I hid it round the back.'

'Crafty.'

He walked off, signalling me to follow round the corner. 'Not because of you, you nit, but to avoid embarrassment.' We rounded the next corner and there, on a bit of concrete hard standing next to the old milking parlour, stood the surprise. *'Et, voilà.* Don't say I never do anything for you. This is far beyond the call of duty, I'll have you know.'

'It is. I'm speechless.' And there it was, Car of the Century (the last one, obviously), a Citroën DS 21, circa 1972. It was gleaming in the sunshine and my heart leapt. Tentatively.

'Obviously I hid it back here because a) it's a bloody Frog chariot and b) it's bright pink.'

'Yes, that could be a problem.'

'Otherwise it's practically mint; wouldn't have accepted it otherwise. I took it in part-payment.'

I opened the driver door with reverence and slipped behind the wheel. Jake was right, the leather seats, the dash, even the carpeted floor looked exactly as they had the day the car had rolled off the assembly line forty years ago. Only some criminal had sprayed the bodywork rasp-berry ice-cream pink. The interior smelled of flowery perfume.

'How much?' I asked.

'Nothing you can't afford.'

'That's very cheap then. It needs respraying.'

'No shit, Sherlock. It's already booked in. Come back in a couple of days.'

Three

A recurring delusion of mine is that there is time to do it all: the painting and the private-eye work, looking after Mill House and the mill pond, having a meaningful relationship, cooking, cleaning and mowing the grass. I forget that most people who have multiple careers, a large house and three acres of land and yet look wide awake in the afternoons also tend to have a lot of help, hired or otherwise. My own help consisted of a largely undomesticated Annis, herself always busy in the studio, an increasingly part-time Tim and two lazy black-faced sheep who were supposed to keep the grass down. All of which meant that my own attempts at Renaissance Mannishness frequently ran into trouble. It never stopped me trying, though.

There had been no word yet from Constable Whatsisname about Dealey's address so I spent the rest of the day drawing the junk in the outbuildings from odd angles with a view to using them as the basis for a painting. A bit more abstract perhaps but still fundamentally figurative, though without the sheep. I was pretty sure I wouldn't get sheep past Simon Paris.

By next morning I still hadn't heard from Watt so I started transferring my drawings to the canvas. Since I would be sure to invoice Griffins insurance for this waiting time it felt doubly

21

blissful – decent light, free warmth, a new painting, and I was practically getting paid by the hour. In the outbuildings, bright sunlight had been slanting through the gaps in the slatted walls, creating bright patches of light alternating with deep, mysterious shadows. I would carve the lights out of the canvas by painting the shadows first. To this end I mixed a large amount of a deep, cardinal purple that for some reason was called *caput mortum*, which translates as 'death head' or if you are an alchemist, 'worthless remains'. In my case it was prophetic since it remained unused on my palette. My brush hesitated for a second over the canvas while I took another glance at the preparatory drawings I had arranged on the floor, which gave Annis time to burst through the door with the cordless phone in one hand and a piece of paper in the other.

'I just took a call from Sergeant Whatsit, he gave me this address. And it's Jake on the phone for you.'

I quickly scanned the note, it was Dealey's address and it had a Bath postcode. Then I took the phone.

'Your Frog carriage awaits, swivelling headlights and all. I got it back early.'

'Brilliant,' I said. 'How much?'

He told me. Annis could see from my face that I was listening to a hideous sound in my ear; she stood whistling tunelessly and rolled her eyes to the rafters. 'Can I pay you in instalments?' I begged.

'Certainly. In that case I can let you have the front seats and the off-side rear wheel.'

'All right, I expect I'll scrape it together somehow.' I terminated the call.

'The DS reborn,' said Annis. 'Praise be, whatever the cost, as long as it gets you off the Norton. Just as well you got a second assignment then.'

'What second assignment?'

'The one I called you about yesterday? You said to accept. I left you a note on your office desk.'

'I never look at notes on my office desk. I never go in my office.'

'Perhaps now's a good time to try it: the job starts tomorrow.'

'Tomorrow? Doing what?'

'Babysitting Guy Middleton.' Annis was slipping out of the door already. The sun lit up her strawberry hair. She was beautiful and had a pencil behind her left ear. Perhaps the drawing bug had bit.

I ran after her through the overgrown meadow. 'The TV guy with the hair and that?'

'Yup.'

'The one who presents the archaeology programme? *Time Tunnel*?'

'*Time Lines*. Yes. It was the production company that called. The details are on your desk.'

'And they want *me*?'

Time Lines, according to people like Tim who didn't live at the bottom of a valley and had TV reception, was the upstart UK History satellite clone of an excellent Channel 4 programme with a similar name. A blatant copy of the format, it aimed to be glitzier, glossier and more idiot-friendly than the original. It was now in its sixth

23

year and Guy Middleton, who previously had been the heart-throb doctor in an endless hospital series, was its hugely popular and populist presenter. To look the part he had sprouted a ponytail, cultivated an Indiana Jonesish dress sense and he delivered his lines with a seductive voice. Now, why would he need babysitting?

I tramped up the stairs into my office and called them.

'At last! We'd almost given up hope,' said a male voice that sounded about eighteen years old but turned out to belong to Cy Shovlin, the producer of the show. '*Time Lines* is coming to Bath and we want to hire you as personal minder to Mr Middleton during the filming. The dig starts the day after tomorrow, but we'd be grateful if you could meet with Guy tonight for an informal chat. We'll call you and let you know where and when, so please keep your evening free.' I still hadn't said more than *hello* at this point and could easily have gone off to fry some eggs or something and the voice wouldn't have noticed; he simply went on pouring TV speak into my ear about locations and shoots and digs. Eventually he said something interesting. 'We agreed your fees with your secretary. I must say they were higher than we'd been led to believe but Guy asked especially for you so there we are. I hope you're worth the money. We'll draw up a contract and I'll get you to sign it tonight, all being well. Have I got your mobile number? Oh yeah, it's here, I'll call you on that to let you know. See you tonight. Good to talk to you at last.' The line went dead. I imagined that by the time I put down the receiver he was already bending someone else's ear. So that's how they earned their money, by talking at twice the normal speed and not letting anyone ask you unnecessary questions. The question on my own mind right now was: just how unexpectedly high *were* my fees?

From below I heard Annis slam the front door. I leant out of the tiny window that overlooked the yard. 'I talked to them. I'm meeting with Guy Middleton tonight!'

Annis looked up, one hand on the door handle of her Landy. 'Aren't you the lucky one!'

'That's what I'm wondering – how lucky am I? What kind of fee did you negotiate?'

'Twice your normal, hon.'

'Bloody hell. And they agreed?'

'It's telly, that's chicken feed to them. But a new Citroën for you. When are you picking it up?'

'It's ready now.'

'Come down, I'll drive you.'

I clattered down the stairs like a Labrador puppy who'd heard rumours of walkies and even remembered to grab my credit cards on the way out.

Annis mumbled her usual incantation over the steering wheel – according to her the Landy wouldn't start without it – and turned the key. It coughed into life and we were off.

'So you'll be on a *Time Lines* dig, you jammy bastard.'

'Looks like it. Don't know how jammy until I get there. Could be dead boring.'

'Rubbish. You like all that stuff. You would watch it too if we had telly. Admit it.'

'Probably.'

'You're meeting the man tonight? Lucky you have a stylish car again. I was afraid the goggles would leave permanent white rings round your eyes, like a reverse panda. What are they going to dig up? Did they say?'

'I forgot to ask.'

This, apparently, was *just typical*.

Insects buzzed in the afternoon sunlight when Annis turned the Land Rover into Jake's yard. The man came out to greet Annis. Or was it the Land Rover he was greeting? It was hard to tell with Jake. 'She run all right?' Not, *how are you, how have you been*, you'll notice.

'Fine, but she's not looking forward to the winter,' Annis said. 'Where's the French miracle then?'

On the hard standing round the back stood the transformed DS in gleaming black, without a blemish or even a hint of pink. 'I have to admit, it's a thing of beauty,' she said. 'Happy Honeypot. Right, I'm off.'

'Is that all you have to say? Don't you want to sit in it?'

'It's exactly like your old one, hon; nice, but very familiar. I'll see you later.'

'Where are you off to anyway?'

'Ridge Farm to borrow a couple more sheep. I think the two we have are full.'

I did the necessary business with Jake, arranged classic insurance over the phone and drove out of Jake's place feeling like a new man. Having checked that my mobile was on and even had some charge left (yeah) I drove in comfort and style back to Bath. I traversed the city with the windows down and Beethoven's third on the radio and drove out the other side since I had decided there was time to check out Mr Dealey.

Dealey had moved to a good-sized bungalow at the bottom of a quiet cul-de-sac in Combe Down, once a small village, now a suburb of Bath just a stone's throw from the Midsomer valleys. Whatever Mr Dealey's faults, ostentation wasn't one of them. It was hard to imagine a more sober neighbourhood. I could see that keeping the house under any kind of covert surveillance would not be easy since the street was quite short, on a slight incline, and had no traffic but twitching curtains. Could this in fact be the birthplace of neighbourhood watch? The two large windows at the front of the address had Venetian blinds. A big red Honda, matching the one in the photograph I had, was parked in front of the closed garage. The garage looked narrow and was probably not large enough to allow a wheelchair user to get in and out of his vehicle. There was no grass in front of the house, all was wheelchair-friendly tarmac right up to the front door with a shallow ramp and a folksy knocker in the shape of a lion's head. This was going to be difficult. Knocking on Dealey's front door would be useless; he'd get into his chair before answering it. And if he was faking his injury he'd hardly come skipping out of his door to nip down the shops. Unless he was also very forgetful. I probably sat in the car at the top of the street for longer than was wise but so far Mike Dealey had no reason to be suspicious. From now on though every visit had to be far

27

more clandestine. I turned the car around and drove home the long way round simply for the fun of it.

Mobile reception was also intermittent in the valley but I could just make out the same voice, belonging to Cy Shovlin, the producer of *Time Lines*. Did I know the St James's Wine Vaults? Could I meet Guy Middleton and himself there at nine? I did and I could.

So I did.

The St James's Wine Vaults had vaults and they sold the odd glass of wine but otherwise the place was a regular pub. I recognized Guy Middleton instantly. He was wearing his trademark hat even in here. The fact that you never saw him without it made me wonder if it was hiding a bald patch on his middle-aged head. He was sitting at a table by the window opposite a short-haired man in his late twenties who was wearing a shirt the colour of milky tea and they appeared to be having an argument that involved a lot of finger pointing on the younger man's part. Middleton was drinking beer, the younger man bottled lager. I armed myself with a pint of Guinness, put on my best professional face and made my way over. As soon as I was spotted their argument evaporated and TV smiles appeared like the sun from behind rain clouds.

'You must be Chris Honeysett,' said Middleton. 'Welcome, sit yourself down.' I did, with my back to some punters who were taking pictures of him on their mobiles. 'This is Cy Shovlin, our producer.'

We all shook hands. 'So, *Time Lines* has come

to Bath,' I said. 'And you want to hire me to do what exactly?'

Guy Middleton breathed in but Cy got in there first. 'We are shooting at a secret location just outside Bath,' he said, looking around as though fearful of being overheard, despite the music and the babble of voices. 'The whole project will take us a week, with possibly one or two extra days, not sure yet, depends on weather and things, for shooting scenes in town, Roman Baths, establishing shots, history gaff, that kind of thing. During this time we want you to be a minder to Guy, make sure he doesn't get mobbed by fans or abducted by aliens.' Just then a woman in her thirties turned up at the table, carrying in front of her a *Time Lines* book that bore Middleton's name and picture on the cover but which no doubt had been ghost-written for him. She had spotted him through the window, run home to fetch the book and was still out of breath. 'Not now,' Shovlin said to the woman. 'Can't you see we're busy here?'

The woman made a face, half-apologetic, half-pleading. Middleton smiled with unfeasibly white teeth. 'No, no, it's OK,' he said in a suffer-the-children manner and signed the book with the proffered biro. He dismissed the profuse thanks. 'Not at all, not at all.'

'Well, that'll be your job from now on,' Cy said when the woman had disappeared. 'You'll tell them to get lost and Guy will contradict you and say *no it's all right* which makes him feel like Jesus and looks like he always has time for the public he so despises.'

29

'Shut up, Cy,' Middleton hissed.

Cy ignored him. 'Security is important at any shoot but with the cuts and thousands of frontline police withdrawn we've been told we can't even have a single bobby on a bicycle to discourage trespassers. Fortunately we're just outside Bath on a large private property so we should be reasonably safe. But if we hire a normal security firm – we've done this before – we might as well advertise; they go and brag in the pub about it or tell their kids or whatever. And the longer we can keep the location of the dig a secret the better. For a variety of reasons. I have a contract here.' He produced a four-page document from a file on the table. 'You'll be hired as a freelance by the production company and if you sign it that means giving away the location to anyone is a breach of contract, you understand?'

'Sure, no problem,' I said. 'Mind you, if you yourselves are sitting in a pub in Bath it won't take people long to find out what you're up to.'

Guy waved it away. 'Of course they'll find out. But it might take them two or three days to find where we are and where we're all staying. And that bit of peace and quiet is priceless, believe me.'

'Absolutely.' Cy was multi-tasking, reading and answering the fifth mobile message on his BlackBerry since I had sat down. 'Our adoring public can be a real pain when they decide to get their arses off their sofas. We get all sorts: love-sick women, archaeology nutters, souvenir hunters. We had a streaker last time – shame we couldn't use that shot really; Guy's expression

was priceless. Right, initial all and sign last page.'
He held contract and pen out to me.

I didn't bother to read any of it, just made my
mark and signed. Cy whipped it away into his
folder. 'We'll want you from tomorrow morning.
Bright and early at the Roman Baths for some
historical background stuff. Guy will be delivering his opening PTC. We'll be trying to—'

'Delivering his what?' I asked.

Middleton to the rescue. 'PTC. Piece to camera.
You'll pick up the jargon, don't worry. By the
end of the week you'll talk *like you've worked
in telly all your life.*' This last bit appeared to be
directed not at me but at Cy.

Cy didn't miss a beat. 'Yes, quite. As I was
saying, we'll be doing establishing shots and
PTCs in the Roman Baths three hours before the
public are allowed in so the crew will be in there
at six and you'll meet Guy there at *six-thirty*,'
he said, with an emphasis that in turn appeared
to be aimed at Guy, not me, though it did make
me swallow hard.

'Six-thirty, right,' I said happily, as though
sparrow's fart was my favourite time of day. I
checked my watch. I would have to fall unconscious *immediately* to get the Honeysett-approved
amount of shut-eye.

'Six-thirty sharp,' Cy added as he got up and
gathered his things.

I made to get up too in order to drive towards
my bed but Middleton shook his head and said:
'Stay. My round.'

I stayed; it was his round. When he returned
he was carrying our pints and what looked like

31

a triple Scotch which he dispatched in a couple of gulps. 'That's better,' he said.

'Mr Middleton . . .'

'Guy, call me Guy. We're all one happy family on this team, as I am sure you have noticed.'

'Problems?'

He impatiently twirled the empty whisky glass on the table. 'Everyone in telly is now about twelve years old which can get a bit tiresome.'

I looked at him closely now and saw the tell-tale signs of stress under his eyes. Or perhaps it was just tiredness after having travelled here from who-knew-where. 'Guy, why hire me? I mean, as opposed to anyone else.'

'Oh, didn't they mention it to you?' His eyes met mine. 'I own a couple of your paintings,' he said, brightening up a little. 'Two big blue ones, I'm sorry I can't remember the titles, they've got pride of place though in my holiday home in the Lakes. I love your stuff. Bought them here in Bath, in fact, three, four years ago. They told me you were a private eye at the gallery. And I thought: why not hire someone with an artistic temperament rather than an ex-copper – that's what most PIs are, I'm told. Who wants to hang around with coppers? Cheers.' He lifted his pint and I mine. He returned his own half-drained to the table. 'But that's not the only reason I wanted a private detective rather than security guards. There's something else I want you for. Apart from what's in your contract. I've received threats lately.'

That explained the stress then. 'What kind of threats?'

'Well, what do you think? Death threats.'

'*Guy Middleton, I'm going to kill you?*'

'Even cornier than that. *Your days are numbered* said one. *One day soon they'll have to dig you up*, the last one said.'

'And these take the form of what, letters?'

'Yes, I've had letters. But the really creepy ones are the notes. I find those anywhere. At work. Or under my windscreen wipers. Had my car scratched twice, too.'

'That could just be inverted snobbery. I assume you drive a good car?'

'When I'm working it's the Range Rover, it's good for all the bloody fields and bogs we end up in. X-type Jag, otherwise. But it was the Range Rover they scratched both times. Once just zigzags, the second time it said "DIE". Right across the bonnet, the bastards.'

'Could be a crazed fan. Or someone at work you upset. Does anyone spring to mind?'

Middleton flicked a dismissive gesture with his hand. 'Nobody and everybody. TV is stressful, it's a competitive business, people rub up against each other, there are endless arguments and plenty of backstabbing and jealousies. So, no, nobody comes to mind and then again it could be everyone.'

'OK, you got some through the post but you also find notes at work. Then it's probably someone quite close.'

'That's what worries me. If they can get close enough to stick notes on my car they can get close enough to stick a knife in me! I tried not to take it seriously at first. But it's beginning to get to me. Letters by post I can deal with – every TV star gets crank letters – but knowing someone has got that close to me that they can stick notes on my car, that unnerves me. It's bloody scary.'

'It's supposed to be. What did the police have to say?'

'Police? Are you mad? It would become public knowledge like *that*.' He snapped his fingers between us. 'I can't afford to. That's not the kind of publicity the programme wants, believe me. I'm *adorable*, you understand. Nobody hates me; people send me flowers. Which they do, of course. *And* cakes *and* chocolates. All of which get incinerated as a matter of course.'

'They do? Even cake?' Were these people mad?

'Edible stuff sent to celebrities is always chucked away; there are too many nutters around to risk it and celebrities can afford to buy their own, after all.'

'I suppose you're right.' But still. *Cake!* I mean, really. Perhaps I should offer my services as a food taster. Cakes a speciality.

'So, no. No police and utter secrecy.'

'What about your producers, what about Cy? What do they think?'

'Same, I haven't told them. It's between you and me. And I want you to find who is doing it.'

I pondered this for a moment while I sipped my Guinness. Just assuming for the moment that these were empty threats, designed to scare, that would be fine. But in the unlikely case that they were not – what could I realistically do to prevent Middleton's demise? But naturally for a double fee and un-incinerated cake I'd give it a go. 'OK, it's your choice but I'm not sure it's a good one.'

'Keep it under your hat all the same.'

'Do you have any of these letters here?'

'No, I chucked them away.'

'Shame.'

'Not at all. They're vile things and I threw them away as a gesture of defiance. The notes I found under my windscreen wipers I crumpled up there and then and chucked over my shoulder, in case they were watching.'

'You mean you acted as though you didn't care.'

'Absolutely. I'm not an actor for nothing.'

'I'm not so sure that's such a good idea either.'

'Why ever not? I'm not giving them the satisfaction.'

'Let's for a moment assume they're just trying to harass you, to frighten you. If they are watching and it looks as though they haven't succeeded they may turn up the wick and try something even scarier.'

Middleton grunted and shifted uncomfortably on his seat. 'Yeah, all right, I hadn't thought of that.'

'If another one turns up, keep it. I'd like to look at it. And try to look harassed when you read it. Are they handwritten?'

'Some were – printed in capitals, though, no joined-up writing. Others were computer print.' He picked up his empty glass. 'Another one?'

'Not for me, thanks. It's my round anyway. I'll get you another but I really have to get home now.'

'All right, piss off, then. I'll buy my own, don't

35

worry. I bet I make ten times what you earn. I'll see you at the Roman Baths in the morning.'

'Will you be all right getting to . . . where are you staying in Bath? If that's not a secret?'

'Course not. Royal Crescent Hotel, just round the corner. Only for two nights, mind; after that we'll all be out there somewhere.' He waved an arm at the dark window. 'In the wilds of Somerset.'

Four

'Hnn? Whaaa . . .? What's going on? What's that hideous noise?' Next to me Annis burrowed deeper under the duvet.

I myself fumbled blindly with my mobile, which was making increasingly shrill bleeping noises until I had silenced the unfamiliar sound. 'It's called an alarm. For people,' I yawned like a hippo, 'who have to go to work.' Neither of us had heard an alarm clock for years. How did people live with it?

'What time is it?' said Annis from very far away.

'Five.'

'Bring me a cup of tea in about two hours.'

'You'll have to fend for yourself. I'm in television now, the golden hour and all that.' I dragged myself out of bed and opened the shutters a crack. 'The sun's actually just up, you know. Amazing.'

Annis snatched my pillow and piled it on top of her head. 'I'm so very, very happy for you.'

I nearly fell asleep again standing up in the shower but by the time I had plunged the cafetière and was warming my croissant in the oven I felt almost normal, except that the early light had such a quality that I opened the back door simply so I could look at it. It lent a certain beauty even to the straggly herb garden that was giving room to herbs and weeds in democratic measure. I piled my croissant high with rose petal conserve – I had brought half a suitcase of it back with me from Greece – drained the cafetière and drove into town.

Not only had *Time Lines* managed to borrow the Roman Baths for a few hours, they had also wrangled reserved parking for their vehicles at the end of York Street for the morning. There were vans and cars and a Land Cruiser in the green and gold *Time Lines* livery. I stuck my car at the end of the line.

It was very quiet here in the centre of town – perfect for filming, I supposed – and the warm early light playing on the sandstone buildings was in itself nearly compensation for the early start.

Six-thirty exactly. The doors to the baths were closed. In answer to my knocking, a sleepy and monosyllabic employee opened up for me and pointed the way past the silent tills and racks of audio guides. As I turned right and started down the stairs I could smell the warm sulphurous air that had pervaded this place since the beginning of time. Even though I hadn't been here for years I still remembered it well, the smell and the museum layout. Not that it was possible to get lost in the museum. It had been designed as a one-way walk-through for funnelling hordes of visitors past the exhibits, down to the baths and out through the gift shop. I took my time, revelling in luxurious, tourist-free quietude.

All the lights and displays had been turned on for the benefit of the TV crew, giving the empty museum an eerie, abandoned air. Here and there life-sized film projections of actors in period costume, sitting, standing and chatting silently, added to the ghostly feel of the empty rooms. As I progressed I could hear voices – English, not Roman. I found the first of the TV crew by the overflow of the Sacred Spring, just inside the museum building. A camera on a tripod was pointing at the ancient stonework of the arched culvert from which hot water gushed into an equally ancient drain. Minerals in the water had stained the stonework bright orange and the scene was atmospherically lit from below. A sad-eyed, middle-aged sound recordist with headphones clamped to his ears kept shaking his bald head at the man behind the camera.

The camera operator, a man in his thirties with a sharp nose, dark hair and long sideburns looked up. 'Are you . . .?'

'Chris,' I confirmed.

'Hi, I'm Paul. Guy with you?'

'I was supposed to meet him here.'

'We all are. OK, erm, we need some quiet for this now. Emms is outside, through that door.'

'OK. Emms?'

'Mags Morrison. The director. Red hair, lots of it, can't miss her.'

I stepped through the door, shedding two millennia in the process. The green waters of the Great Bath steamed gently in the cooler morning air. Surrounded by a colonnaded archway paved with uneven flagstones worn smooth by a million feet, the rectangle of the bath itself was open to the sky and watched over by life-sized stone figures. This didn't need projections to transport me back in time; it was doing fine on its own. Then I heard voices and spotted the twenty-first century encamped in a dark doorway. Camera, sound equipment, monitors, cables, people with clipboards, thick files and several laptops.

As promised by Paul the cameraman there was a woman with henna-red hair. Dressed in sweater, jeans and walking boots she had her hair drawn back into a long ponytail clasped by a black plastic butterfly grip. Behind her I saw Cy crouching in the shadows in front of a laptop. They had set up shop at the west end of the baths. Behind them thousands of coins, thrown there by visitors, glittered at the bottom of a circular plunge pool.

I walked over to introduce myself to the director but she beat me to it. 'Hi, I'm Emms, I'm the director. Mags Morrison, really, but Emms is fine. You must be Chris Honeysett. Cy described you well.'

'Did he?'

'Well, the long hair, ancient leather jacket and stuff . . .' We shook hands while I worried about *stuff*. 'Welcome to *Time Lines*. You've met Cy over there. The others are busy. You'll get to know them if you hang around long enough.'

Cy, who was now standing with a phone clamped to his ear, looked in my direction rather than at me when he said: 'You're late. And so is Guy. I'm calling the hotel again.'

Emms shrugged. 'There's plenty of time as long as we shoot within the hour. After that the sun will come round and we'll lose this shot.'

'Hi, it's Cy Shovlin again,' he said into the phone. He nodded impatiently as he listened. 'Yes, I'm sorry about that, but could you try his door again for me, please?' He wandered away along the rim of the pool as he waited for an answer.

'Problems?' I asked.

'No, not yet,' Emms said. 'We always call Guy to make sure he's up and running but this morning he's not answering and the staff at the hotel said they got no reply from his room. You met him yesterday?'

'Yes, we had a drink.'

'*A* drink? Skip it,' she said before I could answer. 'You're a painter as well as a private investigator, how does that go together?'

'Oh, really well,' I lied as though I'd planned it and not simply slid into it by accident. 'They complement each other.'

Cy came striding back into the sunlight. 'They tried his door again and there's no answer. Honeysett, that's your baby from now on, making sure he's on location, on time. Go up there and drag him out of bed and deliver him here. Use all reasonable force,' he added with a cold smile. 'Call if there's a problem. You got my number?'

The town had come to life in the last thirty

minutes and traffic was building up but Bath is a compact place and ten minutes later I was parking the DS in the centre of the crescent in front of the Royal Crescent Hotel. No neon signs here to mar the Palladian splendour, just a couple of potted plants and a doorman with top hat and tails. 'Can I help you, sir?' he asked, rightly guessing perhaps that I would turn out not to be a guest.

'Yes, you can. Don't let anyone stick a ticket on that car, I won't be long.' At reception I explained the who, why and what-for and they found me a manager. She was a concerned forty-year-old in a suit and she walked upstairs with me to the second floor.

'Mr Middleton is a regular guest at the hotel. He always takes the John Wood Suite. I do hope nothing has happened to him.'

'A few double whiskies may have happened,' I said and started pounding on the door with my flat hand like police officers like to do.

When the manager had had enough of the noise she unlocked the door herself. 'We don't like doing this except in an emergency.' She opened the door and allowed me to go in first.

And I found Guy Middleton. He had never made it to his four-poster bed. He lay half naked and slumped on the sofa facing the fireplace.

The manager remained by the door as I went to look at him. 'Is he all right?' she asked.

On the floor beside the sofa lay an empty cut-glass tumbler where it had fallen from Middleton's grasp. His mouth was half open. He was snoring. 'He's alive, anyway.' I shook him, without getting

41

a response. Remembering Cy's permission to use reasonable force I pulled him upright by one arm and patted his face. And again a bit harder. His eyes remained shut but he at least made some kind of protest sound. 'A large cafetière of coffee, I think, would be helpful,' I suggested to the manager. She agreed and left.

I noticed that Guy didn't have a bald patch after all. I also noticed there was a bottle of complimentary mineral water standing untouched on a side table. I opened it and poured some of it over the man's head. His eyes opened and swam around unfocussed. This was entertaining so I poured some more.

'Hey!' Middleton tried to say something else but only said 'hey' a couple more times. Eventually his eyes found me.

'Right, time for a shower, Guy. You're late.' I managed to hoist him up and get him to his feet, then launched him in the right direction. He ghosted towards the bathroom, walking under his own steam now, like a very old man using very old steam. He didn't utter a word. While he showered I called Cy. 'He's in the shower. I'll deliver him in half an hour.'

'Arse!' was Cy's first reaction. 'The pisshead's done it again. He'd better hit the ground running when he gets here.'

When Middleton emerged from the bathroom in a hotel bathrobe he didn't look like a runner. A walker, perhaps. He walked straight past me. 'I know what you're thinking; you think I got paralytic last night. You're wrong, Honeysett. Some bastard spiked my drink.' He picked up a bottle

42

of whisky from the little period table by the sofa and thrust it at me. Covering the normal label was a handmade one of the same size, cut from printer paper. A crudely drawn skull and crossbones sat above the hand-printed legend 'POISON'.

'Explain?'

Middleton spoke while he dressed himself as though his clothes were made from woven lead. 'I did have a few last night. But I wasn't being stupid with it. Well, no more stupid than normal, if I'm honest. When I got up here I wanted another drink. I had that bottle of single malt in my shoulder bag. Got it out and saw someone had stuck that *poison* thing on it.'

I opened the bottle and sniffed it. A fine whisky smell. 'And you drank from it?'

'I thought about it for a while first.'

Oh, of course. 'You get threatening letters, then someone sticks a "poison" label on your Scotch and you think about it and then decide to drink it anyway?' Before I could tell him what I thought about it there was a knock at the door. I opened it and a waitress delivered a cafetière of coffee, two cups and some biscuits on a red tray. Cafetière, cups, tray and girl were all as beautiful and immaculate as you'd expect at just under £500 a night. I poured two cups and handed one to Middleton who was still *sans* trousers but making progress.

'Two thoughts came to me, and both made complete sense last night. A bit less this morning, naturally. The first was that if someone wanted to kill you they probably wouldn't warn you about it with a sticker. You see, it could have been just Cy trying to send me a message about my drinking – he's always on about it to me, the sanctimonious little git. One bottle of Becks and he needs to have a lie-down.'

'How would he have managed to get at the bottle? Are they all staying here?'

'Shit, no, the rest of the crew are staying in third-rate accommodation all over town. Unlike them I had top hotels written into my contract.'

'How, then?'

'Oh, we all met up at the Wagon and Horses near Avebury on the way here yesterday. Most of us, anyway, the archaeological team and some of the production team and myself. They do make good coffee here, is there any more?' I poured him another cup and sat it on a side table while he pulled on his boots. I held out the plate of biscuits but he made a face as though I had offered him maggots. 'We had a working lunch there and then we all went on to our destinations. Some of the archaeology guys are already camping at the location.' He tapped the side of his nose. 'Still a secret. So anyone could have got at my bag. I had it with me at the table.'

'Not just Cy then.'

'No, but he's the one going on about my drinking. I had one drink of that last night and felt myself slipping away.'

'Perhaps sleeping tablets then. How are you feeling now?'

'A bit slow but not too bad. Splitting headache but I took some painkillers. If I can keep the coffee down I'll get through it. How do I look? That's much more important.'

44

Actors. 'Nothing five minutes in make-up won't cure,' I said truthfully. 'You said two thoughts occurred to you last night, what was the other one?'

'The other one,' Middleton said as he slipped on his jacket, 'was that since it was a thirty-six-year-old Glenfiddich and I'd paid nearly a grand for it ten years ago when I could still afford such things, I was going to try it sooner or later anyway.'

'Whoever is doing this has a fine sense of humour. Because they probably knew you would try it anyway.'

'What they wanted was to make me feel stupid. Which they succeeded in doing.'

'And they wanted you to miss a morning's filming.'

'Which they failed to do. I'm ready. Let's go.' Middleton strode from his suite, head held high. I poured the biscuits into my jacket pocket and followed him.

I drove towards the Roman Baths as fast as traffic would allow. 'What would Cy have to gain by spiking your drink? Surely it would ruin his day as well.'

'He wants to find a good enough reason to get rid of me. He's not exactly coy about wanting me gone; he thinks the show needs a younger presenter and preferably one with better tits. This stuff goes out in the States and the network over there put that particular flea in his ear. He's got a few fleas of his own, naturally, like all those kids brought up on computer games.'

'Can't he get rid of you in a legitimate way?'

'My contract is watertight. As long as I continue to deliver there's no way they can replace me.'

'Anyone else who might like to see you gone?'

'No idea. Finding out is *your* job.'

Was it? I was beginning to wish I had read through the contract before I signed it.

The same monosyllabic guard let us in and I led the way downstairs. 'Have you been here before?' I asked Guy.

'Only as a very small kid. I barely remember it. I've seen it on telly though. Warm in here, isn't it?' The projected Romans still spooked wordlessly on walls and in niches.

It happened just as we approached the spotlit golden head of Sulis Minerva in its narrow glass vitrine. Out went the lights with a distant bang, plunging us into total darkness. Behind me Guy sounded panicked. 'Shit, what's happened? Oh shit, shit, shit. Honeysett, where are you?' He suddenly sounded very small. His groping hand found me and grabbed my leg.

'I'm here, hang on.' I dug around in my leather jacket and laid my hands on my tiny Maglite. I pointed the feeble beam behind me. Middleton was crouching on the floor against the Plexiglas edging of the walkway. He looked genuinely scared. 'You all right?'

He stood up now, letting out a long breath. 'Yes. Yes, I'm fine now, just don't go anywhere with that torch. Terrified of dark places, is all. Always have been. Not always easy in this job. Dark outside – fine. Dark inside – panic.'

'Yes, I can see that could be a bit tricky.'

'They shoehorned me into some dark and evil

Roman sewers up in York once so I could talk about Roman poo. I had nightmares for days after that. I'll spare you the details.'

'Much obliged.'

Without a fanfare the lights came on again and the ghosts sprang back into their niches.

We made it through the museum without further incident. As the last level came into view Guy laid a hand on my arm. 'Look, you won't . . .'

'I won't,' I promised. 'Presumably they all know you're scared of the dark?'

Guy just semaphored with his eyebrows then breezed into the arms of the *Time Lines* crew. 'Sorry, chaps and chapesses . . .'

It turned out that one of the technicians had shorted half the museum when they relocated to the east end. Damp plugs, was the verdict.

The atmosphere at the Baths was edgy. The sun had travelled around too far for the planned shot so everything was being moved to the east end of the outdoor area. It looked fussy to me but I supposed they knew their job. I had done mine by delivering Guy, who immediately got into a short sharp argument with Cy which was broken up by Emms who sent Guy off to have his make-up done. Guy had made me swear I would not mention the spiked drink to anyone. Everyone just assumed he had had too much to drink the night before. All except one, perhaps. If one of them was responsible for tampering with his whisky then not mentioning it was a show of defiance on Guy's part that was nearly as admirable as his recuperative powers. But was it wise?

Fifteen minutes later Guy emerged, looking on top form. Despite the bright sunlight the wall-mounted flares were lit for an extra touch of the picturesque. Another five minutes of discussion and he was in front of the cameras, delivering his opening piece, setting the scene and theme for this *Time Lines* episode: Roman invasion, battles, dramatic changes, temples, offerings, new foods, luxurious bathing, under-floor heating and plumbing. *The Romans – where would we be without them?*

What on TV would look like one seamless speech, delivered with confidence and apparent depth of knowledge, was a painstaking and slow process, constantly interrupted by adjustments, small changes in the wording, change of camera angle, pace of delivery. One minute Guy was standing, being framed against the backdrop of the green waters, the next filmed from across the other side, seen walking, talking and gesticulating.

Emms stood by the monitor, rehearsing, checking, changing. She had the kind of author-itative voice I always imagined directors to have. 'That was good, Guy, but can you do that again, only a tad faster this time so you finish on "lead plumbing" before you get to the next column or you'll disappear from view at the critical moment . . .' To me it seemed a maddening procedure but everyone appeared to have endless patience with the process. With only minutes to spare before crocodiles of tourists descended on the place the shoot was wrapped up and everyone was nods and smiles again. The moment he was released Guy strode out of the colonnade and disappeared up the stairs towards the exit – his first day's work done. Cy took me aside.

'That was another typically unnecessary, typical Guy Middleton delay. This show would be a lot easier to produce without a prima donna at the centre. Tomorrow morning we'll start later, around eight, at the site of the dig. The archaeologists have to make up their minds about things before Guy is needed. It's a week-long shoot so it's nice and relaxed. Looks like we're going to get some rain during the week but we should be fine. We rarely stop for rain unless it's a real deluge. Make sure Guy makes it there by eight. It's only four, five miles outside Bath; you can leave just after seven from his hotel. He'll have his own car and he knows the way. You'll follow him there.'

'Still keeping it a secret?'

'No offence. Not that I don't trust you, but you could be talking in your sleep for all I know and the owner of the place would give us a mountain of grief if he found himself beleaguered by sightseers in the morning. He hates the great unwashed even more than Guy does.'

'Oh, by the way, is there a Mrs Middleton at all?' I asked. I had been wondering.

Cy smiled as he walked away. 'There've been a few. But the last one walked out on him a few years back. Because he can't keep it in his pants!' he called loudly across the pool as though hoping Middleton might still be able to hear him.

On the other side of the pool Paul the cameraman was taking last-minute stills shots with an

SLR camera, his long lens pointing directly at me. He waggled one hand in acknowledgement, of what I wasn't sure. I waggled a hand back and left the Roman Baths complex through the gift shop. It was time for a bit of wheelchair watch.

Five

You're thinking of setting up as a private eye? Learn to make interesting sandwiches. Invest in the right technology, too: your most exciting gadget will be your Thermos flask. Ah, the glamour of it.

You'll be sitting in your car a lot or standing around waiting and watching the people someone suspects of doing this, that or the other. Especially the other. Because mostly it's infidelity, sometimes runaways, and often insurance work. If your insurance premiums have gone up relentlessly then I can offer you two reasons. One is the boundless greed of insurance companies, the other is the army of so-called injury lawyers advertising on TV, encouraging chancers to make false claims for injuries that never happened, or happened elsewhere. Crack your ankle playing football in the park? We can help. Find a bit of uneven pavement and sue the council. Faking a life in a wheelchair however was in a different league altogether. It was in a different league not simply where the prize money was concerned but because it required a life-long commitment to deception.

Because you never know who's watching. As I was staring at Mike Dealey's bungalow from the incomplete shelter of a substation at the top of his street I wondered whether Dealey – always considering he was in fact faking it – was planning at some point to have a miraculous recovery. Presumably though, the size of the payout had been tailored to a projected lifetime on wheels, with all the pain and frustration that brought. Would he have to give back part of the money if he was suddenly capable of walking again? I didn't know. Forgot to ask. *Typical*, as Annis would say.

There was the other possibility of quietly slipping away unnoticed, to Spain perhaps, or somewhere else where you are whoever you say you are. Change addresses a few times, then lose the wheelchair, settle down under a different name, a few hundred grand richer. It was an elaborate scheme and strewn with possible pitfalls. Not the least of which was someone grassing you up to the insurance company by sending them a picture of you, taken while you absentmindedly stepped out of your wheelchair to stretch your legs.

It was a very quiet neighbourhood and simply standing here would eventually attract someone's attention. I couldn't park in the cul-de-sac itself; I'd get rumbled even more quickly there if this surveillance went on for a while. Once Dealey knew someone was after him he would be too careful to make any mistakes and short of using illegal means I'd probably never prove he was faking it. The proof I obtained had to stand up in court as well as being admissible in the first

51

place, which meant I couldn't exactly set fire to his house and see if he came running out. Tempting though it was; one per cent of three-quarters of a million buys a lot of firelighters.

I withdrew to the car I had left around the corner. He'd never make a mistake round his own house; the neighbours would instantly notice. I would have to wait until he went out. Since it was a cul-de-sac I'd definitely spot him when he came out in his car. If he came out.

I snaffled a smoked salmon and cress sandwich. Drank another cup of tea from the flask. Nibbled broken hotel biscuits from my jacket. Fiddled with the radio. Stopped fiddling with the radio. Always kept a sharp eye on the top of his street so I could follow him the moment his red Honda appeared.

I woke up with a start at the noise of school kids calling to each other from opposite pavements. Damn it, school was out. How long had I snored behind the wheel? I had slept at an awkward angle, too; it hurt to straighten my neck. I sat up, checked my watch: half past three. I had slept for two hours. Dealey could have been out and come back for all I knew, doing cartwheels past my car each way. I went and checked on his Honda. It was still there, and it didn't look like it had moved. Of course, just because his car was there didn't mean *he* was. For all I knew he could be on the Costa del Sol, sitting by the pool and painting his toenails. I slouched back against the tide of chattering school kids and sat behind the wheel, brooding on the tediousness of the job. I shook my flask; there was enough left for a cupful and I'd need it to wake up properly. I had poured a brimful cup, shaking the last drops from the flask, when the red Honda appeared and turned left into the main street. Bum. I was facing the wrong way, too. And had a brimful cup of hot tea in my hand. I sipped some of it, too hot still, poured some of it back into the flask, some of it over my trousers. Started the car. I had to do a U-turn first, trying not to squash dopey kids wandering into the road.

Now where had he gone? I drove down the road until I came to a double roundabout choked with school-run traffic and no red Honda. I briefly considered another U-turn to explore some of the side roads I had passed but the tea was cooling in the wet patch on my trousers, making me feel more than a bit stupid and anyway, I couldn't possibly leave the car in public looking like I had just copiously wet myself. Well, there was no hurry. I was sure to catch Dealey some other time.

Wasn't I?

The sun rose on the first day of the dig and I was awake to watch it creep over the edge of our valley. At first, leaving from the Royal Crescent Hotel just after seven had sounded quite civilized but in reality it meant I had to be up before six, not something Mill House was used to. Last night Annis had decamped to her own room, unwilling to share my early alarm misery for a second time, so I groaned and harrumphed all alone into the shower and grumbled on my lonesome downstairs to the kitchen.

Another culinary addition from my sojourn in Corfu was Greek coffee, which is just what you need to wake you up at unholy hours. I had brought back a *vriki*, a long-handled little pot, and now brewed cups of strong sweet coffee at the slightest provocation. Accompanied by a five-minute egg, croissants and quince jam it made the early start almost bearable.

In front of Middleton's door at one minute to seven I took a deep breath before I knocked. I had a moment's doubt, wondering what state he might be in, but I worried unnecessarily. He yanked the door open wide, still in his dressing gown and towelling his hair, and left me to close the door while he went back into the bathroom.

'Shan't be a moment; plenty of time, though,' he called back. He kept on talking but his voice was drowned out by the whine of the hairdryer. There were the remnants of a continental break-fast on a tray. A different bottle of Scotch had kept Guy company on the sofa last night, not a thousand-pound Glenfiddich this time but a more modest ten-year-old Laphroaig. I held it up to the light – he had made quite a dent in it, nearly halfway down the label, and by the looks of it he had drunk alone. Yet when the dryer stopped and he came back into the room he looked fine, certainly a lot better than the day before, and his mood was more upbeat.

'As long as we get there on time they won't pester us much this morning,' he promised. I wondered if this was the 'royal we' or whether he now considered us an item, him and me against the rest of *Time Lines*, at least one of whom definitely wished him ill.

'Are you now allowed to let me into the big secret? Where are we going?'

'Oh, good Lord, no one's told you yet.' He was dressed now and flinging a last few things into an open suitcase. 'Tarmford Hall is where it's happening. Suspected Roman villa, no less, that's why we have a one-week special on. Of course if it all goes tits-up we'll pack up early.'

'What's so special about the place that even yesterday Cy wouldn't tell me?'

'Tarmford Hall? Owned by Mark Stoneking. He bought it quietly a few years back.'

'The rock musician? Of Karmic Fire? He's still alive then.'

'Alive, immensely rich and eccentric. That's the best way to be, don't you think?'

'One of those keeps eluding me.' I watched Guy stash the bottle of Laphroaig in his shoulder bag.

'That's why we had to be more secretive than usual. He's quite keen on his privacy where the general public is concerned, doesn't mind mixing with us media types though, it seems. We're all staying at the Hall, plenty of room, by all accounts. It's quite a pile; I saw it briefly from the outside.'

'Is he still making music?' Karmic Fire had been huge in the seventies, churning out nine albums of rock music vaguely inspired by Eastern sounds and religions. And even though any survivors of the group were probably using walking frames now, compilations, 'best ofs' and 'previously

55

unreleased tracks' seemed to keep at least the brand going. Annis quite liked them, had two of their albums – recorded long before she was born – and would be dead jealous to know I was at a rock legend's house. I would let her know and rub it in at the first opportunity.

Guy picked up the phone. 'Is he still making music? No idea, you'll have to ask him. Not my kind of sound. Not that he'd have to; I'm sure he gets by.' He spoke into the receiver. 'Would you pick up my suitcase? And I'm ready for my car now . . . Oh good.' He hung up. 'Car's out front.'

A moment later a porter arrived and he followed us down with Guy's suitcase.

We swanned out of the front door into the early-morning sunshine. Suitcase stashed in the back of Guy's Range Rover and the porter tipped, Guy fiddled briefly with his sat-nav, then we set off in convoy down the cobbled crescent. Right from the start Guy drove like an idiot. This was predictable since he also wore his wide-brimmed hat in the car. He caned the big four-litre engine as though it ran on water and had used his horn three times by the time we made it to the Circus two hundred yards further on. He kept this up all the way through the city and up Wellsway. Even when we turned off the Midford Hill and on to narrow country lanes he still drove as though on a broad one-way street, simply blaring his horn then surging through the blind bends. I hung back far enough not to get embroiled in any accident but his luck held and the head-on collision he was surely looking for didn't happen.

Tarmford was a small village five miles south of Bath. It was picturesque, with a pub, the Druid's Arms, beside a village green and duck pond. They had somehow managed to hang on to their post office-cum-grocery store and a red phone box – the picture postcard stuff Somerset does so well.

Guy whizzed past the place, splashed through the ford of the tiny River Tarm and soon took a left into another narrow lane. A high freestone wall appeared by the side of the lane and it was some time before we reached a wide wrought-iron gate with rusting scrollwork between the bars.

Guy was out of the car, thumbing the button on the intercom. Nothing happened for a few moments, so I got out myself. Had I not known better I'd have thought the place was deserted. One of the two carved-stone urns on either side of the gate had half its shoulder missing; weeds and ivy grew out of it. The gate itself was in need of repainting and the circa 1980s security camera on top of the wall above me looked dead. But then the intercom croaked, Guy said the magic word – *Middleton* – and soon the ghostly gate groaned open by itself. Beyond it lay a long, curved drive lined with horse chestnuts and as I followed Guy in I got an early glimpse of architecture at the end of it. Both Guy's Range Rover and the fabled suspension of my Citroën made light work of the rills and potholes in the much-patched drive. By the looks of it someone had given up patching it in the third quarter of the twentieth century.

Mill House, with its three acres, ramshackle outbuildings and the barn on top of the meadow, was a big place and difficult to keep up, but manor houses are in a different category altogether. One look at the many-angled roof which was probably the size of a rugby pitch and I realized that here repair bills weren't just difficult to pay but took on the magnitude of natural disasters. The house itself was massive and looked complicated and of several periods, with a tower here, some crenellations there, a wing jutting out on the right and stuck to the end of it a coach house, now a six-bay garage by the looks of it. A dozen cars and vans of all shapes and sizes stood in front of the house, yet there was still space for a few more on the gravelled forecourt. We parked our cars at luxuriously wilful angles and got out.

Guy Middleton, in wide-brimmed hat, faded waxed hunting jacket, khaki trousers and decoratively worn-out boots, looked ready to raid tombs. He shouldered his leather bag that I knew contained his whisky and I wondered if he was ever parted from it. 'Not bad, eh?' Guy said to me as I caught up. He made a theatrical gesture. 'All this for one ageing rock star. What's he do with it all?'

'You can ask him,' I said, nodding my head at the man who was just then stepping out between the columns of the stone porch in the centre of the building.

Mark Stoneking. It was unmistakably the same guy who with Karmic Fire had rocked huge audiences all around the world, yet he looked older than any rock star should, even in blue jeans, purple tee-shirt and black trainers. His hair had receded at the front but was still long at the sides and back and darker than was plausible at his age. He was tanned on face and arms but no more than a man with a fifty-foot verandah during an English summer ought to be.

'Welcome to my humble abode.' He stretched out a bony hand and shook ours. I wondered if he used the 'humble abode' line every time he opened the door. 'Good to meet you, Guy. You look just like you do on telly.' He turned to me with questioning eyes.

Middleton obliged. 'Oh, this is Mr Honeysett; he's looking after me on this shoot.'

'Chris,' I offered.

'Mark. The others are already on the verandah, come in, come through.'

We followed him into the lofty, two-storey hall, equipped with all the clichés you could ask for – a grand curved blue-carpeted staircase, sinister daubs in elaborate gilt frames every few steps, a lugubrious long-case clock under the arch of the stairs and grey marble floors strewn with well-worn rugs. Dark doors off to either side. The walls were painted wine-stain red and together with the long blue tongue of the stairs made me feel like I had stepped into the toothless mouth of an enormous chow chow. Once the door had closed behind us the foyer became a dim and echoing space. 'This way.' Stoneking waved us on down a shadowy passage and into a long gallery at the centre of the house. We passed a much less grand set of stone stairs. 'You can leave your bag here,' Stoneking said to Guy. 'Carla will take it to your room.'

Guy patted the bag. 'I'll hang on to it. It's got stuff in it I'll be needing soon.'

Through open double doors we came to a long bright drawing room. This looked much more like it had been furnished by a rock star and less like it had come with the house. It had an inglenook fireplace, three leather sofas grouped around a knee-high, intricately carved Nepalese table, several armchairs and a scatter of tables and rugs. The paintings on the pale green walls were bland contemporary fare. In one corner stood a gleaming Yamaha grand piano. There were four hi-fi speakers in walnut cabinets that were so large that I first mistook them for cupboards. It was an uncertain mix of styles and centuries but extremely bright with tall sash and enormous French windows, the latter wide open to the verandah.

Guy made all the diplomatic noises about the interior while rolling his eyes at me. '*Extraordinary* place, Mark . . .' Stoneking seemed pleased by what he took for approval. I just nodded at stuff, like the enormous china elephant and the five-foot carved-wood golliwog holding a tray.

As we followed him on to the verandah where the production team were sunning themselves at two tables, the scale of the place began to sink in. Beyond the verandah stretched a vast lawn, gently sloping towards clumps of trees and unkempt hedges a hundred or more yards away, with just a glimpse of glittering water beyond. The verandah faced west and the lawn was bound on the north and south sides by dense woodland. To the far right I could just make out the long roof of a greenhouse above a dense hedge. Odd statuary and stone carvings were dotted about the place and the verandah was punctuated by waist-high stone urns covered in green algae.

The realm of the fabled Stone King.

Chairs were found and we joined the *Time Lines* team who were drinking coffee and working their way through a large plate of shiny bagels. I sat between producer and director, Cy on my right, Mags 'Emms' Morrison on my left. 'Don't mind if I do,' I said to Stoneking who nodded invitingly at the spread. I poured myself some coffee. Upwind from us, Guy shared a table with Paul the cameraman, the bald sound man and two others, as far away from Cy as he could manage, I assumed.

'I'm glad you're doing your job,' said Cy, making a show of checking his watch. 'He looks halfway awake at least.'

'He was quite chirpy when I found him,' I said loyally. I wasn't exactly enamoured with Guy but I somehow preferred him to the uptight producer.

'Makes a change. The first day is always quite a happy day, of course. Everyone hopeful and the script intact. It's when that lot really get going that it gets bloody.' He gestured towards the lawn.

The archaeology team were advancing, far outnumbering the TV crew. They walked about in groups, surveying, pacing out and measuring, or sat talking in small huddles on the grass. A woman with very short, very blonde hair dressed all in blue and holding a map appeared to be the focus of attention. Not being a follower of the programme I wondered who she was.

Emms answered my question. 'That's Andrea, the chief archaeologist and team leader.'

I was busy piling cream cheese on a bagel and decorating it with slices of cucumber. It's an art. 'So what happens?' I asked.

'They'll decide where they'll investigate and what they think they've got. Then we make them discuss it all again but more concisely for the camera. After that we record absolutely everything interesting that happens. We have a script ready, based on what the archaeologists *think* is out there and that will get rewritten when we find out what's actually there. Then it all starts. It's a long journey from here to the finished programme you'll see on your screen.'

Stoneking sat forward in his chair, listening to every word, glancing often at the figures on his lawn. He looked eager as a child. A woman appeared from a door near the other end of the verandah, late thirties, with dark hair in a pony-tail and sparkling stud earrings, carrying a tray. She wore a white apron over a blue flower-print knee-length dress and approached our table.

Stoneking tested the weight of the coffee pot. 'More coffee, Carla, I think.' She wordlessly took the pot away.

I had despatched my bagel. 'All right if I have a wander about before it all kicks off?' I had vaguely aimed the question at the entire table.

Stoneking said: 'No, go right ahead, man.

Actually, I'll come with you.' He drained his cup. 'Can't believe it's happening at last.'

'It's very brave of you to let that lot dig up the place,' I said when we were out of earshot.

'Rubbish, nothing ever happens in this damn place. No, I can't *wait* to see what's under there, it's exciting. A whole week of it, how good is that?'

We traversed the lawn at an angle towards the south end. 'You're not sad about the lawn?' I asked.

He wrinkled his nose. 'Sam will be. He'll be livid, in fact. My gardener. Only he's . . . well, he's away at the moment. I wrote to him, telling him what's happening and he hasn't replied, which probably means he's sulking. He'll be back in a short while, I hope. Nah, to me it's just grass. They'll take it up, they'll put it back. Mind you, I've cut it myself since Sam went and even with the sit-on mower it's one hell of a job. I never realized.'

'How big are the grounds?'

'Ninety acres – it's not all lawn, thank the gods. Most of it is woodland, of course. There's another forty acres of farmland which I rent out. It's paradise, really.' He lifted his eyes to the dark line of trees and hedges and paused for a moment. 'If you like solitude,' he added like a man who hated solitude. We came to a series of broad and shallow stone steps where a couple of young diggers, a man and a woman, had parked themselves with their wheelbarrow while the bigwigs made their decisions. The woman was reading a paperback novel which she lowered as we approached.

63

'Morning,' Stoneking said and they both got up from where they'd been sitting. 'As you were.' The two sat down again. 'You're part of the team? I'm Mark.'

'We are. I'm Julie, this is Adam,' said the woman. Dark hair showed under her frayed straw hat. A green and gold *Time Lines* tee-shirt, baggy shorts and work boots completed her outfit. Her friend sported an identical tee-shirt, jeans and well-worn boots. He had a first-edition goatee beard and tightly curled blond hair. 'We're diggers,' said the woman.

'We're just foot soldiers; we do the work while the rest of them talk,' confirmed Adam happily.

'Not just you two, I hope,' I said.

'Lor' no,' said Julie, pointing across the lawn. 'There's eight of us diggers. We're a big circus. There's us and then there's geophys – two of them are students on loan from Bristol Uni – so that's ten of us in the woods already.'

'In the woods?'

'Yes,' Stoneking confirmed. 'They're all camping down near the lake. I'm afraid there was only room for the star performers at the house. No offence, guys.'

'We're used to it,' Adam said evenly.

'Too right, we are,' Julie said. 'Field archae-ologists are paid really badly, so we're practically always under canvas. It's a scandal, really, but we all knew that when we started. And it didn't stop us, did it?'

'Nope,' agreed Adam.

'So what's happening now?' I asked.

Just then a very large white van nosed

backwards past the far end of the great house, bleeping reverse-warnings as it went. It stopped in the lee of the north wing.

'The catering van's arrived, that's what,' Julie said. She stuffed her paperback into a back pocket. 'Excuse us, most important matters to attend to.' They both pushed off towards the van.

'Pretty,' said Stoneking.

'Which one?'

He snorted. 'You're right, both of them, really. They're so damn young. How old do you think they are?'

I looked at their slim shapes retreating up the lawn. 'Oh, twenty-five, twenty-six, perhaps?'

'Blimey. I think I had made my first million by then and was busy spending it on crap. And all *they* want is to stand in a hole and dig up stuff.'

'Yes, where did you go wrong?' I said.

Stoneking laughed. 'Quite, quite.'

I nodded towards the catering van that was setting up at the edge of the house. 'You're not feeding them then.'

'Too many of them. I mean Carla, my house-keeper that is, Carla's fine about serving breakfast to everyone who is staying at the house but the rest of the meals are all provided by the caterer. I might throw a dinner or two for a few of them at some stage and they can have afternoon tea if there's time for that but I'm not running a restaurant. Carla would kill me. And I can't afford to piss her off. I can't live in this bloody pile without her.'

We had reached a shady clump of old and twisted trees I didn't recognize. 'What are these?'

65

'Ancient sweet chestnuts. Aren't they fantastic? Probably older than the house.'

'Yes, I meant to ask, how old is the house?'

'Oh, ancient. Bits of it anyway. It's been messed about with for hundreds of years. Added to, mostly.'

'Listed?'

'Only about ten per cent of it,' he said happily, 'or I wouldn't have been able to put in the pool and decent bathrooms and things. The Cunninghams, the family who owned it since Victorian times, were quite a weird bunch. They were spiritualists and into all things gothic, and they were vegetarians, which wasn't at all considered normal in those days. They made so many alterations between the wars, pulling stuff down and rebuilding it, that it's hard to fathom what's original and what's fantasy. I had no idea how strange the place was when I bought it. Nothing here is quite what it seems.'

'Like for instance . . .?'

'On the first-floor gallery is a door that doesn't open. It has no keyhole but it won't budge. Eventually I got a tape measure and figured out that the door is a fake. There's no room behind it. It's just there to confuse people. I mean, there is a room behind it but you enter it through a different door. It's just a visual joke. Like up there.' He pointed up to the house. 'See that window right up there? Third from the left? The one that looks a bit darker than the others? That's a fake too. No room behind it; it's where a service staircase goes up. The place is full of stuff that doesn't add up. That's where the gothic feel

66

comes from. You see all those gargoyles and urns everywhere around the roof? Those weird stone figures and eagles? All added in the 1920s. Some of it isn't even British. They'd go round Europe and India and buy up anything that took their fancy, then drag it into the house or stick it on the outside or just plonk it in the garden, like this one.' We were passing a four-foot terracotta griffin half-swallowed by ivy. 'Nutters. And they're all still here, too.'

'What do you mean?'

'You'll find out.' He stopped for a moment and breathed in deeply. 'I don't know, I might get myself buried here when the time comes. I don't fancy a crowded cemetery.'

'So you can haunt the place.'

'The place already has a full complement of ghosts.'

'Naturally.'

'Ha! You may mock.'

I could hear running water. We took a left through an arch in a hedge that was in dire need of trimming and there beyond it lay the ornamental lake, fed by a lively cascade of water tumbling over suspiciously picturesque rocks at the edge of the dense woodland. At the lake's centre was a tiny wooded island and a small rowing boat made fast to a rickety landing stage near the inlet seemed to invite exploration. Ducks were skirting the reed beds.

'Quite a duck pond.' It was probably thirty times the size of our mill pond at home and again it struck me that scale made all the difference.

'Yeah, I come down here a lot.' He waved an

arm towards the woods on our left where a less than picturesque row of green portable toilets marked their fringe. 'The archaeologists are all in the woods with their tents. I just hope they don't set fire to the place . . . Hang on.' He stood still, listening. From up behind us in the distance came the growling sound of an engine. 'I bet that's the mini digger they use; they must be ready to start. Come on.' He walked back quickly, loath to miss any of the goings-on.

He had been right, a yellow digger – not as mini as all that – was crawling along the lawn. Any other lawn owner would have greeted the sight of its caterpillar tracks on the grass with dismay but to Stoneking it spelled entertainment. Shortly afterwards a much larger vehicle arrived at the hall. It was a cherry picker for those overhead camera angles. An unimpeded route on to the lawn would have been on the north side, only that already had the catering van and its paraphernalia established on it. No matter, Stoneking personally waved the big Iveco lorry straight through a flower bed at the south end where it left broad tyre marks. What was his gardener's name again?

Two girls in identical checked shirts and khaki shorts were now walking their geophysics equipment up and down a marked-out area, scanning the ground. It was another hour before the filming got underway and the activities on the enormous lawn took on a shape TV audiences would have recognized. Stoneking had infected me with his enthusiasm and I stayed close to listen. Enthusiasm was what the director wanted too, and she got it.

Guy Middleton and Andrea Clementi, the team leader, did a lively question and answer session about what they were expecting to find.

'So, Andrea, do you really think there could be a Roman villa under here?'

'Well, there has been a small excavation here already, done by amateur archaeologists in the late nineteenth century, and that is the conclusion they drew from their finds, which included coloured tesserae and some substantial stonework.'

'Do we still have any of those finds?' Guy asked, as he had been told to.

'Unfortunately the drawings and all those finds are lost. But just *look* at the geophysics results, Guy.' She produced the A3 printout she had held hidden under the map of the estate. The cameras zoomed in, and Guy wowed at the geophysics results as though he had never seen them before.

'That's extraordinary. Could those really be walls . . .?'

And so it went on. Most of it had been scripted or discussed before, some of it had to be repeated, and yet it all sounded fresh and quite convincing every time. Mark Stoneking himself had refused to be mentioned, nor did he allow Tarmford Hall to be named, but he was constantly there, just out of shot, as close as the TV crew allowed. A decision was made to open two trenches; Andrea herself marked out the areas with spray paint and the mechanical digger moved in. It wasn't long before the real diggers, the low-paid field archaeologists that included Adam and Julie, were beginning the task of painstakingly scraping away the centuries with their trowels. The spoil heaps that were building up on tarpaulins nearby were being swept with a metal detector for anything that might have been missed.

Lunch was called at one o'clock and predictably it was first call for the production team and celebrities. And their minders. The catering was provided by a woman called Adèle who everyone called Delia. She was the very picture of a jolly cook who enjoyed her own food a lot and was assisted by her nephew Jamie, a spotty teenage boy with bad posture and translucent ears. We took our place in the queue where I stood in line behind the director.

'There seem to suddenly be a lot more people, where did they all come from?' I asked her.

'Of course, you only met about half of us,' Emms said. 'There are so many people working behind the scenes. Mark here kindly found us what we call an incident room in the upper floor of the coach house.'

'It's really just a garage now,' Stoneking said modestly. I made a mental note to check out what the rock star had parked in it.

'All the information goes to the incident room, where we have computer operators, graphics people and so on. It's where all the finds get logged, too. If we get any,' she added, crossing her fingers.

The lunch served from the catering van turned out to be above-average canteen food and I ended up eating quite an acceptable piece of fish and a mountain of salad on the lawn, watching the real diggers at work. Once the mechanical digger had hit archaeology, no matter what the producer would have preferred, the machine had stopped and shovels and trowels had taken over.

When the *Time Lines* elite had finished their lunch and drained their wine glasses the diggers downed tools and took their turn in the lunch queue. Guy was already in discussion with Cy, Emms and Andrea again, going over schedules and scripts. I took myself off for a walk in the grounds.

The catering van was at the north end so I decided to explore that side first. The digging and most of the geophysics had concentrated on the other end so I felt sure that I was in nobody's way as I ambled down the gentle incline of the majestic lawns. A paved path of weathered York stone appeared to my right, the width of two wheelbarrows, and soon it ran along a high and dense hedge. I followed the pavement through a clump of trees. Weeds and algae had colonized the path beneath, making me wonder how long the gardener's sabbatical had been going on, when I heard a grunting noise of effort coming from just out of sight where the hedge curved sharply to the right. The grunts were cut short by a slap of feet and seconds later someone jogged right to left across my path and immediately disappeared again behind the next line of hedges that screened the lake from view. Doubtless he never noticed me. I'd not seen him before but from age and attire I had him immediately listed as a digger. A digger who was skipping lunch.

When I turned the corner to the right I saw the beginnings of an explanation. A simple but tall iron-grill gate barred my way through an opening in the hedge that ran on for another twenty yards or so to the next corner. Through the gate I could see into an enclosed area which at its centre had a long Victorian glass house. There were sheds, cold frames, water butts and several upturned wheelbarrows. Long snakes of terracotta pots of all sizes, stacked one inside the other, sheltered on the ground in the lee of the big greenhouse. Here was the working heart of the gardens, kept out of sight and, as I noted when I tried the gate, under lock and key. So my jogger had perhaps climbed out of that area and jumped down from the top of the gate. Because he was a closet gardener? Being naturally nosey, a prerequisite to detective work, I briefly considered scaling the gate but it really had been quite a generous lunch and I decided to postpone my climbing trip. There'd be more than enough time for acrobatics later.

I wandered off in the direction the climber had taken with little hope of catching up with him. The series of hedges with their staggered gateways were designed to delay walkers in three successive garden areas, each with some absurd statuary in its centre, before allowing them to arrive at the lake they had only been able to glimpse thus far. When I got to the shore of the lake I spent a few minutes sitting on a mossy slab of stone under a large fig tree, enjoying the view. The sound of the stream splashing on the far side, the sun glittering on the water and the little island in its centre all stirred Treasure Island impulses in me. I might have followed them had I not noticed that the rowing boat had disappeared from the rickety landing stage.

Back on the lawn the first excitement was simmering. Coloured tesserae, inch-sized cubes from a Roman floor mosaic, were beginning to appear in the smaller trench furthest from the house. Filming was in full swing now, with Paul, the main cameraman, following all the action, helped by his melancholic sound man, closely shadowed by Emms and watched over by Cy. A second camera was mounted on top of the now-extended cherry picker, recording from above and operated remotely from a laptop on the ground. I had never given it much thought before then but realized that all these man hours, all that equipment, all that expertise could not come cheap, even taking into account that the diggers were underpaid and some of them even volunteers from local university courses.

Being new to it all, the afternoon seemed to fly by. I made sure I was seen always to keep an eye on Guy and the people surrounding him to justify my extortionate fee. Middleton seemed to go through a considerable dip in energy levels after lunch and kept making mistakes.

'No, no, it's "at the end of the *first*, beginning of the *second* century",' Emms corrected Middleton impatiently. 'Do concentrate, Guy, we'll have to do the whole sequence again. Go back to the far end, Guy, and watch for the signal. Paul, that looked good. Let's do it again . . .' I was delighted that the director really did shout 'action!' and each time she did I had to fight the impulse to hold my breath as I felt nervous for Guy to get it right.

The day's filming and digging stopped at six-thirty. Everyone looked tired but satisfied with the day's work and I could hear mention of the Druid's Arms, the pub in nearby Tarmford. I was no longer needed, with everyone heading for bathrooms, tents or the lake and, in Guy's case, probably a bottle of whisky. Cy pointed at Guy's retreating back and called to me: 'Seven o'clock, all right?' It seemed even here I was expected to drag the man out of bed in the morning. I suspected that Cy was trying to make a point: Guy was unreliable and difficult and needed special, expensive attention.

Back home at Mill House I faced a new dilemma.

'What do you mean you can't tell me?' Annis challenged my assertion in the kitchen, a vegetable peeler suspended above the carrot she was holding.

'It's in my contract. I'm not to tell anyone.'

'Anyone out *there*,' she said, pointing at the window with her carrot. 'I'm sure they didn't mean me.' She started whittling thin strips of carrot into a salad bowl.

Of course I was dying to tell her where I'd been all day. In fact I already knew I would eventually; I just thought I'd drag it out a bit. 'I'm afraid they mean absolutely everyone. If they find out I told you that's breach of contract and they won't pay.'

'I won't tell anyone you told me. I want you to get paid. Very much so.'

I watched the carroty strips fall. 'Perhaps. I'll have to think about it.'

'Think fast, you've got five seconds,' Annis said, whittling faster.

'Oh, all right. It's a place called Tarmford Hall. It belongs to Mark Stoneking.'

'From Karmic Fire?'

'Yup.'

'Is he there?'

'Yup.'

'You met him?'

'Had lunch with him on the lawn.'

'Oh, no, I think I hate you.' She dropped the peeler on the table and walked out. I heard her stomping up the stairs. 'I can't *believe* it! He doesn't even like Karmic Fire!' Two minutes later the sound of Karmic's first album pounded through the ceiling.

It was a karmic kind of evening, with the pounding beats of both albums making conversation difficult. I promised to get the albums signed and eventually quiet returned to Mill House.

Until it was rudely interrupted at five in the morning by the phone ringing beside the bed. I knew with absolute certainty and without opening my eyes that it was too early for conversation, so I ignored it. Annis couldn't. She crawled across me and picked up. 'Hnn? . . . Really? . . . Yes . . . OK, sure.' She hung up and collapsed on top of me. 'That was Guy Middleton. He wants you there immediately. He's found a horse's head in his bed.'

Six

A horse's head? At five in the morning? Was he mad? I dialled one-four-seven-one but got the message 'Caller withheld number'. Oh, great.

Five o'clock. In the morning. I'd never get used to that, I decided, no matter how pure the smell of the air or how rosy-fingered the dawn. *Nobody* got up this early. Except perhaps farmers and nurses. I dropped an egg into boiling water. Truck drivers and postal workers. I shoved my croissant in the oven. Fishermen and bin men. I stirred the coffee in my *vriki*. Airport staff and police. And bakers, I supposed. Oh all right, it looked like most people were up by now anyway, so I might as well get over it. I built my breakfast and ate it staring out of the window, blinking once every five minutes like a lizard.

It was twenty past six by the time I pressed the buzzer on the intercom at Tarmford Hall. It seemed to take forever for the gate to be opened remotely without a word from the speaker.

I found Guy pacing up and down in the echoing hall, waiting for me. He was dressed but his hair was wild. 'You took your time; I called over an hour ago.'

'I came as soon as I could.'

'I very much doubt that. It can't take you – what,' he checked his watch, 'an hour and a half to get here and if it does then that's simply not

76

good enough.' He was still pacing and hardly looked at me.

'Calm down, Guy, I'm here now. Tell me all about it. My partner said something about a horse's head. Did she hear right?'

'Come upstairs and I'll show you.'

I followed Middleton through the passage into the downstairs gallery and up the stone staircase. It was cool at the centre of this large house, so isolated from the warm weather outside. The staircase wound gently clockwise and was only dimly lit. It landed us on the first-floor gallery, a long and broad passage, mirroring the one below. An assortment of worn rugs and carpets covered the uneven floorboards. Monstrous pieces of carved furniture stood lugubriously between dark doors. I could hear a radio play upbeat pop music behind one and I thought I could hear someone singing in the shower behind the next.

'Stoneking's bedroom suite is that one at the back there, but I'm in here.' Guy pointed at the door as though afraid to open it. It was the last room before the corridor turned sharply towards the north tower. There was no lock, just a medieval-looking grip and latch. I pressed it, released the catch and went inside. It was a good-sized room with a double bed of mahogany, a medieval-looking built-in wardrobe and an armchair by the ample fireplace. The door to the bathroom stood ajar. I checked there was no one in there before turning my attention back to the room. The velvety curtains over the mullioned window were half-drawn or half-open, depending on your temperament.

The bedclothes were pulled back and left hanging over the side and there, on the pillow closest to me, was the object that had scared Guy into calling me.

'A drawing? Just a drawing of a horse's head?' It wasn't a bad drawing at that, though quite unlovely, done in thick felt tip pens on a piece of A3 paper. One wild eye appeared to be rolling back into the head in panic and a red serrated edge at the neck indicated that the head had been severed from the body. There were blood red drops falling from its flared nostrils. 'You got me out of bed for that?'

Guy remained standing in the doorway. 'What difference does it make whether it's real or on paper? The message is the same. And the damn thing wasn't there when I went to bed last night so someone actually came into my bedroom, *while I was asleep*, and put it there.'

'True.'

Middleton came in and closed the door behind him. He spoke more quietly but with the same urgency. 'If they could do that then they could also have killed me.'

'But they didn't, Guy. Look, if they really wanted to harm you, would they bother with this kind of . . . prank? Someone's just trying to scare you. It's a wind-up.'

'Well, if they're trying to scare me then they've managed it, I don't mind admitting. This is just too close for comfort now.'

'Are we keeping this secret again?'

'Bit late for that. I'm afraid I made rather a lot of noise when I saw the thing. Emms has the

78

room next door and she came over to see what was going on.'

'What did she have to say?'

'She laughed. Had I upset any children lately, is what she said.'

'She has a point. As a threat it's a bit cut-price. But then horses' heads don't grow on trees.'

'No shit. Can you please take this seriously? The fact remains that someone came into my room in the middle of the night *and put that there.*'

'I am taking it seriously. But you're alive and that probably means they have no intention of actually killing you.'

'Perhaps they were simply not ready.'

Middleton had a point. Killing people wasn't that easy. Well, it was, but killing them and getting away with it wasn't.

'But at least it narrows it down,' he said grimly. 'It must be one of the production company. Someone who is staying in the house. And that narrows it down considerably.'

'So who is staying here? Let's make a list.'

We made one on the back of an extortionate phone bill I found in my jacket. Cy, the producer; Emms, the director; Paul, the cameraman; the sad-eyed sound man; a computer mensch; that ink-stained graphics chappy – Middleton couldn't remember all their names – were all on this floor. The rest, as far as he knew, were all camping in the woods.

Guy spent two minutes in the bathroom and emerged with his hair tamed into a ponytail but otherwise he looked exactly like a man who

hadn't got much sleep and had been badly frightened. It seemed that despite his rugged persona
and sonorous voice he was the nervous kind –
suspicious, afraid of dark rooms, jumping at
shadows. Or perhaps he had reasons to be scared
that he wasn't sharing with me.

'There'll be breakfast in the dining room now,'
Guy said as we went downstairs.

'For the chosen few?'

'Yes, but I'll see if we can squeeze you in.'

The dining room was adjacent to the large
drawing room and about two-thirds of the size,
which still left room for a table that could seat
fourteen in comfort. Stoneking sat at the head of
it, working through a full English while a
respectful two places away from him sat Emms
who was making do with scrambled egg on toast.
Along the wall opposite the French windows
stood a monstrous sideboard which held the kind of
breakfast buffet in silver dishes I had only ever
seen in period movies. Good mornings all round.

Stoneking was wide awake and in an irrepress-
ibly good mood. 'Guy, Emms just told me
someone tried to spook you with a drawing on
your pillow. Stupid prank. My apologies. None
of the rooms here lock. Some don't have locks
and those that do don't seem to have keys.'

Guy checked out the breakfast dishes on offer.
'Yes, well, I'm not amused.'

'Don't let it get to you,' Emms said. 'Remember
when they filled my wellies with toads? That's
archaeologists for you.'

Guy made no answer and I went to check out
the buffet myself. I dropped sliced bread into the

toaster, then loaded up with scrambled eggs, fried mushrooms and grilled tomatoes.

Soon the rest of the production team dribbled into the room: Paul, the cameraman who had restless eyes even in the morning; the bald-headed sound man who speared four sausages for his breakfast; Cy, already gluing his mobile to his ear, and the computer and graphics blokes who looked like they were joined at the hip and who talked to each other in clicks and murmurs. Carla came in to check all was in order and we all murmured our contentment and compliments. I sat down next to Emms and thought that, like Poirot, I had all the suspects gathered in one room when the housekeeper burst my bubble. It appeared Stoneking had entertained the crew in the drawing room last night and the French windows had been left wide open. This morning Carla had found two diggers comfortably asleep on the sofa. 'They hadn't even taken their boots off,' she complained.

'My fault,' said Mark, 'I forgot to check the doors. Plain forgot. Probably had one too many last night.'

The discussion soon turned to the shoot ahead and to the changing weather. It had clouded over during the night and today rain was a possibility. As I snaffled my free breakfast and poured myself more orange juice I wondered if I was not enjoying myself too much. Was it just that someone was determined to wind up the less-than-loveable Middleton, a man who couldn't even be bothered to remember the names of half the people he had worked with for years? Or was someone here, in this room or out there in the woods, determined to first thoroughly scare Middleton and then do him real harm? I would have to find out before anything happened to my charge that would make these questions academic.

The field archaeologists had breakfasted around the catering van and were ready and willing at eight. Soon after they had returned to the trenches there was genuine excitement. Adam in trench one, the smaller one furthest from the house, had uncovered what was without doubt a floor mosaic. *Time Lines* was in business. Lines were written for Guy and with the happy diggers in the background he revealed the discovery to camera.

'What we had hardly dared hope for this early on in the dig has just appeared at the bottom of trench one. Just look at the delicacy of that work. Andrea, am I right in saying that this is high-quality workmanship?'

The camera moved in. Water was sprayed on the small area so far revealed. The colours were pinks and blues and did look amazingly fresh after so many centuries underground.

'We seem to have come down on the edge of the mosaic,' Andrea explained. 'You can see the bands running parallel here so we'll expand the trench in that direction,' she pointed towards the house, 'as well as lengthening it to where Julie is standing.'

'It's going to be big,' Guy marvelled.

'It's going to be big,' Andrea confirmed. 'Bring in the digger.'

The mini digger was driven by Dan, one of the field archaeologists with a licence for heavy machinery. While he walked off to get the machine Paul repositioned the main camera and Cy zoomed in the camera on the cherry picker from his laptop. The digger was parked on the edge of the lawn. It seemed an age before its engine came to life and when the noise reached our ears it sounded odd. Seconds later the whole machine disappeared in an enormous cloud of thick grey smoke which didn't clear. Soon we could hear that Dan had cut the engine.

'What the hell?' Cy clapped his hand to his forehead. 'Not the digger. Not that.'

There were ironic cheers from the diggers in the trenches. Windmilling his arms Dan emerged from the smoke, coughing. He jogged towards us, several times looking over his shoulder at the now clearing smoke cloud.

'What's happening?' Cy demanded.

'No idea, I've never seen anything like it. And it doesn't sound at all happy.'

'Can you fix it?' Cy asked.

'I doubt it,' Dan admitted.

'Useless,' Guy hissed.

Dan went on the defensive. 'I'm not a mechanic, Guy. I'm a field archaeologist who happens to have a digger licence. I can do basic maintenance but I don't do repairs.'

Guy looked disgusted. 'If you had done basic maintenance this probably wouldn't have happened.'

Cy pointed. 'Guy? Shut up. Dan? Get a mechanic out here.'

Emms clapped her hands for attention. 'Right, listen up! The mini digger is out of action and we don't know how long it'll be before it's

83

repaired or we can find a replacement, so it's good old shovel power now. We can't just sit on our hands. Besides, it makes good telly.' An ironic cheer from the diggers, with trowels raised in salute.

Cy turned to Emms. 'Makes good telly for about thirty seconds and takes forever.' To Paul he said: 'Try and squeeze some excitement out of that. I don't suppose you got a shot of the smoke?'

Paul turned his back on him to reposition his camera. 'Of course I did, what do you take me for?'

Guy slouched past me towards the house. 'It's a bad omen, that. That digger never goes wrong. One-week special? It'll be a three-week special at this rate. I need more coffee or something . . .' His voice trailed off.

'Honeysett? A word.' Cy waved me aside and Emms joined us away from the trenches where Andrea was now measuring out the dimensions of the new trench.

Cy was about to open his mouth but Emms laid a calming hand on his arm and he subsided. She threw a glance towards the house where Guy was just crossing the terrace. 'I'm not sure how else to put it but I think Guy is falling apart on us.'

'Someone is trying to scare him; he's just worried,' I suggested.

'He went completely hysterical over a childish drawing! You weren't there; he was shaking all over and howling. Anyway, we need Guy to be calm and able to work. It's bad enough that half of the time he's working through a monumental hangover. But he really has gone downhill recently.'

'He has been quite impossible for the last three episodes,' Cy said, hugging a clipboard to himself.

'Yes, and he's getting quite irrational. First he said he wouldn't stay here another night, then he changed his mind and said he wouldn't feel safe anywhere else. The long and the short of it is, Guy wants you to stay at Tarmford Hall at night as long as we're filming here.'

'Would he like me to sleep on a blanket outside his door or will I be allowed to curl up at the foot of his bed?'

'I know it's an imposition. We've already spoken to Mark and he's found you a lovely room. Just be here, that's all we ask. That's all he wants. It would reassure him immensely knowing that you're around. He trusts you.'

'This is turning into a twenty-four-hour job – that's not what I signed up for.'

'Actually you have,' Cy said with too much glee for my taste. 'I sent you a copy of your contract, it's all in there.'

I knew I should have read the damn thing. 'What else is in that contract? Am I supposed to hand wash his smalls? I can't be a twenty-four-hour guard dog. I do have other things to do and was hoping to have a private life as well.'

This time it was me who was being treated to Emms' calming touch. 'But naturally you'll be able to take time off during the day for your personal affairs. Just help Guy to get through this week, make him feel safe and looked after.'

'And try and get him to take more water with it,' Cy said. 'I'm sure his drinking has got worse. Why we are lumbering the show with an ageing soak like him is beyond me. Anyway, you won't be needed for a bit while we sort out this bloody digger so perhaps now is a good time to get your jim-jams or whatever.' Cy walked off.

'I know it's quite an ask. And we had hoped it wouldn't come to this, but . . .' Emms squinted at the house and let out a long breath. 'Guy has always been one of those actors who subscribe to every silly superstition going and he brings his own bag of problems too. He sleeps with a nightlight on, you know. Scared of the dark. Scared of this, scared of that. He's always been a gloomy sod but recently he's become, I don't know, a bit paranoid, if you ask me. You can see it in the way he looks at people. Do try and perk him up a bit. He trusts you because you're not one of us.'

Did I have a choice? Apparently not. Annis had it right from the outset – I was a babysitter to the star of *Time Lines*, a star that from this angle looked like it might be on the wane. Off I went in search of Stoneking who according to Emms had 'found a room' for me. Nice to have a few lying about in case of emergency.

The drawing room was deserted, so was the dining room. I hesitated in the lower gallery, for a moment wondering where to try next, when I saw a movement in the corner of my eye. There at the shadowy north end of the gallery stood an old woman, motionless. Looking straight at me. Her white hair was held in a French plait and she was dressed in black. She was holding a broom, not the witchy kind but an ordinary one with a green plastic handle. I was about to walk towards her when I heard footsteps coming down the stair behind me. It was Carla, carrying a bulging laundry bag. When I looked back down the gallery the old lady had gone.

Naturally.

'Carla, I'm going to stay here too from tonight. I'm told there's a room for me somewhere?'

'Mark told me, I've just got it ready for you. Do you want me to show you?' She dumped the linen bag at the bottom of the stair and led the way up to the height of the upper gallery where she opened an unobtrusive door in the wood panelling. It revealed another, much narrower and ill-lit staircase with much-worn wooden treads. 'It's a bit of a climb, I'm afraid.'

'Servants' quarters?' I was beginning to feel just a tiny bit miffed. 'They must have been quite fit in those days.'

Carla briefly paused on the stairs so she could give me a well-timed look for emphasis. 'They still are.'

'I saw an old lady with a broom earlier; don't tell me she climbs these stairs.'

'No, I'm the only madwoman in the attic.'

'So who was it I saw earlier?'

'Old woman? No idea, you must have imagined it.'

'I quite clearly saw—'

Carla snorted with pleasure. 'I'm only kidding. That was Mrs Cunningham. Olive to her very few friends.'

'Not a ghost, then, I *am* relieved.'

'Not Olive. Quite solid, in fact. But the place is definitely haunted. You'll find out if you stay here. The Cunninghams owned the Hall until she was forced to sell it. But she retains the right to live out her life in the granny flat in the north wing, right next to the pool.'

Pool. Of course there was. There would be a helicopter pad somewhere. 'She was staring at me.'

We reached a narrow corridor, largely unadorned and flimsily carpeted with a narrow worn runner. 'She does that a lot. Thinking. Remembering, probably. I'm not sure she sees what we see. You probably won't see much of her, though. She made it quite clear she disapproved of the TV circus, as she described you.'

'I'm not actually part of the circus.'

'Really? That's good. I'm not really a servant, either. Here we are.' She opened the second door along. 'I put you in here. I hope you'll be comfortable; it's quite a nice room, no *en suite* though. Bathroom's at the end of the corridor and naturally you're welcome to use the pool, where there are showers too.'

'Thanks. No, I'm not TV; I'm just here to look after Mr Middleton while he's in Bath.'

'Rather you than me, I think.'

'And you're here to look after Mark Stoneking. What's that like?'

'Delightful,' she said. It sounded almost as though she meant it. 'If you need anything, give me a shout. Though, please, not literally.'

She left me to get acquainted with my new

home. It was a cosy attic room where a queen-size bed left just enough space for a narrow wardrobe and a small writing desk and chair by the little window. There was a tiny fireplace with a grate wide enough for three lumps of coal. From the window I could see the lake, the woodland and the glasshouse roof but had only a partial view of the lawn. Now all I had to do was go and get my jim-jams, as Cy put it.

As I drove out of the front gate, which closed behind me with a gothic groan, I reflected that with twice my usual rates, pool, a baronial breakfast each morning and upmarket TV catering for the rest of the day, staying at Tarmford Hall really was no hardship; though naturally I would have to make sure it sounded like that to Annis.

On the way there I drove through Combe Down and snuck up on Mike Dealey's place. I was just in time to see him park his red Honda in front of his garage. It was my first good look at my prey. He still had the walrus moustache from the picture but had probably put on some weight since then. He was wearing baggy blue jeans and trainers and a faded black tee-shirt. The driver seat swivelled sideways. Out came the wheelchair from where it had been stashed behind the seat. Dealey opened it up and with no doubt well-practised movements swung himself into the seat. It looked like an uncomfortable manoeuvre and I thought I saw him wince. I called Haarbottle at his office. 'I'm still patiently staking out Dealey's place,' I told him, as though I'd been doing nothing else all week.

'Any luck?'

Dealey pulled a Co-op carrier from inside the car. 'Not so far; he hasn't slipped up once. But don't worry, I'm sticking to him like glue.'

'I'm glad you're on the case and keeping in touch. Naturally, as a company, we have to justify the expense of a private investigator and weigh this up against the very real—'

'Oh, there's movement,' I lied, 'got to go.' I watched Dealey lock his car, propel himself to the house, up the ramp and into the house. The blinds were down and there was nothing more to see. I drove home. Dealey would keep. Naturally I would look stupid if the next time I checked he had moved to Brazil, so I'd swing by from time to time just to make sure. But my priority today was telling Annis in no uncertain terms just how much I hated having to stay at Mark Stoneking's mansion all week, eating free food and rubbing shoulders with the stars.

I found her in the studio by following the noise. Annis was staring at a blank canvas on her easel, loaded brush in hand. The paint looked suspiciously like the *caput mortum* I had left unused on my palette. On the floor our little ghetto blaster – designed for the smaller ghetto – strained to do justice to Karmic Fire's megalomanical soundscapes.

'I downloaded the rest of their albums!' she shouted.

Oh, *great*. 'Great!' I shouted back.

'Horse's head all cleaned up?'

'It was just a drawing!' I bellowed.

'What?' She relented and turned down the din.

'It was just a drawing but it shook him

nevertheless. Mainly because it meant someone had been in his room while he was asleep. Now he wants round-the-clock protection.'

'Will he get it?'

'You're looking at it.'

'Kidding!'

'I'm afraid not. They want me to stay the nights there. I said no but apparently it's in my contract that I'm obliged to if it's deemed necessary. And they're busy deeming. They found me a dingy little attic room to sleep in.'

'Bum. Does that mean I won't see you all week?'

'No, I'll get time off for good behaviour. Right now they're trying to fix the digger which broke earlier so I've come to pack a few things. I'll leave you to your first stroke.'

'Sod that,' she said and dropped the brush on to her palette. 'I've been staring at it for an hour and nothing's happening. Maybe this canvas is too small.'

'Erm . . .' As I looked at the six-by-eight foot canvas my face must have betrayed a flicker of doubt.

'Yeah, I know, but I feel I want to spread my wings.' She stepped outside into the sun and windmilled her arms to demonstrate. 'I want to break out of the confines of the canvas and *soar*.' She illustrated her feelings by running down the meadow, arms spread wide. 'And I need more coffee!' she shouted.

Leaning in the bedroom door frame with a fresh mug of Blue Mountain in her hand she talked about the importance of scale in relation to

91

movement in her paintings while she watched me throw what I considered a few essentials into my holdall: trousers, shirts, tee-shirts, socks, underwear, sweater, painkillers, toothpaste, electric toothbrush, charger for electric toothbrush, mobile phone charger, clockwork radio and last – because I had hoped Annis might take her eyes off the bag for a moment only she didn't – but not least: my swimming shorts.

Annis spluttered into her coffee. 'Swimming shorts? Oh, right, you poor downtrodden over-worked and put-upon shamus! Of course, there's a pool, isn't there? You managed to wangle a week at a luxury manor, waited on hand and foot, free gourmet nosh and hanging out by the pool all day. Leaving me in this bleak hovel with a blank canvas and a cupboard full of pinto beans! With nothing but sheep for company. *Typical!*'

Bleak hovel? Since when? 'It's not quite like that. And I'll be popping round here whenever I can.'

'Forget the popping. I want you to get me invited to Stoneking's manor. I'm part of Aqua Investigations too, you know? And I bought a new cozzie in Corfu that needs airing.'

I took the mug out of her hand, put it on a shelf and pulled her into my arms. 'Yes, I remember it well, what there was of it. I'll do what I can to get you into the Stone King's castle and make you part of the quest. In the meantime, would you like to say goodbye properly? Let me get this bag off the bed.'

Seven

More cars and vans had arrived at Tarmford Hall. A lot more. The generous half-moon of gravel was covered with vehicles and like several people before me I had to park on the grass, far enough from the entrance to the house to make lugging my few essentials a bit of a chore. Not to mention the endless flights of stairs up to my eyrie in the loft.

It was warm in my little room and as I opened the window unfamiliar sounds drifted up from the unseen lawns below. There was clanging and hammering and shouting, more than I imagined the repair of a single digger should warrant. I simply dumped my bag and made my way downstairs.

Time Lines was a much larger outfit than I had ever imagined. There was a constant coming and going between the car park, the excavation site and the so-called incident room above the coach house. Only when I stepped on to the verandah did it become clear what had swelled the numbers in the car park – the Romans were here.

On the terrace, as expected, the cream of *Time Lines* were tucking into their lunch. Less expected were the newcomers. To my far right, on the northwest corner of the lawns, near the stand of ancient chestnuts, camped a Roman army.

'A legionnaires camp.' Stoneking beamed up

at me. 'Cohort Italica, re-enactors from Bristol, complete with tents, giant catapults and what-not. Dozens of them, by the looks of it.'

Emms hunted a tiny tomato round her plate with a fork. 'We've used them before, for the cameos, they're quite authentic.'

Middleton, at the next table, grumbled at his lamb chops. 'I hope their tents are rainproof or they'll get authentically soaked. It looks like rain.'

'They know their stuff but they're extremely boring people to meet,' Cy informed us. 'During the week they're plumbers and post office counter staff, yearning to be ancient Romans. They spend all their spare time talking in cod Latin and polishing their *pilums*. But they look good on camera, I give them that.'

Emms cornered her tomato and stabbed it. 'All re-enactors are the same, they just like playing soldiers, as though that's all there was to history.'

Andrea seemed to speak to no one in particular. 'No one seems to re-enact hard-working normal people. Trades people, farmers, domestics. It would be much better to show some of that part of Roman life.'

'That's visually undynamic. It's not what our audience wants,' Cy began.

'It's not what your teenage mind *imagines* the audience wants,' Middleton sniped.

'The audiences you're thinking of have long died of old age or boredom,' Cy countered.

As they began a fresh argument I was urgently drawn away by the gravitational pull exerted by the catering van where I joined the queuing diggers. The Roman legion had brought their own food and were cooking it on a couple of small camp fires amongst their tents. Delia the caterer noticed my late arrival. 'You've joined the lower ranks then?' She dropped a couple of thick lamb chops on to my plate. 'A shrewd move: bigger portions for the real workers.'

'Especially now that we're digging the whole thing by hand.' Adam was balancing a veritable mountain of chips and salad around the corner of the van. I followed his example and joined him and his mate Julie on the grass. At the other end of the lawn stood the injured yellow beast with its engine cover up and a mechanic with his head in its innards.

'The digger is still out of action, then?' I asked.

Julie smiled broadly. 'Long may it last.' She pointed her fork at Adam's pyre of chips. 'Is that all you're having? Chips and salad?'

'Nah, there's three chops under there somewhere.'

'Do you mean you *like* digging everything by hand?' I asked.

'Oh, absolutely. That's proper archaeology. We're only using the digger to get to what interests the TV people. Andrea, you know, the chief archaeologist, she's always argued against the digger but telly is telly; they won't stand around and wait for us to do it properly. Even now we're just hurrying through the layers as though only Roman finds mattered.'

'If they want to film Roman, Roman is what they find,' Adam said knowingly. I could have sworn his goatee had just become goatier.

'You don't mean they're cheating?'

Adam shrugged and stuffed enough chips in his mouth to excuse him from answering. I looked at Julie.

'Don't look at me,' she said. She checked that no one was within earshot, then spoke quietly. 'I'm not saying they're *faking* it. It's just that we do seem to find amazing stuff on this programme. Not like the poor chaps on Channel Four, sometimes they have no luck at all, which is only to be expected. But *Time Lines* is always very lucky. So very, *very* lucky.'

A few playful trumpet blasts came from the direction of the legionnaires' camp.

'I hope they don't do that all day,' Julie said. 'Archaeology is quite peaceful most of the time. I mean where the noise levels are concerned, of course. That lot just never grew up.'

'I hope they'll all get legionnaires' disease or something,' said the cheerful Adam.

'What exactly is legionnaires' disease?' Julie asked.

'No idea. But if they want to play at being legionnaires then it's only fair they should get some. For authenticity if nothing else.'

When I rejoined the TV crew their argument seemed to have been concluded, or perhaps just adjourned. Guy was nowhere to be seen. Clouds were threatening rain and the air was still and humid. Emms and Cy were standing on the terrace with a Roman centurion called Brian who stood in the heat wearing a full legionnaire's outfit, shiny helmet, armour, sword and dagger. Cy was frowning at the sky. 'I wish we could film this stuff somewhere

where they have dry seasons,' he complained. 'Or decent summers.'

'Try Hollywood,' Emms said drily. 'It would suit you. You could mock it all up in the studio.'

Cy ignored her. 'Right, let's try and get some Roman shots in the can while the archaeologists are dithering.'

Brian the centurion pointed behind us. 'At last, the Britons have arrived, late as usual.' Brian's accent was pure Somerset. Just then a group of a dozen or so noisy and lightly equipped ancient Britons swaggered hairily on to the lawn, shaking round shields and hurling insults and derision towards the orderly camp of Cohort Italica.

'You bring your own Britons to conquer, then?' I asked Brian.

'Oh yes,' he explained earnestly. 'At first the members of the Cohort took turns to be Britons but in the end no one wanted to do it, it's not what we joined the Cohort for. But this hopeless rabble love it. Looks like they stopped off at the pub again, too.'

It was true that a definite whiff of cider had arrived along with the wild-haired, bearded natives. 'And naturally you defeat them every time?'

'Well . . . we let them win sometimes so they don't lose interest but history is on our side, as I'm sure you know.'

'I remember it from school.' I also remembered Boudicca putting up quite a good fight for a bit.

One of the hairy Britons detached himself from the rabble and came swaggering towards us, grinning broadly. Emms, I noticed, smiled in anticipation while both Cy and Brian the

97

centurion viewed his approach with a look of distaste. Like the rest of his gang the approaching ancient Briton was dressed in an assortment of colours, some striped, some checked, with wild hair and a beard to match. He had a sword at his belt and carried a round shield with a much-dented central boss. He brayed at Brian. 'Ha, if it isn't Gluteus Maximus, in the flesh. Prepare to have your arse whipped, Roman dog.'

'Hello Morgan, less of that,' said Emms with mock sternness. 'You're late. And possibly drunk. But you look very convincing. Good of you to come.' She turned to Brian, who seemed uncomfortable in his Roman skin. 'Let's have a wander over there and thrash out the details of what we would like you to do for us.'

With Brian the Roman on the left and Morgan the Briton on the right Emms walked up to the north end of the lawn where Paul had already set up his camera. Brian walked with ramrod dignity while Morgan did seem to sway just a little. To me, Brian and his cohort looked like people dressed up as Romans; their helmets were too shiny, their swords too bright, their tents too clean. By comparison Morgan's noisy band of warriors looked terrifyingly real. Many had painted blue stripes of woad on their faces. Their clothes looked worn and in need of a wash and their weaponry seasoned in battle.

Next to me Cy shook his head disapprovingly. 'Bloody piss artist. No wonder he and Guy hit it off so well last time we had the re-enactors round. Guy is public school and RADA and Morgan is a council-estate motorbike nut but they found instant common ground over a bottle of Scotch. Keep an eye on Guy today; they're bound to booze all night, those two.'

'Seriously? The fastidious Middleton and the hairy Briton?'

Cy walked off to join them. 'I know. But they're soul mates underneath. They're both bloody barbarians.'

There seemed to be no better place to be right now than the verandah so I stayed where I was. Stoneking had the same idea. He appeared from inside, carrying two deckchairs. 'Here, grab one of those and we'll watch the battle in comfort.' We set them up at the end of the terrace, closest to the impending action. 'Looks like we're the only two people here who are not working.'

'Speak for yourself. I'm busy keeping an eye on Guy Middleton.'

'Yes, I wondered about that. What are you, his PA or something? I used to have a PA but found what I really needed was a housekeeper.'

'No, I'm just his minder, and only while he's in Bath.'

'And why does he need minding?'

'You know what it's like, being famous. I just make sure everything runs smoothly for him, keep the nutters off him, see he comes to no harm.'

'Ha! You may have your work cut out. Right now he's surrounded by heavily armed nutters.'

Stoneking had a point. Guy was doing a piece to camera with the Romans and Britons squaring up to each other behind him. 'I'm not required to stop bullets for him. Or spears, in this case.' I briefly wondered if I still got paid if anything

99

did happen to Middleton. Not that I was the least bit mercenary about it. One day I'd really have to read that contract. Guy had now finished his PTC and walked towards us.

'Looks like it's about to start,' Stoneking said. 'This should be quite a good scrap. I've seen them do something like this before. On telly, of course, a couple of series back. I hope it won't get rained off. Look at those clouds.'

Since early morning dirty rainclouds had begun to crowd the sky, becoming darker and more threatening by the hour. Down here not a breath stirred and the atmosphere was getting sweaty. 'Presumably the real Romans didn't stop for a bit of rain. And it might lend a bit of authenticity to the re-enactment.'

Guy had heard me. 'Quite, I agree,' he said, turning round to look at the battle ground. 'Those bloody Romans could do with a bit of mud between their toes; they're all too squeaky clean. It's all that Roman efficiency and precision crap that attracted them to it in the first place, you know. They need to get their hands dirty if they want to be convincing. It's what I told Brian, too: you're a bunch of anal twits and need to loosen up, but he wouldn't listen. I bet they all iron their bloody underpants before they come out. But those Britons, they're as real as it gets. Half of them are hairy bikers like Morgan. And they really know how to throw a party, too. Ah, here goes. Any more armchairs around?'

Stoneking unclipped his mobile from his belt and started texting. 'I'll get Carla to bring one out for you.'

A battlefield had been staked out and the Britons and Romans had a last discussion about the scenes with Emms and Paul, the cameraman. The bald soundman, obviously a pessimist, was already protecting his recorder with clear plastic against the possibility of rain. The discussion seemed to get quite involved, with lots of arm waving and pointing. We heard Morgan's braying laugh. Then Brian pushed Morgan. Morgan staggered briefly backwards, then charged forward, head lowered, and smacked Brian with his shield. Brian sat down heavily on his behind to a burst of laughter from the crowd of Britons who were standing in a huddle at the edge of the field of battle. I saw a plastic flagon of cider being furtively passed around. There was a brief, angry exchange as Cy helped Brian up but we were too far away to hear what was being said. Emms was making calming gestures. Eventually the commanders withdrew to their respective sides.

'This should be good,' said Guy. 'Those two really do hate each other; they're like cat and dog. Ah, thanks, Carla.' The housekeeper had arrived with a deckchair and set it up for him. 'Here we go, it's started.'

Carla remained to watch. She positioned herself behind Stoneking, her hands resting lightly on the top of his deckchair. She seemed more interested in studying the rock star's hair than watching the impending battle. At the Roman end of the battle-field military commands were shouted in Latin, with a definite West Country lilt. They were answered by an incoherent bellow from the rabble of Britons. The Romans advanced towards them in a tight line, shields touching, helmeted faces peering above them, like a row of riot police at a violent demonstration. This kind of formation would have allowed the real Romans to advance despite a hail of stones, arrows and other missiles raining down on them. Only our Cohort Italica (Bristol Division) had been too busy shuffling into position and shouting commands to notice that half a dozen Britons had separated from the rabble and stolen into their rear. When the shout to draw swords – *gladium stringe!* – was followed by the command to commence the attack, the legionnaires were concentrating on their front while six Britons fell on them from behind and kicked them in the back of the knees. At the same time the rest of Morgan's rabble charged into the Roman front line. Brian's battle plan fell apart. Now it was every man for himself. Cy monitored the static camera on the side lines, Paul got in close with a handheld camera. The bald sound recordist looked uncharacteristically happy between his headphones. The noise was impressive. There was much shouting, some of it in cod Latin, most of it pure Somerset. Steel clashed brightly with steel, thumped on wooden shields, shield bosses crashed into armour. Several warriors went down. Then, without warning, the character of the fight began to change. A kick in the shins here, a few bright drops from a bloody nose there. Mock sword fights were abandoned and shields used like battering rams. Fists swung and connected. Combatants, locked in hand-to-hand struggles, fell and rolled wrestling on the ground. Brian was sitting on the grass, looking dazed under a dented helmet. All around him noses were being butted and beards pulled. In the middle of it all I spotted something unexpected. The old lady I had seen inside the house the day before had appeared on the battlefield without anyone having noticed her approach. In a black high-neck dress Olive Cunningham was walking straight through the melee, swinging her walking stick across a Roman behind here, toppling over a pair of wrestlers there. She smote a Briton from behind who wheeled around to answer the blow. Confronted with the white-haired geriatric he made the mistake of hesitating and was rewarded with a firm poke in the solar plexus. The old lady carried on straight towards us.

Emms tried to guide her cameraman backwards to safety while he kept filming but herself stumbled over a defeated Briton trying to crawl off the battlefield. Both ended up on the ground. A flagon of cider was thrown and bounced off a Roman helmet. Cy was vainly shouting at everyone to stop, just *stop*.

Stoneking was on his feet. 'It's turned into Asterix in Britain!'

'They definitely stopped acting,' Guy said. 'What's the old lady up to?'

'She'll tell you in a moment,' said Carla, 'I've no doubt.'

Another two minutes and it was all over. The Romans withdrew from the battlefield, carrying one of their number but leaving much gear of war behind. The Britons appeared victorious, though none of them looked exactly unscathed. Several were limping and one of them was crawling on all fours. Morgan called to him: 'Can't you walk, Terry?'

The crawler didn't look up. 'I've lost a bloody contact lens!'

At the excavation trenches all pretence of work had stopped the moment the fight started and now cricket applause drifted across the lawns. Cy stared furiously at the old lady who had walked straight through his scene. For a moment he looked as though he thought of confronting her, then chose a simpler target. He stomped after the Britons who had obviously started the brawl. Paul was examining his camera for damage and Emms sat on the grass crying with laughter.

The old lady reached the terrace without further incident. I got up from my deckchair and so did Guy, out of politeness as much as in recognition that the woman was furious and knew how to use a stick to make her point. Stoneking, who had been standing, sat down. 'Can't you see you ruined the take, woman? Did you have to totter straight through there? What do you want?'

Olive Cunningham was a tall woman but I doubted she had ever been beautiful. Noticeable, impressive, perhaps she had been called 'attractive' in her day. When exactly that day had been was hard to tell. I guessed she was at least eighty but her voice was as firm as her stick-swinging arm. 'I am perfectly in my right to walk where I want, *Mr* Stoneking. But I am not at all sure you have the right to turn Tarmford Hall into an amusement park. I appeal – I was going to say to your better nature but you do not appear to have one – I appeal to you to send these people home and stop this, this . . .' Her no doubt well-prepared speech faltered under the pressure of real emotion. 'They are desecrating the place. Those dearest to me are *buried* in these grounds and the dead deserve respect. And peace. And what do they get? People digging holes everywhere, a campsite, drunken brawls. If Sam was here it would break his heart. He may be a villain but he understands the Hall. Tarmford Hall is more than just a pile of stones, Mr Stoneking. It is a living thing and you have been torturing it from the moment you took possession of it.'

Stoneking made an impatient gesture. 'Look, we have had this talk, Mrs Cunningham, and there is no point going over it again. It'll all be over in a week and peace, as you choose to call it, will return to the place, all right? In the meantime go away, turn on the radio and do some knitting. Come out again next Sunday – you won't even know they've been here.'

Carla's hand reached towards Stoneking's shoulder but she withdrew it when he stopped talking. There was a heartbeat's pause before the old lady said: 'Oh, I'll know they've been here. We'll all know it. And we won't forget it.' She straightened up and walked off towards the house.

'I'd best get back to the kitchen and organize tonight's VIP dinner,' said Carla. She quickly followed the old lady inside.

Stoneking impatiently crossed his legs and brushed imaginary fluff from his jeans. 'Stupid old bat.'

'Not too keen on us then, the old lady,' Guy said.

'You can say that again. She's been on at me about it ever since I made the mistake of mentioning this thing to her. She even threatened me with lawyers. All piffle of course. Living in the granny flat doesn't give her any rights. She has the right to totter about the grounds and through the house if she has to, but that's about it. She can be a real nuisance. She always pops up where you least expect her. If you want to keep her out of a place you'll have to padlock it.'

'She must be quite old, though,' Guy mused.

'She should be seventy-nine or eighty now.'

'You don't exchange birthday cards then?' I asked.

'No, and I'm beginning to suspect she lied to me about her age. I mean who can tell with old people? She could be seventy-five. And live till she's ninety-five. Hell, twenty years with her ghosting about! I don't think I have twenty years left in me. In fact I'm sure I haven't. My God, she could outlive me, what a thought!'

A rumble of thunder reverberated through the grounds, reflected back at us by the bulk of the house. The hall loomed behind us now against a sky the colour of wet slate. A certainty of heavy rain was in the air and everyone hurried in preparation for it. The archaeologists covered the enlarged trench with a movable khaki tent they had prepared for this moment, and everyone not involved in that made their way towards the house or the campsite in the woods, depending on their status. Delia shuttered the catering van. The Romans had already withdrawn into their camp but the Britons were still struggling to pitch their simple tents at the edge of the lawns, as far from the Romans as possible. The TV crew packed up and Cy came over, carrying laptop, scripts and a fistful of cables. 'That was a total disaster; I doubt we can use any of it. We'll have to re-shoot the thing. That bunch of pissheads were completely out of order.'

'You hired them,' Guy said quietly.

Cy ignored him and turned to Stoneking. 'And that old woman ruined what was left of the shots. Who is she? Sorry, she's not your mother, is she?'

'The madwoman in the attic,' Guy offered.

Stoneking launched into an impatient explanation as the first drops fell. We got out of our armchairs a little too nonchalantly because a few seconds later the heavens opened with a crack of thunder and by the time we had sprinted across the verandah and through the French windows our clothes were soaked. Raindrops hammered on to the terrace and bounced up again eight inches into the air. The storm was getting nearer, lightning and thunder following each other ever more closely.

'Reminds me of the monsoon in Sri Lanka,' Stoneking said.

Emms was the last of the privileged few to make it to the house. 'I'm soaked to the skin,' she said. 'I'll have to go and change.' She splished across the carpets, her red hair clinging close around her head.

'I hope those Roman tents are waterproof,' Cy said.

'I hope they'll get a mudslide,' was Guy's contribution.

I stood by the window and watched the rain.

I liked watching heavy rain. I liked listening to it thrumming the ground and washing the windows, as long as I was dry and cosy inside. But not everyone, I saw, minded being out in the rain. At the furthest edge of the lawn, barely visible through the curtain of raindrops, a hooded figure walked quickly in the direction of the hedge that screened the greenhouse, then disappeared from view among the trees.

Eight

'I've no idea what half of them are. I'm not a great reader, I'd be the first to admit.' Mark Stoneking gestured at the floor-to-ceiling shelves full of books of all sizes. Many of them were leather bound and the whole collection looked as though it had been amassed over the last 150 years. There were gaps on several shelves, some of them quite large.

Guy ran a dust-testing finger through one of the gaps. 'Have you been flogging off the valuable ones?'

Stoneking frowned. 'Things aren't quite that desperate yet, Guy. The books belonged to the Cunninghams and came with the house, just like most of the furniture, the gloomy paintings and all the junk. If you see something weird, or utterly useless, then it came with the house. In fact, if it's older than 1960, then it came with the house. But Olive took all the books she wanted first, as we had agreed. Actually I think she still comes in here and takes books – not that I care; I've not seen a single one I'd want to read.'

Tea was being served to us VIPs in the library while the rain drummed against the windows and the thunder rumbled on. I had the decency to spare a thought for the poor of the parish who were sheltering under canvas, though not a long one. Such is the anaesthetizing effect of luxury on the conscience. It was dark enough for the lights to be turned on in the large but gloomy room. The library was comfortably furnished, with several armchairs and side tables. The place looked like it had been kitted out by the props department of a 1950s B-movie company, with a selection of Indian religious statuary, faded photographs of the Raj and glass cases full of dried scorpions, skewered butterflies, giant bugs and birds' eggs. There was a stuffed baby alligator on the mantelpiece, a muzzle-loading rifle on the wall above it and beside the fireplace several swords in an elephant's foot. The books on the walls were mainly nineteenth-century tomes on obscure subjects with titles like *The History of Magic, Islands of the Occult* and *On Sledge and Horseback to Outcast Siberian Lepers*.

'A place like this house should really have a ghost,' Andrea said, examining the specimen on show with a fascinated disgust.

'Oh, but it has,' said Carla, who was serving tea and coffee. 'And it's right over there in that glass case.' She nodded at a mahogany display case between the windows.

'What ever can you mean?' said Emms, pulling

a sceptical face, but both women rose to inspect the case, and so did I.

'I don't see any ghost,' Andrea said.

Carla joined us at the case. 'It was before the First World War. A ghost started appearing in people's bedrooms at night and haunting the corridors. Usually accompanied by an eerie green glow. It was the ghost of a young woman. Eventually the Cunningham family brought in a priest to exorcize the spirit. The exorcist captured the ghost and imprisoned it in that little glass phial there.'

'Tosh and nonsense,' Emms said.

'Quite hard on the poor ghost,' I added.

'That depends,' said Andrea. 'What's the liquid in the bottle?'

'It's holy water,' Carla said.

'Let me see that.' Guy pushed between the women and stared down at the little glass phial which was stoppered and heavily sealed with red sealing wax. It was resting on a prayer book in the centre of the collection of other curios like ivory-handled knives, pocket watches, dried beetles and small animal skulls.

'Don't tell me, Guy,' said Andrea. 'You're scared of ghosts as well.'

Guy's nose twitched. He turned to Carla. 'It's just a bit of nonsense, right?'

Carla shrugged. 'One person's nonsense is another person's family legend,' she said, throwing a look across the room where Stoneking was sitting unmoved. Then she went back to serving afternoon tea.

Guy's face looked ashen in the grey light that

110

struggled through the windows as he returned to his chair. Cy, Paul the cameraman and the bald-headed soundman, whose name I still didn't know, were talking shop again with serious faces while Andrea the head archaeologist and Emms the director started playing 'thunderstorms I have seen'. I was sitting near the fireplace with Stoneking while Guy sat apart from all of us in a narrow armchair by the window, looking peeved. All of us, whether peeved, talking shop or swapping Tuscan thunderstorm stories, found time to stuff ourselves with strawberry tart or sticky chocolate cake or, as in my case, both.

Despite the talking and cake munching I detected an odd tension in the room, as though we were all half listening out to something other than our conversations. The sky darkened even further and then all at once we stopped talking, as though by a pre-arranged signal. Everyone looked up. It went very quiet in the room, the only sound the swishing of the rain. The hairs on my arm were rising up as though pulled by a magnet and beside me Mark raised a hairy hand to show me the same phenomenon. The lights winked out, thunder crashed, the windows rattled and the ground seemed to shake. Guy let out a short scream and knocked over his coffee cup. A few seconds later we could hear another, more earthly crash outside.

Stoneking had jumped up. 'That was a lightning strike. It must have struck the house. I'll go and check if there's any damage.'

'Sounded like there was,' I said and made to follow him, but Guy was by my side and grabbed

111

my arm to hold me back. With the lights gone, the shadows of dusk had risen in the room even though it was not yet five in the afternoon. But there was enough light to see he was frightened. 'Come with us,' I told him.

He did. Armed with umbrellas from a stand in the hall we left by the front door. We followed Stoneking, who marched around the building, stopping from time to time to peer up into the rain and thunder, looking for damage in the roof. On the north side, just beyond the swimming pool extension, we found it in the original roof. On the ground lay some crumbled sandstone masonry and a raft of ceramic roof tiles, all broken. Stoneking cursed fluently and inventively as he kicked at the debris. He pointed up into the gloom. 'It hit one of the lightning conductors near those chimneys and knocked a few thousand quid's worth of tiles off the roof.'

'But at least we're not on fire,' I offered.

He gave me a disgusted look. 'Glass half bloody full, is it?'

The lights came back on, both inside the house and in the loft of the coach house where the incident room was. 'Lights are back,' Guy said with relief. 'I'm going back inside; I'm getting soaked even under my brollie.'

'Don't blame you,' said Stoneking. Wind gusted around us, making all of us fight with our umbrellas. Stoneking closed his and swore some more. 'Bloody useless things.'

Just as mine was threatening to turn inside out in a fresh gust of wind, a fast-moving shadow in the corner of my eye made me squint up towards the roof. A dark shape was hurtling towards the ground. I shouted a warning: 'Guy, watch out!'

Guy wheeled around towards me but it was too late: a huge decorative stone urn crashed at his feet, making him stagger and fall on his back. We rushed towards him, squinting up to see if any more of Tarmford Hall was on its way down, and helped him up.

Stoneking swore incoherently.

'That was bloody close!' I said unnecessarily.

Guy looked dazed. 'Tell me about it! It knocked the umbrella out of my hand, *that's* how close it was. Bloody hell, look at my clothes!' Like all three of us he was wet but as an added bonus Guy was covered in dirt and sandstone grains from the exploded urn. 'I couldn't be muddier if I was staying in a tent with the damned diggers.' He was shaking with shock or with rage or both.

Back inside we splished across the hall, leaving damp prints on expensive rugs. The door to the library was open, the room empty apart from Carla who was collecting cups and plates. 'They all went to watch the lightning after you went out,' she explained.

On our way upstairs to change into dry clothes Guy never stopped bitching. 'Things aren't right, Chris, things aren't bloody right. I could have been killed out there. Why the hell did you not stay inside with me as I asked? Why did I listen to you? You're working for me, remember? Next time I ask you to stick with me you stick with me, clear? It's what you get paid for. I don't know. This has got to be one of the worst digs we've filmed for a long time. If not ever.' He stomped up the stairs ahead of me. 'I'm seriously thinking of moving back to a hotel . . . problem is . . . I'd have to . . . pay for it myself this time . . . and drive here every . . . sodding morning.' Eventually he ran out of puff near the top of the stairs and shut up to catch his breath. I peeled off through the narrow door and climbed the servants' staircase. 'Top floor, feather dusters and maids' outfits,' I announced when I got there. The corridor was empty. I caught my breath by the middle window, which offered me an angled view of that part of the roof from where the urn had been dislodged. Gargoyles, decorative urns and other stone-carved nonsense sat at equal intervals along the parapet so it was quite easy to spot the gap where the one that nearly did for Guy had sat. How unlucky to be right under it when the thing decided to return to earth. I looked down to where I was standing. At my feet a strip of the threadbare carpet was wet. I tested the window – it opened easily and more rain landed on the carpet. For a moment I stood as though transfixed while the rain sprayed in. Someone had recently opened this window. And then closed it again. I took a deep breath. This was where Honeysett was going to earn his money. I climbed through the window on to the sloping rain-slickened pantiles. Did I mention I don't like heights? And that I like watching rain from inside?

The incline was gentle enough here for me to keep upright, at least in theory, but the tiles were so slippery with algae and rain that soon I was slithering towards the parapet and clawing at them with my fingernails. Fortunately the proportions of the roof were as generous as the rest of the house. When eventually I landed at the lead guttering and sank ankle deep into the rainwater flowing through it I found it was three feet wide and fairly level. Up here the wind tore at me from several directions at once. Lightning danced and thunder crashed above me. Not ten minutes ago lightning had struck this very roof – what had I been thinking? I was wet to the skin and my shoes had filled with tepid rainwater. The sky looked green with menace. I tried not to look up and definitely not down. The tall trees all around moved so violently in the wind that the horizon appeared to be shifting. From where I had landed I could see where the urn had disappeared. I could just make out the rusty smudge that had once been the iron rod that had secured it to the crumbling sandstone. I held on to the parapet and moved cautiously forward, sloshing against the current of rainwater in the gully. I passed a sinister terracotta eagle with part of its beak missing and a moronic looking apelike figure carved in stone. I grabbed hold of its coconut-shaped head to steady myself. As I did I could feel it move a fraction of an inch. When I got to the place where the urn had stood I wished fervently that I hadn't bothered. There was nothing to see apart from its absence. I ran a wet hand over the rusted remains of the iron rod. I thought I could feel a sharp edge but there were no telltale signs of sawing or levering, just a single scratch where the heavy urn had tilted over the edge. I made myself look down, bending as far over the top of the two-foot wide sandstone parapet as I could without tumbling over it myself. The smashed urn lay directly below like a frozen explosion. If anyone had climbed out here during this storm on the off-chance of flattening Guy with a lucky shot then he was either quite mad or an unbearable optimist.

I began sloshing back to where I had slithered down the roof. The rain was slowing a little now. It made little difference. I couldn't have been wetter had I jumped into the pool. When I reached the point below the window I looked up just in time to see the light go out in the corridor. It was replaced by an eerie green glow as I became aware of a dark shadow above, then the sash window rattled shut. The green light disappeared. 'No, hey, leave it open, I'm out here!' I began scrabbling up the tiles on all fours but my haste made me slip back several times. By the time I reached the window and clawed at its frame there was no one to be seen. It had probably been Carla who, on her way to or from her room, finding it open and not thinking anyone mad enough to climb out, closed it. The window wouldn't budge. I pressed my face against the pane. There was no one on the other side but I could see that the little snick that locked the two parts of the sash had been engaged. Holding on to the wet frame with one hand I felt around in my jacket pocket with the other and eventually closed my hand on my pocket knife. The extended blade was just long enough to budge the snick at the third attempt. I heaved up the lower half and gratefully tumbled through it.

I spent a few moments sitting on the carpet and thinking unpleasant thoughts. Here I was in an

English country mansion during a thunderstorm and there was an outside chance that someone had helped that stone urn off the balustrade in order to flatten Guy Middleton with it. Why else had the window been opened during a rainstorm? It was hard to believe but I had unwittingly strayed deep into Agatha Christie country. I hastily shut the window and sought refuge in my room.

I changed into dry clothes and calmed down a bit, though I was seriously thinking of going down one floor to fill my tooth mug with Guy's single malt. It might help me think. What also might help me think was Annis. When I finally got a couple of wavering bars on my mobile she had the solution. 'It's obvious. All you have to do is get them all into the library, say you know who did it and they'll break down and admit everything and explain the how and the why. Either that or they'll make a sudden dash for the door. Make sure you have Superintendent Needham waiting outside with a moustache.'

'Good thinking. Problem is: no one's actually been murdered yet so that probably won't work.'

'Details. Though only a matter of time, surely. But seriously. Do you think someone is trying to kill him?'

'Not sure. Could be. I'm rapidly going off him myself. But I mean, it's such an unlikely scenario, this. Assuming for a minute that thing was actually pushed off the parapet, then whoever did it would have had to sprint up the stairs after we had left the house and get out there, then wait in the storm, on the roof, on the off-chance that Guy wandered back that way. And heaving a stone ornament from the roof is the most stupid way of trying to kill anyone. Unless you have an awful lot of practice at it. And with a moving target it's almost impossible to do. It only works on telly.'

'A lucky shot, perhaps. What about the rain-water under the window?'

'Someone could just have had a look as I did. Probably Carla. The window was so streaked with rain I had to open it to see properly. I didn't see any wet footprints or anything on the carpet. They could have taken their shoes off as they got back in, I suppose.'

'Oh all right. Just two thoughts, hon.' Here we go. 'One – I assume that's not the only window they could have used? Two – umbrellas. If I were standing up on the roof looking down and you lot all had umbrellas up then you would all look the same.'

'Stoneking had given up on his and closed it by then.'

'That still leaves you.'

'Exactly. You wouldn't chuck bits of building down if you didn't know who you were killing.'

'True. Unless it doesn't matter who you flatten.'

'The whole thing seems absurdly unlikely. I think it was just done to scare him, with murder as a possible bonus. And I think he really is scared now.'

'I'm not surprised. At least you did your job looking after him and managed to shout a warning.'

'The opposite, actually; I nearly got him killed. I dragged him out there in the first place and when I shouted, he stopped to look and the damn thing very nearly squashed him. Had I shut up it would have missed by quite a margin.'

'Bum. Well, make sure you keep an eye on the roofline, hon, in case more of the ruin rots down on you.'

'I suppose that's why he let *Time Lines* dig up his lawns in the first place; he needs the money to stop the place from collapsing. They probably pay quite handsomely.'

'Just make sure they pay *you* handsomely.'

'You bet. But this job is turning into a nuisance, never mind the cakes and luxuries.'

'Did you say *cakes*?'

'Not me, must be a bad line.'

'You need some competent help with those. Why haven't you wangled me an invite yet?'

'Possibly because there's no such word as "an invite". If you mean an invitation – I'm working on it.'

'You're a pedant. You're my favourite pedant, of course, but still a *nit-picking nuisance*.' As I terminated the call I realized I'd forgotten to ask who her second-favourite pedant was.

As for Guy, even as I went off the man I was beginning to feel sorry for him. Someone obviously disliked him enough to want to mess with his mind, leave nasty notes, spike his drink and scratch his car. He'd been scared when we were left in the dark at the museum and quite shaken by having a generous portion of masonry land at his feet. Even if it had been an accident, which was by no means certain, the man had every right to be a bit upset. I went downstairs to see if he had got over the shock yet.

The thunderstorm had moved on, now a distant rumble in the east, but heavy rain continued to fall from a sky so dark it looked like tree bark drawn in charcoal. Middleton's room smelled strongly of whisky. A depleted bottle of Laphroaig stood on the mantelpiece. When I had left Guy on the stairs he had looked pale; now he looked flushed. 'There'll be no more filming today,' he said. 'And if it goes on raining like this there won't be any tomorrow either. I've decided to go for a swim, try and relax a bit. Did you know there was a pool downstairs? Steam room, sauna, Jacuzzi, the lot.'

A half-drunk Guy Middleton and a swimming pool, now what could possibly go wrong? 'I'll get my cozzie.'

'Good man.'

I'd never been hugely impressed by conspicuous consumption but a heated indoor swimming pool was a luxury I agreed with. As soon as we stepped through the modern door at the end of the lower gallery we left gothic revival behind and found ourselves in the twenty-first century again. Here, white walls, bright wood and terracotta tiles, illuminated by recessed lighting and large skylights, created a completely different atmosphere. The unmistakable smell of chlorinated water pervaded the air and the echoing sounds of watery pursuits brought back memories of humbler pools at public swimming baths for me.

While the rest of the mansion was strictly roll-top baths and brass fittings, here everything was aggressively contemporary. The showers started automatically as soon as we stepped into the cubicles and stopped as we left them. Lighting brightened as we walked on through the corridor and dimmed behind us.

The pool house had no windows but a pitched roof of blond timber and glass. The white walls were unadorned, with groups of wicker furniture and a dozen or so palms in giant pots making up for the plainness. The pool itself was a turquoise triangle of wet loveliness. A woman in a blue one-piece bathing suit and white swimming cap was doing a competent crawl towards our end as we entered. When she reached our side and turned for another length I saw that it was Carla.

'Perfect shape for a housekeeper, don't you think?' said Guy. Both of us, I noticed, had instinctively pulled in our less-than-perfectly shaped stomachs. I jumped in, closely followed by a belly-flopping Middleton. We ended up doing a sedate breast stroke next to each other while Carla torpedoed up and down at twice the speed. 'Always wanted a heated pool,' Guy said. 'No point having an unheated one in this country, is there? But a couple of expensive divorces ballsed that up good and proper. And other unforeseen expenses.' He put on an angry spurt of speed, took a loud breath and dived across towards the advancing shape of Carla. With some effort he managed accidentally to collide with her. Carla pushed herself away from him. She tread water for a couple of seconds. I could see she was saying something to Guy but couldn't catch it and my lip-reading skills weren't up to it, which meant she hadn't said anything obvious. She didn't wait around for his insincere apologies. Quick as a

121

dolphin she turned and with a few strokes reached the edge of the pool where she pulled herself effortlessly out of the water. She left the pool house without looking back.

'That was subtle,' I said admiringly. 'Do they teach the underwater grope at RADA?'

'Oh, shut up and mind your own business.' He was very flushed now and made for the side of the pool himself where he held on and tread water to get his breath back. I did a couple of lengths to make myself feel virtuous but only managed to confirm to myself how ridiculously unfit I had become.

Guy was out of the water and stood dripping over me. 'I'm going to sweat it off. Come on, let's find the sauna.' He padded off towards a couple of doors with brightly lit windows by the narrow end of the pool.

I called after him. 'I hate saunas; you won't get me into one of those.'

He opened first one door, looked inside, then tried the other one. 'How about the steam room then? Not quite as insane.' He disappeared inside.

Reluctantly I followed him in. One Istanbul Turkish bath experience had been quite enough for me. It had done nothing to endear me to the weird notion of steaming oneself like a bundle of mustard greens in the sweaty company of hairy men. I was just about to point this out to Guy when I saw that he had found company of a more smooth-skinned nature. In a corner opposite us sat Andrea, the head archaeologist, wrapped in a small white towel. On her the sweat looked OK, but even through the steam and despite her polite expression I could see she was disappointed by our intrusion and possibly wished for a larger towel, too. Guy launched into a detailed account of his recent masonry adventure and Andrea crossed her legs and kept her comments short.

Damn it was hot. The heat stung in my nostrils and sweat made me blink. This had to be a hundred per cent humidity; any more and we'd drown. I was beginning to feel a little claustrophobic. The room was only a modest eight by eight feet and had enough steam in it to drive a train. I gave it another polite minute, then made my move.

'Sorry to interrupt, Guy, but I'm done to a turn. I'll see you at dinner.' This time I didn't imagine it: Andrea looked less than happy. My desertion made me feel unchivalrous but she looked fit enough to fend for herself, towel slip permitting.

After all that exertion and heat treatment I felt quite justified in spending a couple of hours simply lying on my bed with the clockwork radio on and studying the tiny flower print of the wall-paper. The rain stopped and the sky grew lighter and eventually the sun broke through the edge of the cloud like a second dawn. Just as my stomach had finished working through the cake and cream and began growling for more it was answered by a very faint dinner gong; the privi-leged few were being called for a VIP supper and for once I was one of the chosen.

It looked like I was the last to arrive in the dining room. None of us had made a great effort to dress for the occasion, which seemed almost regrettable, since the dinner table with its silver and crystal, its gold-rimmed dinner service and flower arrangements, cried out to be matched by evening dress. Not that I had brought any. There was no starter but a generous abundance of well-cooked food: two legs of lamb spiked with garlic and rosemary, roast potatoes and colourful dishes of simply cooked vegetables. That reminded me of the greenhouse, hidden away and gated behind the hedge.

'Do you grow any of this yourself?' I asked Mark.

'Lord, no, what for? We're surrounded by farms, I get it delivered. And there's a farm shop not five minutes from here.'

'I just thought you might when I saw the big greenhouse.'

Mark made a dismissive gesture with the carving knife. 'Yeah, well, Sam usually grows a few tomatoes in there and raises plants for the beds, but that's as far as it goes.'

Lamb was being carved and dishes handed around. Emms looked down the table. 'Guy isn't here. He didn't go out, did he? Anyone seen him?'

It appeared that no one had. I had been too distracted by the prospect of food to even notice his absence. Cy looked across at me. 'Chris, sorry, but could you see where he's got to? If he starts skipping meals and gets *all* his calories from single malt he'll be even more impossible to work with.'

My stomach felt quite murderous when I agreed to see where he had got to. This babysitting and shepherding was beginning to feel like real work. I took the stairs two at a time and rapped at his door. No answer. 'Guy? Dinner is served . . .'

I knocked again, waited a polite half-second then slowly opened the door. He was not in his bedroom. The bathroom door was closed. I went and knocked again before pushing it open. There was some sort of resistance and I had to push hard to get it open. I stuck my head through the gap. A damp towel had fallen to the floor and wedged itself under the door. I yanked it free and chucked it at the towel rail. No sign of Middleton. I clattered down the stairs, the smell of roast lamb in my nose. In the drawing room I opened the French window and looked up and down the terrace. At the north end a snake of archaeologists and technicians in a fantastic variety of rain gear and rubber boots queued for their supper by the catering van. A thin curl of smoke rose from the Roman camp but there was no sign of our Celtic heroes, which was hardly surprising since the pubs were open. No Middleton here either.

I stuck my head in at the library. 'Guy?' The overstuffed room still smelled vaguely of coffee and cake and a hint of lavender. I closed the door. Lavender?

I opened it again and stepped inside. Olive Cunningham stood very still behind the door, a book in one hand, her stick in the other. She was dressed in black, with pearl earrings her only adornment. Her hands tensed around book and stick; she wore no rings. I opened my mouth but she got there first.

'They used to be ours, you know, and he doesn't even read. Not sure he can. Who are you? Why aren't you at dinner?' It was less a question than an accusation.

'I'm Chris Honeysett. I'm trying to find Guy Middleton.'

'Then you must be the only one.' She gave me a withering look as she walked past me and out of the door. 'And you need a haircut, young man!' she called from the hall.

Young man, how kind. At least she didn't hit me, I thought when I walked down the lower gallery. Here too I could smell the old lady's perfume but she had once more disappeared. At the end of the corridor I opened the door to the pool house. I couldn't imagine Guy still using it after more than two hours yet there in the dressing room were his house shoes and dressing gown.

'Guy?' My voice echoed unanswered in the deserted pool room. Then I heard a thumping. When I turned towards the steam room I saw Guy, his face contorted with panic and as red as a cooked lobster behind the glass of the steam room door. Someone had wedged a wooden chair under the door handle, making it impossible to open from the inside. I unblocked the door and yanked it wide. Middleton fell into my arms and looked up at me with dancing eyes. 'Where the fuck have you been, Honeysett? I've been cooking in there for hours. I thought I was going to die. Might still do that,' he added faintly. 'I need water.'

'You need to cool down and rehydrate. Lean on me and we'll get you under a shower.'

He did lean heavily on me and breathed loudly with the effort of moving. In the shower cubicle he sat on the floor with mouth wide open, letting the cool water run over him. Between gulping mouthfuls of water he told me what had happened. 'Andrea left soon after you did. Stuck-up cow.'

I briefly wondered what, in Middleton's book, made a woman a 'stuck-up cow'. Presumably the category included any woman who didn't enjoy being groped. 'Could she have done it?'

'Andrea Clementi? Doubt it. Too serious. If she wanted to get back at me she'd write a letter to *The Times*.'

'How long after she left did you notice the door was blocked?'

'It was a while. I like steam rooms, even without girls in them. Always feel quite pure after a steam bath. Opens your pores. Sweats out the toxins. You know what they say – no pain, no gain. So I stayed in there until I really couldn't bear it any longer. I had noticed it was getting hotter in there, too. Tried to open the door and couldn't. I banged on the door, I shouted myself hoarse. On tip-toes I could just see the damn chair wedged under the door. I pushed like mad but it wouldn't budge. And you can't turn down the heat; the controls are on the outside. In that box of tricks between the two doors. The bastard who locked me in there must have turned it up at the same time.'

'That was a cruel prank.'

Middleton wasn't having it. He exploded at me. 'Prank? Are you mad? I could have *died* in there. I thought I was going to have a bloody heart attack it was so hot. I've never been so thirsty in my entire life.' He gulped some more water, his face lifted up, his eyes closed. Then he expelled a jet of it from between his pursed lips. 'Never appreciated what luxury water is. I tried to lick the steam off the tiles in there but it tasted foul and I was sweating out buckets more than I was getting.' He pulled himself up on his feet.

'Feeling a bit better?'

'A bit.' He dried himself and began pulling on his clothes in the changing room. 'I've got a monumental headache but I no longer feel like I'm about to croak. I need painkillers and a drink. A real drink.'

'The housekeeper has cooked dinner for the house guests. Your presence was missed, that's how I found you.'

'Missed? My arse. I doubt many of that lot would.' He had finished dressing. 'And at least one of them was happy to have me steam to death in that horrible cubicle.' He looked a bit pink still but otherwise recovered when he marched out of the pool house. 'And it's your fault, Honeysett!'

I went after him. 'How is this my fault? I mean, I knew it would be, of course, but how?'

'You left me in there. You were supposed to look after me, but instead you left me alone in there.'

'If I'd been in there with you we'd both have got locked in.'

'They wouldn't have done it had you been there too. I'm certain of it.'

'It was me who rescued you,' I complained.

'I need protection. So I won't *need* rescuing.'

I stopped by the dining-room doors but Guy carried on towards the stairs. 'Won't you come and have supper?' I asked.

128

'I need painkillers and a drink and I'm not hungry. I'm going to barricade myself into my room!' he called from the stairs.

I let him go. He had every reason to be fed up and it was probably better for all concerned if he went for a quiet drink rather than vent his feelings in the dining room. I went inside and found everyone digging spoons into dessert bowls. Strawberries and cream. No sign of the lamb.

'Didn't you find him?' Emms asked. 'I thought I just heard his voice outside in the corridor.'

I hesitated a second. What was the form? Was I supposed to keep this secret too or tell everyone about it? It was his story, I decided; he could tell it himself. 'I found him but couldn't persuade him to have supper. He says he has a headache.'

'He's definitely giving *me* one,' Cy said, reaching for his glass of mineral water.

'Carla is keeping some lamb warm for you in the kitchen,' said Stoneking, 'and we'll leave you some strawberries. But only if you're quick.'

To get to the kitchen I had to walk back past the pool house door and take a turn down a darker corridor. The broad door was wide open. The kitchen matched the rest of the house, which is to say it was ancient, with high ceilings, and cavernously commodious. There was a large cast-iron range, no longer in use, and a cream-coloured Aga. The enormous four-door fridge looked to be barely post-war. The scrubbed oak table in the centre could comfortably seat ten though there were only four chairs of the type commonly used to jam shut the doors of steam rooms.

Carla was washing dishes by hand in a Belfast

sink. She saw my reflection in the window glass in front of her and spoke to it. 'You've come for your supper. I've kept it warm for you.' She wiped her hands on her apron before taking the foil covering off a generous plate of roast lamb and vegetables. 'You'll have to fight the mob for the strawberries.' Carla smiled serenely, standing rooted in her realm.

'Stoneking – I mean Mark – is guarding my portion. If I'm quick, he said.'

She kept smiling. I had noticed before that Carla seemed to be looking at the world from a place deep inside herself and that she liked what she saw. 'I was keeping some food back for Mr Middleton too but I couldn't help overhearing,' she nodded towards the open door, 'that he wasn't going to join the others.'

'He has a headache.' I stood, the plate of food in my hands, being smiled at. I had instantly taken to the self-possessed housekeeper but there was an unnerving depth to her eyes that appeared anything but domestic.

'Mr Stoneking cannot be trusted,' she said severely. 'Your strawberries won't be safe while he has access to a spoon. You'd better hurry, Mr Honeysett.' She turned back to the sink and her washing-up.

Everyone was still at the table when I returned and Mark Stoneking was pouring wine from freshly opened bottles from his cellar. I attacked my plate of food with one eye on the remaining strawberries. A golden evening light lay on the gardens now and through the windows I could see people walking here and there. Suddenly

Middleton was there outside the window like an apparition from a gothic novel. He held a whisky bottle in one hand and rapped the signet ring on his other against the window pane. The sash windows were open a few inches to let in air, so when Middleton started shouting we had no problems following his drift. 'One of you treacherous *bastards* in there is trying to kill me! Which one of you is it, huh?'

'Pissed already, well done, Guy,' Cy said to the room rather than the raging Middleton. 'And paranoid now as well.'

Middleton was shading his eyes against the glass. 'Honeysett, are you in there?' I didn't answer, mainly because I had my mouth full. 'Tell Honeysett I'm with the Britons and send him down there.' He walked off and called back over his shoulder. 'I may need a bodyguard.'

I turned my attention to the remaining strawberries. 'Everyone finished with the cream?'

Nine

'Whoever you are, go away. *Quietly*.' Middleton's voice sounded tragic on the other side of the door.

Last night I had failed abysmally in my task to stop Guy from drowning his brains with the hairy Britons. I had found him sitting on a crate outside Morgan's tent, sharing his whisky around and drinking from demijohns of rough cider with

131

names like 'Legbender' or 'Skullcrusher'. I was full of good wine from Stoneking's table and in no mood to argue much with him, especially since he was surrounded by a hirsute bunch of Britons who seemed to have remained in character. They had decided that the first round of fighting had gone to them and were celebrating with the celebrity. The celebrity was showing off in front of his new friends. 'Piss off, Honeysett,' Middleton had said. 'I don't need a bloody nursemaid.'

This morning he sounded like he could possibly do with a nurse. I stopped banging on his door and tried opening it. There was resistance but it was easy enough to push it out of the way. Guy had set the bedside table in front of the door in a feeble attempt at a barricade against night prowlers. 'Leave me alone. I can't possibly get up. I feel truly awful. Tell Cy I'm unwell. I need at least a day to recover.'

It felt cruel yet satisfying in a told-you-so kind of way to rip open the curtains and let the summer sun beam down on the cringing cripple curled up on the bed. 'You can't take the day off; it would give Cy all the ammunition he needs. That's the one way he will be able to get rid of you, if you're not showing up for work because of a hangover.'

'Hangover! There ought to be a completely new word for what I've got.' Middleton sat up in bed, hunched and dishevelled, the loose strands of his ponytail hanging thin and lifeless over his shoulders. He was holding his forehead as though he was afraid it might come apart. A few years ago he had been the soap-star heart throb; this morning he wouldn't have needed make-up for a vampire movie. 'Right now I don't know who I hate more, you or him,' he growled.

'I don't care. Every day I'm getting an earful from Cy about how useless you are and how I'm supposed to make sure you do your job and I'm getting nothing but crap from you. I'm on your side, Middleton. I may be the only one around here and *I'm* only here because I get paid. So stop the baby talk and get on with it or else pack it in and retire. Go and live quietly in your cottage in the Lakes.'

He swung his legs out of bed, grunting as though he'd been stabbed. 'Huh. *Retire*. What on? I need this bloody gig. And I'll have to do it until I'm old and grey.'

Older and greyer, surely. 'Then I suggest you get under that shower and come downstairs smiling. And apologize for last night's little outburst outside the dining room while you're at it. I hadn't told them you had been locked into the steam room so your accusations made you sound more than a bit mad.'

'Oh, bugger. All right, I'll try. Look, Chris . . . You've no idea what pressure I'm under. There's other stuff. Not just Cy or the death threats. Other stuff.' He gave another grunt as he pushed himself off the bed and got to his feet. He shuffled into the shower. 'I might tell you later.'

'I can't wait.' I left him to it and went to get breakfast.

Ageing rock stars know how to live. Fresh

133

orange juice, scrambled eggs, drop scones, smoked salmon and the whole English breakfast thing – Carla had to be up at the crack of dawn each day to build this wall of food in the dining room. The IT blokes were there, murmuring at each other through mouthfuls of croissant; cameraman and soundman were working through small mountains of fried food. Stoneking was sitting in the open window with a long glass of juice. He was watching Emms and Cy carry their cups of coffee across the sodden grass to the tent that had been erected over the larger trench the day before. Andrea was already there, staring inside. The Roman encampment was still in place and so was that of their enemies. It was bank holiday weekend and they would be with us until it was their time to return to reality.

'The trench has flooded, despite the tent,' Stoneking called over his shoulder.

'To be expected,' Paul said without looking up. 'They'll pump it out and mop it up. Take at least an hour, though.'

'Has the digger been repaired yet?' Stoneking asked.

'Nah. Bloke stopped working when the rain started. What a lightweight. Back this morning, he said.'

I had nearly finished my pile of scrambled eggs and grilled tomatoes when Guy turned up. 'Morning, chaps.' He looked quite presentable, considering what state he'd been in twenty minutes ago. 'Where is everyone, I'm not late, am I? Morning, Mark.' He walked over to the window where Stoneking sat. 'Sorry about last night, I got a bit upset.' He quickly explained what had happened to him in the steam room.

'Shit, that would have narked me off too,' Stoneking said. 'Especially after that thing with the urn. You've got a practical joker on your case, Guy. Better watch out.'

Guy went to get himself some coffee and I went to join Stoneking, who was on the terrace now. 'OK to climb through the window?'

'Be my guest.'

'Now you've mentioned the urn – have you had a look at the roof yet?'

'I was up there first thing this morning. Called the roofers already.'

'Did you check out the place where the urn fell off?'

Mark spoke quietly. 'I didn't actually go out on the roof, I'm not completely mad, that's what roofers are for. But I'm pretty sure it was an accident.' He looked over his shoulder at Guy, who was sitting at the table nibbling toast. Stoneking left his glass on the windowsill and we ambled to the edge of the verandah out of earshot. 'The place needs some serious mainten-ance; I do feel guilty. I will get the roofers to check out all the nonsense stuck to the parapet, see if any of it needs securing. Or pushing off, when it comes to it. I mean, this stuff's been up there for an age. You know what they say – what goes up . . . But what's this thing with Guy and the pranks? No wonder Guy's a bit paranoid now. First the note in his bed, now this steam room thing.'

'I think for Guy the falling urn is also part of it.'

135

'I have already apologized like mad to him. But he's not the most gracious man I've met. He has appalling manners. And, I mean, look who's talking here – even I think he's a pain in the arse and I'm not the politest man in the world. It's a rock 'n' roll hangover.'

'Do you rock 'n' roll much still?'

'Me?' He snorted. 'I can't stand rock music.'

'You're kidding.'

'Straight up. Haven't played any for twenty years, don't listen to it. When I do listen to music these days it's mainly classical. Twentieth-century stuff. But three blokes with guitars and a drummer? Give us a break.'

'My girlfriend's a Karmic fan; she'd be devastated to hear you say that.'

He wagged a finger. 'Now, don't go round telling everyone. I rely on the money from all those people who never grew up and are still buying Best of Karmic Fire CDs. No offence to your girlfriend, OK? It was all right, Karmic was all right. But that's nearly forty bloody years ago. I don't even think about it from one year to the next. I think of the guys sometimes but they're all gone now.'

'Sorry to hear that.'

'Why should you be? You never met them. And you might not have liked them much if you had.'

'Do you still play the guitar?'

He held up his right hand for my inspection. It was an old man's hand. 'Arthritis in my finger joints. I haven't played guitar for years. Getting a bit deaf in one ear, too. I've no idea why I'm telling you this. Let's change the subject.

136

Because . . . I have a little proposition. You're a painter as well as a minder, Cy told me. So I looked your stuff up on the internet last night and I really like it. It's got oomph. It's nice and big, too. I love abstract art, see? The crap we had on the album covers? I always hated that shit, even then. So I have a proposition. I was going to soften you up with a bottle of wine first but since we're talking I'll come straight out with it. I want you to do a mural for me. In the same style of your paintings. In the pool house.' Mark could read my expression and before I could open my mouth said: 'I know, it's probably not what you usually do and it's not canvas but I'd give you a completely free hand. Whatever you come up with I'm sure it'll look great.'

'It's not that . . .'

'Look, you're here already, standing around half the day, so you might as well. And I'd pay good money, have no fear. You can charge whatever you want, I mean, within reason, obviously.'

'Mark, the paintings you saw. On the website. I've changed my style since then. Quite radically. I've gone figurative. And I'm still feeling my way.'

'Oh.'

'But I have an idea and I think you're going to like it . . .'

A few minutes later Mark was studying the images on annisjordon.com on his phone. 'Blimey. And are they big?'

'Eight foot. But she'll be delighted to paint larger than that.'

'I really like these images. I like them even

137

better than yours, no offence. And you think you could persuade her?'

'I think I might.'

Mark flicked to the biography page. 'Is that her? Pretty. I always had a weakness for red hair and freckles. How do you know her?'

'It's a long story.'

'Would you ask her for me?'

I checked my watch – it was early here but the middle of the night in Annis Jordan's world. 'I'll ask her later today.'

Despite yesterday's thunderstorm the atmosphere remained close. It was warm already and the gardens steamed in the hazy sunshine. We ambled across to the enlarged trench where diggers were removing the khaki tent, marching it to the tree line at the very edge of the lawn. A small diesel generator was started up and connected to a pump.

Andrea, lowering the business end into the trench, turned to Mark. 'It's very muddy and we don't have enough hose to get it all the way to the lake. It'll make more mess of your lawn.' She pulled an apologetic face. 'Are you sure you don't mind?'

'Hell no, give my gardener some more to moan about but it's only mud. Pump all you like.'

Mark and I retreated as the operation got under way. 'Your gardener. Sam, was that his name?' I asked.

'Yeah, why?'

'It was something the old lady said. She called him a villain, I think.'

'That he is. Or was.'

'He wouldn't be taking his sabbatical at Her Majesty's pleasure by any chance?'

Mark sighed and gave me a brief sideways glance as we kept walking in a loose, purposeless loop around the excavation. 'Not for anything he's done recently. He's been pretty straight since he's been working here. They actually taught him horticulture while he was inside for a few years, and he was doing some of his apprenticeship here with the then gardener as part of his parole afterwards. When I bought the place the old gardener retired. I kept Sam on as a replacement. Never regretted it.'

'So why's he inside now?'

'It's DNA, isn't it? A robbery he never got fingered for back in the day, they could suddenly prove he'd been part of it. Not the big one, an earlier one.'

'Big one?'

'The Bristol Airport bullion robbery.'

I'd have whistled admiringly if I'd known how to whistle. 'Oh, that. *Very* big.' I remembered it well: twelve million pounds worth of gold bars, gone in four minutes.

'He was part of that, he drove the van. Took his gloves off because he couldn't get his chocolate bar unwrapped and left fingerprints on the steering wheel.'

'Classic.'

'Cost him four years. Most of the others got caught too, eventually.'

'It was good of you to take him on. You didn't think it was a bit of a risk?'

'Not really. I don't have any gold bullion lying

about and you could tell he was really into this gardening thing. He's pretty straight now. I get on with Sam. I know where he's coming from. If it hadn't been for Karmic I might easily have gone that way myself. I was quite wild back then.'

'So I heard. When's he coming out?'

'This week if all goes to schedule. He'll go mental when he sees all this. I'll never hear the end of it.' Mark smiled to himself as though he was very much looking forward to it.

The pumping of the trench continued for a long time. Paul was there to capture the effort on camera. His prediction came true: it was a whole hour before they reached the bottom and even then it was only to reveal a mud bath. The smaller trench had been bailed out by hand by Julie and Adam, both covered in mud but looking unperturbed.

Now Guy was there too, in his usual hat and jacket, doing PTCs or at least trying to. Loss of short-term memory is the bane of all heavy drinkers. He kept forgetting his lines or mixing them up. He faltered for the third time. 'Sorry, can I have another look at the script?'

Cy threw up his hands. 'For Christ's sake, Guy, there's only four bloody sentences in the sequence. Do you need an idiot board?'

'Don't swear at me,' Guy protested. 'Anyone can forget his lines once in a while.'

'What do you mean, *forget* them? You never knew them in the first place.' Cy, steaming with righteous anger, stomped a few yards away from the trench. 'Will no one rid me of this turbulent . . .' He looked to the heavens in frustration.

'Beast?' Andrea supplied quietly.

If Guy had heard he didn't let on. He studied the script and nodded. 'Got it now. Definitely.'

'OK, from the top,' said the patient Emms.

Cy spotted me and marched over, pointing a rolled-up sheaf of papers at my nose. 'This is your bloody fault. I asked you to keep him away from Morgan and his bunch. I think he's actually still drunk. He hasn't got a single functioning brain cell this morning.'

I tried to think of the money I owed Jake for the car, of the pool and all that lovely free food, and took a deep breath. I spoke softly. He would just have to imagine the big stick for the moment. 'If I hear "it's your fault" one more time – from you, from him or anyone else in this TV circus – then I'm walking straight out of here back to civilization.'

'We won't pay you a penny if you walk out,' he argued. 'You know that, don't you?'

I shrugged. 'I'm not that desperate,' I lied.

Cy deflated a little. 'Just try a bit harder then,' he grumbled and walked back to the shoot.

'You can't walk out of here,' Stoneking said with a smile. Perhaps he recognized my bluff for what it was. 'Not until you've got that girl to paint my mural, anyway.'

The auto mechanic was back, this time with a mate, trying to get the digger to work. From time to time the engine roared into life, belching out great clouds of white smoke, then it would subside and the head scratching continued. It was just before lunch when the engine was started again. No smoke this time. It sounded a lot better, too.

Dan, the driver, downed his trowel and jogged across. He tested the drive, swing arm and bucket, then turned the engine off. From where I sat on the terrace I couldn't hear what was being said but he seemed to be having a lively discussion with the two mechanics. When they had packed their gear and walked off Dan stood for a while by the side of the digger, staring into space. Then he walked back to the excavation just as the VIPs left for the catering van. I decided to wait for the second sitting and to call Annis. My mobile displayed one flickering bar so I asked Stoneking if he had a landline I could use. He had, and led me into a strange little room near the library. The single window above the solid dark wooden desk looked out over the gravelled forecourt with its collection of cars and vans. An assortment of furniture had been crammed into the room and every surface was cluttered with obscure objects to rival anything I'd seen in the library. Three-foot brass Buddhas rubbed shoulders with African masks. A moth-eaten stuffed fox bared its teeth at a Japanese pufferfish which someone had tastefully turned into a lantern. There were enough African spears and Arab daggers to arm a rebellion. 'It was meant to be a sort of office,' he explained. 'But I don't really need one so it turned into a kind of junk room / gun locker.'

'You keep guns?'

He nodded at the gun locker behind the door. 'With a place this size? You bet. Do you shoot?'

'Reluctantly.'

'You don't fancy joining me in a little rabbit cull?'

'And badly, I should have added. I'd just make more holes in your lawn.'

'Who cares? We're overrun with rabbits and I'm planning to shoot a dozen or so and feed them to you.'

'OK, I'll have a go, but I'm much better at cooking rabbits than killing them.'

'You can cook rabbit? Excellent, you can help with the skinning afterwards.'

When will I learn to keep my mouth shut?

Annis picked up after an interminable time. 'I was busy shooing sheep out of what used to be our herb garden,' she explained. 'They snaffled the lot, I'm afraid, all except the mint.'

'I wonder why.' I explained Stoneking's pool house mural proposition. It didn't need much arm-twisting to bring her round to the idea.

'At last a decent-sized arena! And I get a free hand? He's not going to say the colours need to match his bath towels? He won't want swirly things that remind him of clouds or galaxies?'

'He's actually quite a cultured man, I think. He hasn't displayed any rock star foibles at all.'

'Whatever *they* are. A mural at Mark Stoneking's mansion will look fabulous on my CV. And if he likes it perhaps he'll recommend me to his mates.'

'He hasn't got any. They all died of drugs or liver failure.'

'Shame. OK, tell him you talked me into it. Do I get to stay there?'

'There's a queen-sized bed in my room. I think we'll manage.'

I was just in time to join the end of the foot soldiers' lunch queue and scoop up a generous portion of steak and mushroom pie. I found Adam and Julie, who were eating on a still-damp table on the terrace. 'What do you make of the latest development then, Mr Detective? I think you ought to spring into action right away.'

'What development would that be?'

'You haven't heard? *Sabotage*.' She widened her eyes as she pronounced the word.

'Really? Where?'

'Yup,' confirmed Adam. 'Apparently the digger was sabotaged. Someone poured water into the fuel tank, that's what caused the smoke and all that.'

'Naturally the suspicion will fall on us lot,' Julie said, jabbing her fork into her pie for emphasis. 'Everyone knows we don't like using the digger. So of course it has to be us.'

'Has anyone accused you?' I asked.

'Not yet. But we've been asked to assemble in half an hour for a general meeting. I can hear Cy already. He thinks we're a bunch of dinosaurs. If it was up to him we'd probably be using dynamite as well as a JCB. I think he's far more interested in producing *per se* than he is of producing an archaeology show. For a start he hasn't got the patience for it. Or the vision, or whatever.'

Adam smiled. 'He's definitely run out of patience with Middleton. They're constantly having rows these days. I mean, no one likes Middleton much, apart from the punters, of course, which is why he's here. Cy always hated having to work with him but they're having blazing rows now. It'll end in fisticuffs, I'm sure.'

144

'Let's hope so,' Julie said, dropping her cutlery on to her cleared plate. 'I hope I'm there to see it.'

'OK, who's your money on?' Adam asked. 'Guy or Cy?'

Julie closed one eye as she gave it some thought. 'It all depends on how drunk Guy is at the time,' she decided. 'Guy will put up his fists but Cy will already have paid someone to stab him in the back before he can land a punch.'

Adam nodded wisely. 'Admirably analysed. I concur.'

Soon afterwards Cy assembled his troops on the verandah. It was quite blustery today and after the urn had so nearly – and unfortunately as some would have it – missed the presenter of the show some of the diggers argued that standing around right by the house might not be the safest place. Cy called it a 'load of nonsense' and could they please get on with things?

I was standing among the group of diggers. Behind me, Adam said, *sotto voce*: 'I can't see Guy anywhere. If I were Cy I wouldn't feel too safe standing there. If Guy appears on the roof and puts his shoulder to one of those urn things no one's going to mention it to Cy, I'm sure.'

'Right, listen up!' Cy clapped his hands for attention. 'I'm sure you've all heard by now – the digger was in fact *sabotaged*. Someone poured water into the fuel tank, that's what put it out of action. Fortunately no lasting damage was done, because while the thing's insured I don't think it's covered for water damage. Now, I know some people disagree with the use of the digger but to them I say: you don't live in the real world. Grow up, guys. This is telly; time is money; schedules are tight. If it wasn't for the digger we wouldn't have a programme. And if it wasn't for the programme, most of you field archaeologists would be signing on, so think again. I take a dim view of anyone trying to interfere with the shoot. If I find out who did that they're off the team for good. Fired without pay. Someone also tried to nobble Guy by locking him in the steam room. Now Mr Middleton really doesn't need any help; he's quite capable of sabotaging himself. If whoever did that meant it as a practical joke then look around, no one's laughing.' Someone called 'Ha!' but Cy ignored it. 'The same goes for the re-enactors.' He turned towards the two groups standing at the periphery of the circle. 'We worked quite well together in the past but yesterday was nothing short of a fiasco. Any repeat of that kind of thing and you won't be asked again. As it is, we'll have to re-shoot some scenes today and then catch up with the weapons demonstration etcetera. We'll do the Roman food cameo tomorrow but I'll talk to you about all that in a minute. OK, everyone, that's all I have to say on the subject apart from this: I have my suspicions as to who's responsible and I'll be keeping an eye on them. That's all. Brian? Morgan? A word.' Cy walked off with the leaders of the re-enactment groups to reveal the schedule for the afternoon. Everyone else went back to work.

So much rain had fallen on to the lawn that no sooner had the pump cleared the water than it seeped back into the trench, collecting in puddles on the bottom. But difficulties made good telly, according to Emms, as long as they didn't interfere with the schedule. The digger went back into action. More and more of the mosaic was being uncovered and the excitement began to rub off on me. It looked nothing short of miraculous. There was discussion now about more trenches being opened and soon it would be time for Guy to sound surprised, delighted or sceptical, depending on what the script required.

Cy called me over. 'Chris? Find Guy for us? I can't get his mobile. We'll need him in ten minutes. Erm . . . please?' he added.

I could now add production team runner to my CV but *please* made all the difference. 'And tell him to bloody well turn his mobile on, for God's sake!'

Double rates, keep thinking double rates, I told myself as I jogged back to the house. Ten minutes? The place was so big I would have to hurry to get Guy to the shoot on time. No luck in drawing or dining room. I took the stairs up from the central gallery and knocked on Guy's door. When I got no answer I went in, looked in the bathroom – nothing. I clattered back down the stairs. Had he gone swimming? The pool house was deserted, echoing emptily as I called Guy's name. Five minutes gone. Back through the gallery and into the hall. I was beginning to feel uneasy when I called his name again in the huge hall, the sound reverberating unanswered in the cavernous space. Perhaps I should have kept a closer eye on him. I stepped into the library; it was empty apart from the stuffed, spiked and bottled residents. The little glass-topped display case near the window had its lid raised. Despite being in a hurry, curiosity got the better of me and I went over to look inside. Every object I remembered appeared to be there and the display of knives and beetles had no obvious gaps. Then I saw it. The ghost bottle resting on the prayer book was empty, the stopper with the broken seal lying next to it. That's all I needed, something else to scare Middleton. I stoppered the bottle and lowered the lid of the case.

By now I had become so tense that I actually breathed a sigh of relief when I looked up and through the window saw Guy standing by his Land Rover, his shoulder bag by his feet. He whisked a small sheet of paper from under the windscreen wipers, unfolded the note and stared down at it. I rapped on the window pane and he started, frowned in my direction and hastily crumpled the note into his jacket pocket. I went and opened the front door to let him in but he had got into his car. I jogged across, waving. He had started the engine and wound down the window. 'What?'

'Where are you going? You're wanted on the set.'

'Already? I thought the pumping would take much longer. I was going to, you know, buy a few things. I asked the housekeeper if she could do it but the bloody woman refused point blank.' He swung out of the car, slammed the door and shouldered his bag. When he opened his mouth to speak I cut him off.

'Before you ask – the answer is no. I'm here to make sure you get safely through this week so buying supplies of whisky really isn't in the job description. I'm not letting you out of my sight.' Did I really say that? I hoped with some fervency that Guy wouldn't hold me to it. I ushered him through the house and out the other side. 'What was that I saw you read earlier? Just before you got into the car?'

'Nothing.'

'Sure? It wasn't another threatening note?'

'Look, erm, now isn't the time, OK? I'll tell you later but I'll do it when I'm ready. I have enough on my plate without you getting on my case. When I need your help I'll ask for it, OK?'

'Just make sure you don't ask when it's too late.' I gestured to Cy: one slightly rattling TV star duly delivered.

Guy dropped his bag on the grass and walked straight into the waiting arms of the make-up artist. There was a lot of script to get through. The thunderstorm was discussed in front of the camera, as was Guy's narrow escape from the fallen urn. Ceaselessly mentioned was the significance and importance of the site, the high prestige of what was undoubtedly a late Roman villa of astonishing proportions. Everything, I noticed, was astounding, unprecedented, previously unheard of and never before encountered. All of them were consummate actors: on screen Guy would come across sober and interested and the archaeologists delighted to have Guy around. If one of them had murderous intentions towards him, no jury would convict them on this evidence.

Throughout the afternoon the re-enactors were kept busy too. When not filming the archaeology

149

Emms was busy re-shooting some of the fighting scenes, though she had the good sense not to let them loose on each other in large groups again. Sequences were kept short and many were in close up, involving no more than four actors at a time. She was even-handed in who won which bout, too. An equal number of Britons and Romans went down and the ham acting continued on and off for hours. The most sophisticated weapon of the Britons appeared to have been the bow. Brian the centurion was quick to point out that it had been around since the Neolithic and hence suited Morgan's bunch of cavemen. The Romans however had weapons never before encountered on the battlefields of Britain, one of which was the *ballista*. And Cohort Italica had brought their own working reconstruction of it. It was five foot high and looked a bit like a giant crossbow on a stand. It was made from wood, in places braced with metal plates, and used six-inch metal darts with wooden flights. Morgan the Briton had taunted Brian about it all day with announcements like: 'Gluteus Maximus and Caius Fatuous will now display their awesome weapon, made from two short planks and rubber bands from Brian's own extensive collection.'

The skies had cleared. Emms waited until the golden evening light to film the demonstration of the Roman artillery piece. It was carried to the edge of the lake by four legionnaires. With the help of the rowing boat a four-foot straw target was ferried across and set up on the shore of the tiny island. This had been Emms' idea, since it would look a lot more interesting than siting the demonstration in a field. Brian the centurion, standing by his pièce-de-resistance weapon by the lake, was not happy about it. 'Any darts that go off the mark or fall short will end up in the lake. We'll never find them again. You can't just buy these in a shop, you know, they're specially made for us by a blacksmith.'

Guy, who was standing by to introduce the *ballista* to the viewers, looked at the weapon with contempt. His mood had not improved all day. 'You said the thing was "deadly accurate" if I remember rightly. Says in my script: "It was capable of picking off individual soldiers up to a distance of three hundred yards."'

Brian squirmed a little. 'It all depends on the conditions and, of course, the operator . . .'

Guy licked his finger and held it up to gauge the wind. It had died down during the afternoon and right now it was perfectly still. 'Conditions appear to be ideal. What you're saying is that in fact you're no good with the damn thing.'

'Let's just get on with it, shall we, while we have the light?' Cy said. 'It's not even a hundred yards to the island, Brian, and the target is enormous, so I don't see how you can miss the damn thing.' Paul's camera was focussed on the *ballista*. Cy himself operated a second camera trained on the target.

'Do it in your own time, Brian,' Emms said. 'No need to fumble; take as long as you like, we'll cut it afterwards. And . . . *action*!'

Brian, with the aid of another soldier, lined up the *ballista*. There was much squinting along the top and tapping the side of the weapon. The

151

vicious dart was slid into place. The torsion was racked up, then it was Brian at the trigger. He released the catch and with a violent snap the machine hurled the dart into the lake, just short of the island. Disappointed groans all around. Applause from the watching Britons. 'That was an expensive splash,' Brian's helper complained.

'Shut up or I'll send you diving for it,' Brian hissed.

Adjustments were being made, followed by more squinting. Another dart taken reverentially from the box and fitted. The arms of the bow cranked back, the whole contraption creaking under the tension. Brian was sweating under his helmet. He squinted. He squinted some more. He took a deep breath, pulled the release and the dart flashed the hundred yards across the glittering water and thudded into the target, a hand's breadth away from the bull's eye. Jubilation and whistles. Brian was visibly relieved. 'I think that's as close as we'll get it,' he said, puffing out his cheeks.

'A hugely impressive demonstration,' Guy said to camera, 'of the superior firepower of the Roman army at the time of the invasion of our islands. The ability of the *ballista* to pick off individual commanders from this kind of distance greatly unnerved the opposition . . .'

'Better than chucking stone urns any time,' Brian muttered under his breath as he closed the lid on his box of precious bronze darts.

The footage of the two shots was checked and declared fit for consumption and the next hour was spent taking close-ups of the *ballista* workings from several angles, tensioning, loading and firing without actually shooting off another dart. Stoneking and I watched it all while sitting under a large fig tree and by the end of filming we felt we were both experts. The sun was low in the sky and glittered golden on the water. I had to squint against the light before I could make out the solitary figure standing on the right-hand shore beyond the reeds. 'Mrs Cunningham is watching,' I told Stoneking.

He shaded his eyes. 'So she is.'

'She always seems to be staring at me,' I complained.

He got to his feet and brushed at the back of his jeans. 'Well, yes, we're actually sitting on her grandmother . . .'

'Are we?' I quickly got to my feet.

'Another madwoman. Yes, she lost her cherry in this spot or something, so she had herself buried here. In her nightdress and holding a fig in her hand. She said if there was life after death a fig tree would grow out of her grave.'

'And so it did. How very reassuring.'

'Maybe it did. Or maybe someone planted one on top of her. Either way it doesn't prove a thing except that she was as daft as the rest of the family.'

I looked across the lake but the old woman had disappeared again. Naturally. 'Do you believe in life after death?'

'No. I believe in life before death like a sensible person. Come on, let's grab some TV catering, I'm starving.'

Tonight was barbecue night and there was no first- and second-class dining arrangement. Even the re-enactors, who normally cooked their own food at their campfires, were invited as long as they left their weapons at home. A large barbecue was set up next to the catering van and worked by the spotty youth under Delia's watchful eye. Apart from the predictable barbecue fare there were also grilled sardines to be had and even the vegetarians were well catered for. The smells of garlic, lemon and oregano mingled with the charcoal smoke. Wine and beer made an appearance and soon it turned into a party. Carla attended, in jeans and tee-shirt, looking less like a housekeeper than ever, and everyone apart from the old lady appeared to be there, eating and drinking in the warm evening air. After sunset Stoneking brought out a tray full of candles and lanterns that were soon dotted around the scene. As I stood at the edge of things, breathing in the summer fragrance, drinking some more of Stoneking's wine, I thought I was witnessing one of those English summer evenings that stay on in the memory as a touchstone for all those that follow. I had no idea just how memorable it would soon become.

A bonfire was kindled at the edge of the British territory and wax flares marked the Roman camp further down the lawns. Only one solitary light was showing in the house, behind the drawing-room window, which meant that beyond the pools of flare and firelight the darkness became inky. Here and there the glow of cigarettes or the dance of flashlights gave away the position of those beyond the edge of light. Inevitably someone with a guitar and a repertoire of folksy tunes turned up by the camp fire. I replenished my glass and made the rounds, vaguely looking for Guy but stopping to chat here and there and always keeping an eye on the barbecue. People were wandering about, sitting on the slightly damp grass or standing in small groups. Emms and Paul were strolling in my direction, talking shop. I could see smiles so briefly said hello.

'Not a bad day,' Emms said. Paul nodded his agreement. 'Tomorrow should be good too; we're getting the helicopter for a day and at some stage there'll be the Roman feast.'

'Sounds good,' I said. 'Never been on a helicopter, never had a Roman feast.'

'You can come up in the chopper with me,' Paul offered. 'We'll make lots of flyovers.'

'And you'll get a little taste of Roman food, too,' Emms promised.

'Excellent. Hang on, though. Who's cooking this Roman feast? It's not Brian, is it?'

Emms nearly choked on her wine. 'Ha, no!' she spluttered. 'We have Hilda Carson coming; she's a food historian from Bristol Uni. She's good, we've used her before.'

'Yes,' said Paul. 'She made us some Stone Age food, horribly authentic. I went right off the Neolithic after that gruel . . .'

I spotted Guy at last, sitting on a log under one of the gnarled chestnut trees, right at the edge of the light from the Britons' bonfire. He had a glass in one hand and a bottle of wine in the other. I was glad it wasn't a whisky bottle. Morgan was sitting on the grass next to him, cradling a plastic flagon of cider between his legs. Guy was sipping the wine tonight rather than trying to drown himself in the stuff and that was probably as

155

much as I could hope for. Morgan too seemed a little more mellow today. Perhaps it was the atmosphere of the evening. Out of politeness I squatted down by the tree next to Guy.

'Midsummer Night's dream,' Guy said vaguely.

'Appropriate,' I said. 'These are the Midsomer valleys.'

'Really?' said Morgan. 'I thought they only existed on telly. You know, *Midsomer Murders*.'

'Nope, they're right here. You walked into a dark legend.'

'Yeah? Maybe, but I sat in a damp patch, I reckon,' he said and got to his feet with a groan.

I felt it stir the air as it flew past my head and slammed into Morgan with a blood-wet thump. The giant metal dart knocked Morgan to the ground. He lifted himself up again to stare unbelieving down at his mangled thigh. The dart had ripped right through it, sticking out at either end. Then he started to scream. Blood was spurting in arcs from his trouser leg which was already soaked with it.

'Am-bu-lance!' I shouted towards the party crowd who had not yet grasped that Morgan's screams were no histrionics. 'Someone call an ambulance. *Now!*'

'Oh God. Oh my God.' Guy had sprung to his feet and kept repeating the incantation over and over, mesmerized by the blood. I undid Guy's belt and slipped it from his waist, then pounced on the fainting Morgan. By the time I had fashioned a tourniquet with the help of the belt and Morgan's packet of cigarettes he had passed out.

People crowded around now with candles and lanterns, looking shocked and dismayed.

'Who called an ambulance?' I demanded, making sure they hadn't all left it to someone else. No less than three people had, on their mobiles.

'So did I,' said Stoneking, pushing through the ring of people. 'I gave them instructions and opened the gate for them. What happened?'

'It's the *ballista*. Someone shot Morgan with the *ballista*,' I said.

'Brian! Where's Brian?' several people shouted.

'Then I expect we'll need the police as well,' Stoneking said.

Emms was crouched by Morgan's head, looking worried. 'The thing couldn't have gone off by accident, I suppose?'

'No it couldn't!' said Brian, pushing to the front. 'Someone took one of the darts from the box in my tent, aimed the *ballista* and fired it. And before you ask, it wasn't me.'

The ambulance seemed to be an age in arriving. 'Do you want me to take over?' Stoneking offered. I gladly accepted. I have never been keen on gore and I'd been staring at it for the last twenty minutes. I was liberally covered in Morgan's blood. 'Do we have to release the tourniquet from time to time?' Stoneking asked.

'I have no idea. I'd rather we didn't. He's lost so much blood already.' I could hear the two-tone ambulance siren now. Thanks to Mark's instructions they drove around the house and straight on to the lawn with their lights on full beam. I was on my way back to the house and they stopped next to me. 'Not me, not my blood,' I explained. 'He's down there.'

They gave another squawk on their siren and drove on towards the huddle around the stricken Morgan. I was still crossing the lawn when an armed response unit flashed past the house and stopped their vehicle at the top. They got out of the car and came across to cut me off, dazzling me with their torches. 'Are you hurt, sir? We had reports someone had been shot.'

'Someone was. With an ancient weapon; follow the ambulance. I helped the victim, hence the blood.'

'Is this a party Mr Stoneking is giving?'

'Sort of. You'd better ask him, he's down there.'

'Right, where are you going now?'

'To have a shower.'

They were still blocking my way. 'Do you live here? And can we have your name, please?'

'I'm staying here, as a guest, and the name is Honeysett.'

'Did you witness the shooting?'

'I did.'

'Please don't leave the property; we will need to take a statement in a minute.'

'Later. After I've had a very large drink,' I promised.

'I wouldn't advise that, sir.'

'Yes, thanks, I always call armed response when I want nutritional advice.' Their torch beam followed me for a few more paces before they turned to other matters but before I had even reached the verandah more of Avon & Somerset's finest arrived and poured round the corner. Behind them, at a more sedate pace, owing to his generous shape, followed the very last person you'd want to meet if you're covered head-to-toe in someone else's blood: Superintendent Michael Needham. He pointed a fleshy digit in my direction. 'Hold it right there, Honeysett.'

Ten

'It's not what it looks like, Mike.'

'You've no idea what it looks like,' said Needham. 'I won't shake hands, under the circumstances.'

'You've no idea of the circumstances yet.'

'Touché. Go get yourself cleaned up.'

'If you really think I should.'

'Come and find me when you're presentable again. And don't be too long about it.'

Tarmford Hall seemed eerily quiet; everyone was on the lawn and subdued and not a sound could be heard from inside the building.

First things first: a drink. I walked through the drawing room. There was a tall Chinese medicine chest that served as a drinks cabinet but I wasn't going to leave bloody paw prints all over the inlay work. I walked past it, down the central gallery and turned left towards the kitchen. I know my place. The door at the end of the corridor was wide open.

I now realized that the kitchen was inside the rectangular tower at the north corner and through the window above the Belfast sink I could see past the catering van and glimpse the lights of the ambulance. I switched on the ceiling light and went to the sink where I washed my hands. Then I started opening cupboards. I knew it had to be here somewhere. I opened a small door that I thought might lead into the pantry but it opened on to a narrow staircase. Worn stone steps led up as well as downward in a dizzyingly tight spiral without a handrail. Mm, maybe later. I closed it and opened another narrow door. The pantry. I pulled the string on the ceiling light and found it: Carla's cooking brandy. There was wine, calvados and sherry too but it was the brandy I glugged into a water glass now. I took a sip, then checked the label. Blimey, if this was what they cooked with, how expensive was the stuff they were drinking? I replenished the glass and returned the bottle.

In the attic I creaked along the uneven corridor, past my own door and to the end where the bathroom was. It was unreconstructed Edwardian and had a few personal items like toothbrush and shampoo in it, presumably Carla's. The old roll-top bath had generously old-fashioned proportions. I tried the hot water. Nothing. Not a drop. The tap sighed emptily. Then it groaned. It was obviously thinking about it. It steamed for a bit, then it spat, then a glorious stream of piping hot water came noisily from the flared spout. I put the bathplug in and went to my room. Five minutes later I returned in my bathrobe with my drink, towel and sponge bag. As in the rest of the house there was no lock or bolt on the door. Presumably one was expected to sing

160

in the tub to avoid embarrassment. I would definitely give that a miss. It would *create* embarrassment. I found Carla's bubble bath on the window ledge and added a generous measure to the steaming water, adjusted the temperature from boiling hot to scalding hot and let myself sink groaning into the trembling mound of bubbles. I closed my eyes and instantly the image of Morgan's shattered thigh appeared, blood spraying with the force of his pumping heart.

Morgan had been shot in the same place where he had been sitting when I got there, and the dart hit at the precise moment when he had stood up. Had the damp grass not made him move, had he still been sitting down, the dart could easily have pierced his chest or head. Only a few inches to the left and it would have found Guy's head or mine. I took a large gulp of fortifying brandy. This time there was no doubt in my mind: someone had aimed to kill. This was no stone urn heaved off the roof and hoping for the best. Someone had carefully taken aim, at one of us three, wanting to kill.

Unless . . . I took a deep breath and slid under the water, held my breath until I thought my lungs would burst, then spluttered upright. Bath foam crackled noisily in my ears. Unless it was exactly the same scenario as the urn: a lucky shot, not caring *if* it hit or *what* it hit. I flicked the foam from my ears and blew a blob of it off the tip of my nose.

I heard a creak and looked towards the door. In the dim light from the low-wattage bulb I stared at the dented doorknob – was it moving?

I noticed I was holding my breath again and let it out. Another creak, like someone putting weight on a floorboard, then quickly withdrawing it. Keeping stock-still would only alert whoever was out there to the fact that I had heard them. I made some casual splashing sound, then as quietly as possible lifted myself from the water and stepped on to the bath mat where I dripped for a moment, listening. I thought I could hear tiny sounds on the other side of the door. Softly I stepped closer, picking up a little wooden stool on the way; I held it like a weapon. Then I closed my right hand on the doorknob and yanked the door open. Nothing. The corridor was dark and empty.

Scary bathroom scenes, who needs them?

By the time I caught up with Needham on the terrace the cooking brandy had definitely done its thing; if anything, it had overshot its target. On the lawn and terrace, arc lights had been set up and in their cold glare people were making statements to police officers, both plain-clothed and uniformed. Superintendent Needham didn't look any more pleased to see me now that I was freshly washed. 'You took your time. I said *get cleaned up*, not go for the whole beauty treatment.'

'My room's up there under the eaves, Mike. Look at it; it's a ten-minute hike just to get up there.'

'And while I'm here on official business you can call me Superintendent.'

'Super.' Needham had once offered me first-name terms while his judgement was clouded by too much industrial lager and he had regretted it ever since.

Now he started on a familiar lament. 'I should have guessed I would find you here. If there's anything weird going on in Bath, Chris Honeysett is never far away. A man gets brained with a bottle? No sign of you. But a man gets shot with a two-thousand-year-old weapon and naturally you're standing right next to it.'

'I think I was probably hired to stop any weirdness developing.'

'You failed.'

'I'm not paid to stop bullets for people. Or *ballista* darts for that matter. What brought you out here in the vanguard? You usually take your time appearing. Man's not even properly dead.'

'Well, rock legend and all that. I was still working when the call came in, so I thought I'd have a look.'

'Don't tell me – you're a closet Karmic fan.'

'Lord, no, it was strictly folk music in my day.'

'How sad for you.' The ambulance had long left. 'Any word on Morgan from the ambulance crew?'

'Not one. They got a drip in him and carted him off. OK, then, start by explaining what you're doing here.'

We took a stroll away from the police business on the terrace. Forensics were out in force, examining the crime scene and taking away the *ballista* and spare darts, all of which were being wrapped in copious amounts of clear plastic. A sad-eyed Brian watched them do it.

I gave Needham the long version of why I was here and what had happened so far, including the drugged Glenfiddich episode, the steam room incident, the tumbling urn and the dart in the dark, all of which sounded like episode titles for a 1930s wireless mystery.

He gave it a moment's thought. 'I think what Annis said is at least something to bear in mind. Both the urn and the dart could have been meant for you. It's unlikely but possible.'

'Highly unlikely; I never met any of these people before. I think both of them were meant for Guy Middleton.'

'Well, don't stand so close next time.'

'I was just thinking the same thing myself.'

'You know, when *Time Lines* decided to come to Bath they asked if police could provide security for them. We politely pointed out that we just lost five thousand police officers in the cuts and told them to get their own bleeding security.' He made a sweeping gesture with one arm, encompassing the entire scene. 'And now look at it. The entire nightshift is up here and then some. And I suppose you are the bloody security they hired!'

'Ah, yes, I wondered when we'd get around to the *Honeysett-it's-all-your-fault* bit.'

'I'm not blaming you. Much. You'd need to hire an army to secure this place the way things are at the moment. I had a little chat with Mark Stoneking about his so-called security and it's a complete farce. *That* way,' Needham pointed back towards the house, 'you've got a high wall and a security gate. But the gate has so much wrought-iron decoration it's practically a ladder. *That* way,' he pointed towards the tented camp of the diggers, 'he's got a bit of deer fencing, which then peters

164

out where the farmland begins beyond the lake. Anyone can come in that way if they can swing their legs over a three-foot fence and aren't scared of cows. And at *that* side of his property,' Needham completed the compass by pointing beyond the hedge that hid the greenhouse, 'he's got *bugger all* apart from half a mile of brambles. It may discourage his fans but if someone wants to come and do him a mischief, or any of his guests for that matter, then the door's wide open to anyone with a pair of secateurs.'

'I wasn't hired to patrol the perimeter.'

'I guess not.'

'We've no witness to the shooting then?'

'No one saw anybody near the *ballista*, it was too dark. Wait a minute! There's no "*we* have no witness" – you keep your nose out of this and leave it to us. Oh, why am I wasting my breath? But if you do find out anything you'll let me know pronto. If you know what's good for you.'

'I'm well known for it. And guess who's coming tomorrow to stay here and paint a mural for the Stone King?'

'Really? Why am I surprised? I suppose that Tim Bigfoot chap's not far behind then,' he said and left me standing in the middle of the lawn.

'Big*wood*,' I called after him. 'It's his *wood* that's big!'

Apparently.

The questioning went on, the police took photographs as well as fingerprints for 'elimination purposes' and generally party-pooped around the place for hours. Having been quizzed by the top quizmaster himself and my fingerprints being on file for an awful lot of previous elimination purposes, I was immune to all that. It had been a long day and I had drunk a tumbler of very fine brandy. So I thought I could safely call it a day and go to bed.

Wrong again. I woke suddenly, taking a fraction of a second to realize where I was. For a moment I lay still, blinking into the darkness. What had woken me I didn't know, unless it was the stifling heat up here under the eaves. The tiny window was open but not a breath stirred. I groped for my mobile: four o'clock. I got up and stood by the window. It seemed a little cooler out there and very dark. The lonely twit-twoo calls of a couple of owls came from the woods. Then I heard a clink, quite faint, quite far off. But what kind of clink? There it was again. Metallic or stony? Metallic *and* stony, I decided. No reason why it shouldn't go clink out there, with all those people camped around the place – Romans, Britons and field archaeologists, and most of them armed to the teeth. The police had very nearly confiscated all their weapons. But since they had made no arrest there was still one urn-flinging, dart-shooting maniac out there. Middleton had promised to barricade himself into his room and insisted he would only open the door to me. That was not as daft as it sounded: the only people who could not possibly have fired the dart were him, Morgan and me.

I dressed quickly. There was no way I would get back to sleep lying on my bed in this stifling room, waiting for the next *clink*. And anyhow, there was always that fenced-off greenhouse that was begging to be looked at. Downstairs I padded through the dark drawing room with the aid of my mini Maglite. As I had suspected, the key was in the lock and the French doors unlocked which confirmed Needham's assessment that the security of Tarmford Hall was non-existent. It appeared that as long as it kept Karmic fans out of his hair it was enough for Mark Stoneking. I flicked off the light and, as quietly as I could, slipped through the door into the night. Out here I stood and let my eyes adjust to the dark. The cloud was broken and there were a few stars to pierce the darkness but I moved very gingerly nonetheless. Once on the vast lawn I didn't expect any obstacles and quickly got my bearings. There was the dark huddle of the Britons' encampment, nothing but an amorphous presence on the edge to my right. Further on down the slope were the ghostly white tent shapes of the Roman legion. I gave them a wide berth. Far to the left I could make out the hump of the giant spoil heap near the two trenches and, still thirty or so yards ahead of me, the dark mass of the first hedge between me and the lake. This meant I was probably in the right place to turn towards the greenhouse. I moved right and stopped. There were small noises ahead in the dark, breathing perhaps . . . shuffling . . . the sounds of exertion . . . not joyful exertion, I concluded. I moved cautiously towards it and the sounds abruptly stopped. There was a metallic clang, then a suppressed exclamation and all went quiet. I thought I could see a shape or two dwindle into blackness. If I used my tiny flashlight now it would probably achieve nothing much apart from telling everyone where I was. I was acutely aware that there were still any amount of bows and arrows out in those camps. I also retained the tiniest suspicion that perhaps, just possibly, both urn and arrow had been aimed at me after all. If I wanted to go on playing silly buggers in the dark I had better stagger on without a light. The one thing the torch would perhaps have achieved was to stop me cracking my ankle on something hard and cold. As it was I nearly fell over it. I groped around at my feet and even blindfolded I could have identified it as a spade. There was the black shape of a tree a few paces away so I lent it against that and went on. There it was, the dark loom of the high hedge that surrounded the greenhouse area, curving around at the bottom. I reached the stone-flagged path and found the iron gate set in the hedge. It was still locked so I scrabbled up it as well as I could, swung myself across and dropped down on the other side.

From having seen them in daylight through the bars of the locked gate I could tell what the dark shapes around me were: water butts, stacks of flowerpots, upturned wheelbarrows and several wooden bays that were probably compost heaps. I left them to my right and kept the greenhouse to my left. I flicked my torch on now as it was getting very dark here. The white paint used on the glass as shading against excessive sun made it look like the ghost of a greenhouse; its old-fashioned double door at the end stood wide open.

Nothing smells quite like half a greenhouse full of cannabis plants. I was no expert but these looked tall and perfectly smokeable to me, which probably explained the interest an enterprising field archaeologist took in the greenhouse after dark. Despite his heavy metal background, Mark Stoneking didn't strike me as the pot-smoking type, so presumably these automatically watered, well-ventilated plants were what kept Sam the gardener happy on his rounds. Not that cannabis was the only thing growing there; the staging running along the centre of the glass house was full of flowering plants in pots, some on automatic watering systems and doing well, others had perished and shrivelled in the heat. Behind the greenhouse and half disappearing into the unruly hedge stood a substantial wooden shed. I focussed the beam of my torch on to the door. Its padlock had been broken off, hasp and all, and the door stood ajar. I pushed it wide. Neat rows of gardening tools hung from the walls or stood leaning against them. There was a workbench with hand tools and bays of potting compost. Whether anything was missing I couldn't tell.

I climbed back out of the greenhouse area the way I had come and walked confidently back towards the house by starlight, which was a mistake because my right foot disappeared into a hole in the lawn and I fell flat on my face and twisted my ankle. I sat on the ground rubbing it and shone my torch at the unexpected hole. That was definitely not supposed to be there. It was far too deep and steep-sided to have been dug by an animal, bringing to mind the spade I had run into earlier. I flashed the torch around but its weak beam did not reveal any other holes, nor the author of this one. I hobbled back to the house and into the kitchen, found ice cubes in the fridge, shook them into a carrier bag and packed that around my ankle. Then I hobbled back to bed.

'Nighthawks,' Andrea said. We were standing with our breakfast cups of coffee by the hole I had fallen into. 'We've got bloody nighthawks.'

'And what are they when they're about?'

Cy joined us. 'Thieving bastards, is what they are.'

'For once I agree,' said Andrea. 'Nighthawks are thieves armed with metal detectors who turn up at night on archaeological sites and dig up anything they fancy or can sell on eBay. They're after coins, jewellery, any precious metal or artefact.'

'Metal detectorists are brainless scum. Half of the time they don't even know what they dig up or destroy.'

'Not all of them are bad, Cy; we've had this conversation before. Some do keep records and notify us when they find something. Most are trainspotter-type people. But these chaps – and they are always men – that raid archaeological sites at night are criminals. We'll tell the police of course but I know what they'll say.'

So did I. 'We no longer have the manpower?'

'Yup,' said Cy, kicking at the pile of earth left beside the hole. 'They're too busy chasing after drunks and druggies all night to protect us.'

'Hang on a minute.' Andrea pounced on the pile of earth Cy had kicked and lifted up what looked like a lump of mud to me but made Andrea

170

smile happily. She stood up and rubbed at the lump with her thumb until we could see it was a Roman coin. She squinted at it. 'There you are, fourth century. We'll make an archaeologist out of you yet, Cy; you dug it up with your boot. Chris here probably disturbed them and they didn't have time to find it.'

'They'll be back for it,' Cy said.

'I'm afraid Cy is right. We'll have to keep eyes and ears open for the rest of the week,' said Andrea. 'They always come back.'

Cy was visibly fuming and his hands worked into fists. 'If I get my hands on one of them I'll ram his metal detector where the sun doesn't shine.'

Andrea fluttered her eyelids. 'Aw, Cy, I didn't know you cared.'

When Mark Stoneking heard what had happened he was equally enraged, thumping the breakfast table. 'Letting archaeologists dig up the lawn is one thing, but thieving nighthawks quite another. If I catch any of them I'll let them have a dose of birdshot from my twelve-bore!'

'I wouldn't advise it,' I said, suddenly sounding like a policeman. I would have to watch that. 'Unless you can prove your life was in danger it'll earn you a jail sentence. Mind you, I had some trouble myself a while back, so I emptied the shot out of some cartridges and replaced them with uncooked rice. Hurts like buggery but is unlikely to do much lasting damage.'

He immediately stood up. 'Excellent idea. Any kind of rice?'

'Obviously, Arborio would be apt if you had

171

trouble with Italians but for your average British thief pudding rice will do.'

'I'll go and ask Carla if she's got any. I'm not having these people creep around my house at night digging for treasure. And who knows, perhaps it was one of them who shot at Morgan. Perhaps they were trying to steal the *ballista* and it went off.'

It was a subdued team that returned to the legitimate dig under a sky of lazily moving summer cloud. Last night's incident and the subsequent questioning by police meant that many had had too little sleep and too much to drink. Guy was monosyllabic at the breakfast table and the Britons, who were moving off now, looked glum. There was no more bravado, no more jeering. The Roman legion were tidying their camp and barely gave the departing Britons a glance. Emms called the hospital and announced the news that Morgan was now 'in a stable condition'. 'And how stable is Guy this morning?' she asked. We were standing on the terrace while Guy finished his breakfast inside.

'I'm not his psychiatrist. But if anything can make you jumpy, then having the chap next to you get shot usually does the trick. It didn't do much for my own Zen, I assure you. Are your digs always like this?'

'There's usually plenty happening but this is quite exceptional, even for us. In the past we've had scaffolding collapse, all our tools stolen, a river breaking its banks and putting the site under three feet of water. We've had permission to dig withdrawn halfway through filming because of a dispute among the owners and once the diggers went on strike. You see? I'm no stranger to directing shoots under difficult conditions, but this is scary even by my standards. What do you think? Was it meant for Morgan or Guy?'

'Your guess is as good as mine.'

'The police have put a guard outside Morgan's room at the hospital but haven't offered to protect Guy in the same way, so they must think the dart was meant to kill the one it hit. And I don't see a single police officer here now. Are they just going to let it lie? They haven't arrested anyone for it, have they?'

'They never ignore a violent crime like yesterday's; I wouldn't worry too much about that. They'll be back.'

As Emms went inside to coax Guy Middleton into another day's performance in front of the cameras my attention was claimed by the arrival of Annis Jordan, mural painter to the stars. She had packed the Landy to the gunnels with painting gear and strapped two ladders and planks to the roof rack. I helped her unload and carry the equipment inside.

'So where's Lurch?' she asked as she stepped into the gloomy entrance hall. 'I had expected a creepy butler. Or a footman with staring eyes at the very least.'

'No butler. There's a housekeeper. Carla.'

'Is she spooky?'

'Self-possessed. Very good to look at.'

'Oh, yeah?'

'Oh yes. But she only has eyes for the Stone King. Guy Middleton tried to grope her in the pool. Be warned, that man has roving hands as well as an expensive single-malt habit.'

'Gossip at last.'

Mark Stoneking found us depositing boxes of paints and jars full of brushes in the pool house. I introduced them. Dauber and muso stood among the paint pots and sized each other up; both seemed delighted by what they saw. Stoneking started by telling Annis how much he admired her painting – even though he had only seen them on a computer screen – and Annis told him she had all his albums – even though she had only recently dug them out again. I left the mutual admiration feast before they started autographing each other and went back to the dig.

Guy was in front of the cameras, fluffing his lines. Even the ordinarily patient Emms had a sharper tone this morning as she corrected Guy's mistakes. Middleton was only saved from a roasting by the arrival on the terrace of Hilda Carson, the Roman food expert. Emms came up to greet her but stopped next to me to vent her frustration. 'That's the problem with using actors to speak the lines instead of archaeologists; he doesn't actually understand what he's saying. If he knew anything about archaeology he wouldn't constantly get things muddled up.' She looked me in the eyes, laid a hand on my arm and smiled. 'I've no idea why I'm telling you. Probably because you're not part of it. Don't mind me. Just make the right noises.'

'There, there.'

Her hand remained on my arm. 'I'm sure you could do better than that.'

174

'OK, how's this: Emms, you're *so* right. It must be *very* trying having to deal with an alco*holic* actor because the punters *adore* him when Andrea, the head archaeologist, could do it *standing on her head*.'

'That's much better. Come and meet our food historian. I have it on good authority you're a bit of a foodie yourself.'

'Whose authority?'

'A large police superintendent's.'

'He can talk.'

'Hello, Hilda,' she said. The two women kissed on both cheeks. Hilda was about fifty, a whole foot shorter than the director. She wore a blue and white checked shirt, jeans and trainers and had slight sunburn on her nose and forehead. 'I'm glad you came out to help us again, and on a bank holiday at that.'

'Couldn't have done it otherwise, I'm so busy at the moment. But I love doing these demonstrations, and Roman is such a good period, too.'

Emms introduced us. Before she could explain why I was hanging around the place Mark Stoneking arrived on the terrace to greet Hilda. It appeared they had spoken on the phone.

Hilda buried her hands in her jeans pockets. 'Mark, you said you might be able to provide a few rabbits for the cooking demo. Any luck?'

Mark slapped a hand to his forehead. 'I did, didn't I? Rash words. I'll go and see what we can do. And Chris here promised to help shoot some, I seem to remember. Let's see if we can pot some now. When do you need them?'

The sooner the better, it turned out. In the

cluttered gun room Mark handed me a fine Browning over-and-under shotgun, a mate to the one he was loading for himself. They were engraved with autumn game and worth an absolute fortune. We walked down to the lake along the edge of the wood where the diggers were encamped.

'Broad daylight is not the best time to hunt rabbit,' Mark said. 'Much easier with a lamp at night, but at least we're less likely to kill anyone this way. Place is crawling with people.'

'At least the Britons have left the field.'

'Yes, that poor man,' Mark said. 'I hope he'll be all right. I still can't believe someone here wanted to murder him.'

'Or Guy.'

'Or Guy. Or you, for that matter.'

'It had occurred to me. And unless it was one of Morgan's own troop it means that person is still here. Have you changed your mind about the urn falling from your roof at all?'

'It's beginning to look dodgy now, isn't it?' He pointed. 'Go that way. We'll skirt the lake and the wood for a bit. You can see the diggers' tents up there now.'

To our left, about thirty yards beyond the fringe of the woods, a collection of tents, blue, red, green and silver-grey. Their camp had been set up close to the weed-fringed stream that ran through the length of the wood and then out to feed the lake. Lengths of washing line were strung between trees; clothes and sleeping bags were hanging up to air. Soon the ornamental lake began to narrow and curve a little to the right. Here an area of bracken encroached on the path and reached out towards the lake from the fringes of the woodland. Another hundred yards further and I could see the end of the wood and of Stoneking's private domain, marked by a low electrified fence, designed to keep out sheep or cattle. There were none in the grassy fields beyond.

'This is a good place; we'll wait by those trees there. Our bunnies love this area. It's the bracken, gives them cover from buzzards. But they'll show themselves . . . Oh, there's one right there, see?'

A tiny fluffy thing had appeared at the edge of the bracken cover. 'That's barely a mouthful,' I complained.

'We'll wait.'

'Until he gets bigger?'

I was never a hunter. Occasionally I'd get the notion to shoot a rabbit in the long grass around Mill House but as often as not I was outwitted by the things or simply missed by a mile. There is, however, something primevally exciting about watching and waiting for prey, a deeply buried hunting instinct that awakens as soon as you hold a weapon and see edible critters move about in the wild. Mark had chosen the place well. Not five minutes after our arrival four rabbits were hopping about on the grassy slope between the bracken and the edge of the lake.

'All right,' Mark murmured in my ear. 'You'll take the left, I'll take the right. When you're ready, on the count of three. One . . . two . . .'

On three I squeezed the trigger. Mark let fly with both barrels, killing two rabbits. I killed a bracken.

'You really are quite a lousy shot, aren't you? If you're ever accused of shooting anyone I'll be your character witness.'

'Told you.'

'You can be gun dog then. Fetch.'

I picked up the rabbits, Mark paunched them and we moved on. 'Are you beginning to regret the *Time Lines* thing yet?' I asked.

At first I thought he was ignoring the question but he was merely taking his time before answering. 'I thought it would be great. I mean, I liked the programme. I was thrilled to meet them. But I had no idea there would be so many of them. The diggers. Geo-physicists. And the re-enactors. All the people you never see – sound man, camera man, the technical staff and the caterers.'

'At least the re-enactors will leave tonight.'

'Oh, yeah, and in a couple of days we'll get a busload of school kids to be shown around and they'll stay and wash all the finds that have come up so far.'

'You must have agreed to all that.'

'I didn't read the contract.'

'I didn't read mine either, not beyond the agreed fee. Presumably they'll pay you well.'

'Reasonably well. But if I break the contract and tell them to leave *I'll* be paying *them*. A huge amount. Couldn't afford to.'

'Grin and bear it?'

'Don't know about that; it's not something I've ever been good at. Wait, see what I see?' He lifted the gun, aimed, fired and two more rabbits keeled over. 'That'll have to do; I'm getting bored with this. I want to go back and see whether Annis has made a start on my mural. If I like it I might get her to do the whole pool house . . .'

Back at the dig I found Hilda at the edge of the legionnaires' camp. With the help of some of the diggers and the production team she was setting up her Roman kitchen which she had brought complete in the back of a Land Rover. Was I the only person left who wasn't driving one? A huge iron barbecue had already been set up and lit. There were rustic tables and a lot of terracotta and iron implements, all reproduction but looking ancient enough. Faggots of herbs, mysterious bottles and stoppered jugs promised exotic ingredients and new tastes. I waved the rabbits at Hilda who was now dressed in a brown tunic and cream shirt rolled up at the sleeves and had changed from trainers to leather sandals.

'You got some!' she said when she received my offerings. She was delighted with Mark's murderous efforts.

So was Cy. 'I want the whole thing, the skinning and all that.'

Emms was unconvinced. 'People don't watch *Time Lines* to see animals being skinned. And it'll probably upset the vegetarians.'

'It's living history, blood and guts. We'll show it. And sod vegetarians, they're always upset. Not enough zinc in their bloody diets, or something.'

'We'll do that first then,' Hilda suggested. 'They'll take time to cook.'

'OK,' Emms agreed, 'we'll do the passage about food introductions afterwards. The helicopter is due any minute, too. Paul will go up to

179

do the aerial shots, then return and do the rest of the food cameo. Can you work around that?'

Hilda waggled a vicious-looking knife and smiled. 'I'm easy.'

Paul set up his camera and focussed on the chopping board. Emms waited until everything was in place, then called: 'Action!'

'I was keen to include rabbit in our Roman feast because we take rabbits for granted, seeing them in the countryside, that is, but it was the Romans who first introduced and farmed them. We have a lovely example of a rabbit here and I will show you how to skin it now.' With two swift strokes of her big knife Hilda chopped off the feet. 'We don't want these, but you can keep them if you are superstitious. They're supposed to bring good luck though it doesn't seem to have worked for the rabbit. We take off the head like so.' The knife easily separated it from the body. 'Then you start peeling the fur back, freeing the hind legs, and then you pull.' She stripped the fur off the rabbit's carcass in one swift movement. 'And there you have one skinned rabbit ready for the pot.'

'And cut,' Emms said, appropriately. 'I didn't expect it to be that quick.'

'Forty-two seconds,' Paul said admiringly. 'You have done this before.'

I found myself a knife among the utensils and helped with the skinning of the bunnies, but Hilda skinned the remaining two in the time it took me to do one. While I struggled with it I noticed that we were being intently watched by Delia, the caterer.

180

Hilda had noticed it too. 'Hello,' she said. 'Interested in Roman food?'

I introduced her. 'Delia – sorry, Adèle, everyone calls her Delia – is our excellent *Time Lines* caterer. She feeds the multitudes during the dig.'

'You're a cook, are you?' said Hilda. 'Gosh, I couldn't do that day in, day out; it would bore me rigid. I just do the odd historical demo, the rest of the time it's refectory food for me, too busy with my real job. Right, Chris, joint your rabbit the way I did these and then we can start that dish off. I like to give it at least two hours with wild rabbit, three if they're on the large side.' She turned her attention to the giant barbecue.

Delia gave the Roman kitchen one more critical look, then walked off. 'Everyone needs a hobby.'

The charcoal had burnt down nicely to a steady glow and Paul was ready for the next shot. Hilda started her stew by glugging a historic amount of olive oil into a cauldron, followed by the rabbit pieces and wine from a stoppered jug. Next, in went a slug of vinegar and a faggot of fresh herbs. When she covered the cauldron with a lid the filming stopped.

I was still nosing around the unusual and unlabelled jugs and covered terracotta pots when the unmistakable noise of a low-flying helicopter approached. One minute it was just an ear-popping churning of the air, the next it appeared over the house and lawns like an evil bird ready to pounce. There was ample space for it to land and the pilot picked a likely spot. Even at a distance the wash of the rotor blades was making itself felt.

'We'll go up three times,' Emms told me. 'First

I go up with Andrea and Paul, so Andrea can tell us what she sees and I'll throw together some lines for Guy. Then Guy, Andrea and Paul go up, Paul shoots the chat they have. Then Paul goes up again to take long shots of the area and you can go with him then.'

'Great, ta.' In the sober light of day my enthusiasm for helicopter rides had somewhat subsided. I had always been scared of flying but an enforced flight home from Corfu earlier that year had taken the edge off my terror, since I had quite clearly survived it. Though now that the thing stood churning on the lawn I wasn't so sure this would be fun.

Annis, who had come out to take a break from staring at the blank wall of the pool house, thought it would. 'You survived three hours in cattle class from Corfu to Bristol. This will be a breeze. You'll kick yourself if you don't do it – it's fun.'

'Oh yeah? Been on many helicopter rides?'

'Loads. Parents used to drag me to the Isles of Scilly on a regular basis.'

Stoneking, who seemed to be shadowing Annis now, pulled a face. 'I always hated the damn things. As soon as we got famous that was how we were supposed to arrive everywhere. I never got used to it, felt sick every time.'

The helicopter took off with archaeologist, director and cameraman, sweeping off towards the lake in a climbing turn. It did occur to me that, on an accident- and sabotage-prone dig, putting those three in the air together looked like tempting fate. If that load crashed it would spell the end of *Time Lines*. For nearly ten minutes the helicopter just hovered around above us and soon no one paid much attention. The dig was progressing and the three of us took a walk around, now that we could not get in the way of the filming. Large amounts of finds had come out of the ground, looking like so much rubbish to me; they were piled up in black seed trays waiting to be cleaned by excited school kids but, as Adam and Julie told us, nothing very exciting or unexpected had turned up. 'But I'm sure it will,' Julie said from the bottom of her trench. 'Remember what I told you; *Time Lines* is famous for the unexpected.'

'I think we've had enough of the unexpected already,' said Stoneking.

After a short break for writing lines it was Guy and Andrea who went up with Paul. 'I *hate* the damn things,' Guy hissed as he stomped past us. 'And they always fly them like it's bloody *Apocalypse Now*.'

Their flight looked sedate enough to me until a few minutes later when all of a sudden the helicopter swooped in low over the bottom of the lawn near the last hedge before the lake, then hovered at tree-top height, churning up leaves and making the hedges sway in the wash. Then it swooped off again and came in to land, much sooner than I had expected, considering they were going to film Guy delivering his lines. I ambled towards the landing place since it was my turn next. Even before it had properly settled on the ground Guy jumped from the helicopter and stomped off towards the lake, followed more sedately by a happily smiling Andrea.

'What's up?' I asked.

Paul was changing seats and repositioning his camera. 'Hop in and you'll see. I'll make sure to get a good shot of it, though I doubt it'll appear in the final cut. Buckle up.'

I did. This was me, in a helicopter. With the doors wide open. What had I been thinking? Of course I was going to buckle up, and where did they keep the parachutes on these things? Up it went like an express elevator and swooped round, first towards the hall, then in a tight climbing turn. So *that's* what that felt like. I had often wondered. Could I get off now, please? It was bloody noisy, too.

Paul pointed at the pair of headphones beside me. Once I had put them on I could actually hear what he was saying. 'I don't think Guy is having such a good time on this dig. There he is. Have a look down there.'

I could now see Guy, easily recognizable by his hat, Emms with her red hair and Andrea all standing at the bottom of the lawn near the hedge. Guy was waving his arms around a lot. They were standing in front of an area where the lawn had wilted to a sickly yellow, forming two-foot-high letters. They spelled SORRY IT MISSED YOU. We hovered above them.

'Good effort, don't you think?' Paul said without taking his eye off the viewfinder. 'Done with weedkiller, I expect. Not quite as popular as he was, our Mr Middleton. You should have heard him when he saw it; it was priceless. I think it's quite a polite message, considering what a completely selfish bastard he is. I'd have written

184

something more pithy and anatomical myself.' He spoke to the pilot now and told him to fly a few gentle loops around the entire area. After a while I managed to relax a bit and began almost to enjoy myself. An aerial view really does give a different perspective. The Stone King's realm was even larger than I had expected, though most of it was woodland lying to the north, bordered by enough brambles to start a jam-making business. The ornamental lake looked smaller from above and its island was revealed as no more than a dozen trees with a tiny clearing in the centre. Despite the large amount of people involved in the filming of the dig, from up here they looked thin on the ground. At the next flyover we could see Guy marching across the lawn, still gesticulating histrionically, the easily recognizable red-haired Emms following some ten paces behind. She stopped and looked up at us, then waved and pointed with an expansive gesture at the marching Guy. 'I think she wants you down there,' said Paul, 'to pour oil on Guy's waters. Personally, I'd use petrol.'

Eleven

By the time I got back to terra firma there was no sign of Guy. 'Stomped off in a mega huff this time,' Emms said, 'and for once I don't blame him. That was a very unkind message.'

'Paul thought it was polite, considering.'

'But at least we know now that the dart was meant for him, not Morgan.'

'Possibly,' I said. 'Always assuming that whoever weedkilled the lawn is the same person who tried to dartkill the presenter. Could easily be someone else.'

Emms nodded. 'True. Almost anyone, come to think of it; he doesn't have many fans on the team. But none of it helps *Time Lines* and as much as I . . .' She paused, hunting for a judicious word. 'Disapprove of Mr Middleton's style I wish this nonsense would stop.' She folded her arms across her chest and looked out over the lawn from where we were standing on the terrace. 'Look at it. It could all have been so bloody idyllic and for once even comfortable and luxurious.'

'For some of you,' I said, thinking of the sleeping bags drying on the line in the woods.

'Yeah, I know, I'm a selfish cow. But most of them are young and they wouldn't want to be doing anything else at this time of their lives, really. Can you smell something wonderful?'

'That'll be the rabbit stew. Not ready for a while yet.'

'Right, back to work. Andrea will do the PTC from the helicopter. And she'll do it beautifully,' she said, smiling. 'See what Guy is up to and try and hide his whisky bottle or something. Or alternatively just kick him up the behind, I'm past caring.'

I found Middleton in his room. He had worked himself into quite a state.

'The bastards!' Guy's hands were shaking with rage but were steady enough to pour whisky. 'It was meant for me; the *ballista* dart was meant

186

for me. One of the bastards down there is trying to kill me.' He was standing by the window of his room, looking out through the gap between the curtains, too agitated to sit down.

'You've made enemies,' I concluded.

'I have always had enemies. This is different, I can feel it. Probably one of the people I'm looking at right now, but which one of them, which one, eh?'

'Whoever burnt that message into the lawn isn't necessarily the same person as the one who fired the dart. I wouldn't take it as another threat; I think it's just someone gloating.'

He turned around to face me. 'What makes you say that?'

'If I had shot at you I would write "Sorry I missed you". Instead it says "Sorry *it* missed you".'

'You're splitting hairs. And even if you're right, am I supposed to be cheered by the thought that more than one bastard out there wishes me dead?' He looked round the room, found his jacket and rummaged in the pockets. 'Here.' He held out a piece of crumpled and folded paper to me. 'Here's one person who *doesn't* wish me dead. *He*'s trying to slowly bleed me dry.'

I took the note. It was written in capitals and blue biro on half a sheet of A4 printer paper.

THE USUAL AMOUNT
11 PM
WAIT ON THE LANDING STAGE
ALONE

Guy was right, of course; a blackmailer would not be trying to kill the goose that lays a 'usual

187

amount' of golden eggs. 'How much is the "usual amount"?'

Guy had turned his back on me again and resumed his place by the window. 'Two grand.'

'How long has it been going on?'

'A couple of seasons.'

'How often do you pay him?'

He shrugged. 'Each shoot. And the price went up.'

'You're mad. He'll never leave you alone. And the price will always go up. You'll have to tell the police.'

Guy turned around and gave me a look of contempt. 'Thanks for your brilliant and original advice, Chris. I can afford to pay him; I cannot afford to go public.'

'What has he got on you?'

He looked away for a moment, then gave a curt shake of the head. 'I can't tell you that.'

'I'm probably the only one you *can* safely tell. Client confidentiality,' I lied.

'You promise? It's . . . it's kind of embarrassing.'

'You're willing to pay a blackmailer until the end of your days to avoid embarrassment?'

'I'm paying him to stay out of prison,' he said impatiently. 'It would be the end of my career, what's left of it. I'll have to keep on paying him or else find him and kill him.'

'Steady on. Tell me what he's got on you. Perhaps we can sort something out.'

Guy looked doubtfully at me, then went and recharged his glass. He avoided my eyes, shrugged deeper into his clothes, pinched his nose, sniffed. 'He . . . he's got photographs. Of me with a girl.'

'So? Oh, I think I get it.'

'We did a dig two autumns ago in Gloucestershire. She was from the local school; they came out to help with field walking. And later again washing the finds.'

'She was under age?'

'Chris, I swear I thought she was sixteen. She was *nearly* sixteen, a couple of months and she would have been.'

'Even if she had been sixteen that could have spelled the end of your career if the papers wanted to make something of it. But if she was fifteen that's statutory rape. "*I thought she was sixteen, Your Honour*" won't cut any ice.'

He sat down heavily on the bed. 'I know that. I know that now.' He sighed.

'And someone's got pictures of you with this girl? How?'

He made a helpless hand gesture, palms upwards. 'Must have followed us. By the river. She thought it was romantic . . .'

'So what happened to the girl?'

'Not sure. She kept writing to me for a while then it fizzled out. I think she found a real boyfriend.'

'You've no idea who is blackmailing you?'

'Not the foggiest. Someone on the production team, one of the diggers, could be anyone who owns a camera. I've suspected everyone in turn.'

'The cameraman, Paul?' I suggested.

'Obvious choice, of course. But everyone round here takes pictures, videos, stills, for the production, for the archaeology, for their Facebook pages, for their mum and dad! It could be anyone connected with *Time Lines* and actually, Paul is the one person who never complains when I get things wrong or forget my lines.'

'That's probably because he sells the out-takes. How is the money handed over?'

'Different ways. First time it was under a rock near the dig, once I had to leave it in a lift, once in a pub toilet.'

'You've never been tempted to hang around and see who it is?'

'I tried once. I was spotted. That's when the amount went up. As a punishment for trying. The vindictive bastard.'

'What would you have done if you had found out who is behind it?'

'I don't know. Talked to them. Begged them? Thumped them? Hard to say.'

It sounded genuine to me. If you were being blackmailed by someone you worked with closely day in, day out you would be so consumed with curiosity as to who it was you might not think much beyond finding out. But that would soon change, I was certain. You would want to fight back. Unless you were completely spineless, of course. 'Can you afford to pay? Have you got the money?'

'All in tens and twenties.' He puffed out his cheeks. 'I've written cheques for some pretty big amounts in my life but two grand in notes somehow feels a lot more painful to give away.'

'Yes, blackmailers don't usually take cheques. And you don't get much in return that you didn't already have. Do you want me to follow you discreetly, see if I can spot who picks it up?'

He frowned at that. 'If they find out they'll up the money and I still won't be able to go to the police. I'm not sure it's a good idea.'

'I'm pretty good at not being spotted.' Often because I'm not there, I thought guiltily. Michael Dealey and his wheelchair were leaving narrow tyre marks on my conscience.

'I'll think about it.'

'But let me know in good time.' Since Guy wasn't offering me any I found a glass and poured myself a measure of malt. 'Are these incidents connected? Did they push the urn off the roof as a reminder or something? And your sweat lodge moment?'

'I don't think so. I've always paid up, haven't I? That's other people. Everyone's after me. They're trying to kill me for one reason or another.'

Guy was beginning to sound paranoid but I found it hard to blame him. 'You're saying it as though people don't need much of a reason to kill.'

'Do they?'

I took a breath to give him my 'reasons for committing murder', a short list that has Greed and Stupidity vying for top spot, but I didn't want to give Guy ideas. If someone was really trying to bump him off he probably knew the reason, even if he wasn't conscious of it. 'Think about it, Guy. Who, in this group of people, did you cross enough to make them want to kill you? You must know.'

191

'Look, Sherlock, don't you think I've wracked my brains about it? Don't you think I'd have said if I knew? I've thought of pretty much nothing else for months.'

I finished my drink and set the glass on the mantelpiece next to a vase of silk flowers. 'Okay. Then perhaps you could give some thought to this: what kind of behaviour has brought you to a point where the only person you haven't pissed off enough to feel murderous towards you is me? *Yet*. No one likes you much, Guy Middleton. You're not giving people much reason to.' I made for the door.

'The public love me,' he protested.

'Of course.'

'I get fan mail from all over the world!' He was nearly shouting now as I left his room and closed the door behind me.

'Because they never met you,' I said to the empty gallery.

Downstairs I walked into the pool house to check on progress there. I found Annis on the right side of the pool staring at the empty wall with a mug of coffee in her hand and I found Stoneking on the opposite side of the pool, sitting in a cane armchair, watching Annis staring at the wall. I joined him first. 'I've been banished,' he said in a cathedral whisper. 'This is as close as I'm allowed.'

'I'm surprised she's allowed you in at all.'

'She's been standing there for ages. Is she going to do some painting any time soon?'

'Could be hours yet. Then she might explode all over that wall or she might put three dabs of pink on it and call it a day's work. You're not paying her by the hour, are you?' I walked round the pool to check with Annis.

'It's got potential,' she said.

'Course it has, it's a white wall.'

'Perhaps it has too much potential. I mean where do you start? Over there? Or over there? How wide? How high? Long and narrow? Tall and wide? Where's it going to end? I think I'll need more coffee, hon.'

Nothing had changed there then. Back on the lawn the team had just waved the helicopter goodbye and another cooking sketch was being prepared. For this a few Roman soldiers were fetched to go about their business in the background, walking, chatting in pairs or carrying things to and fro while in the foreground Hilda Carson cooked and talked food. Hilda knew her stuff and could talk straight to camera without a script.

'I won't bother you with stuffed dormouse or similar delights. A lot has been said about the elaborate feasts that the Roman elite enjoyed, but even ordinary Romans, unless they were very poor indeed, enjoyed a diet far superior to that of the Britons at the time. Many of the ingredients we now take for granted and use regularly in our own cooking arrived with the Romans. Before the invasion we didn't have parsley, spearmint, rosemary or sage, marjoram, thyme or watercress. The Romans brought with them apples and pears, medlars, mulberries, sweet chestnuts, damsons, plums and cherries and probably the walnut. And of course they brought their beloved grapes.' She pointed to an earthenware dish laden with out-of-season plastic grapes. 'Yet even more surprising is the long list of vegetables they introduced into this country, many of which we tend to think of as typically British: onions, leeks, cabbages and carrots, but also endives, globe artichokes, cucumbers, courgettes, asparagus, parsnips, turnips, radishes, celery and lettuce. Of course neither the potato nor the tomato would arrive in Europe for close to another fifteen hundred years, so you may well ask: what was British food like before the Romans arrived? The answer is of course . . .'

It was populist but interesting enough to keep me hanging around, though the sight of Hilda wrapping a huge salmon in chard leaves and heaving it on to the barbecue would on its own have been enough to keep me there. She was preparing several other dishes, stuffing herbs into offal, making flat breads and even a kind of fruity custard.

Many of the dishes, which sadly included the custard I had eyed with intent, contained large doses of that most Roman of ingredients: *garum*. In order to make it, take a large amount of mangled fish intestines – oily fish only, please – stick them in a big glass jar, pour over a couple of inches of salt and some herbs – as though that made much difference – add a dash of water and leave to fester in strong sunshine for a few months. If you drop the jar it will wipe half the value off your house faster than you can say negative equity.

The very thought of the stuff made me want

to heave so I noted carefully which recipes were *garum*-free. Another two hours went by before all the dishes were ready and lined up in a photogenic display on the tables. I had fetched Annis from the pool to make sure she got more than coffee into her system; she had at last managed to get some paint on the wall, to the delight of Mark who came poodling after her at a respectful distance. Guy made an appearance too. He had been persuaded to stop sulking long enough to speak a few lines for the camera at the opening of the feast before the VIPs, which – off-camera – included Annis, me and Stoneking, started demolishing the display. What began as tentative sampling soon turned to serious scoffing; Hilda's Roman cookery was exceptional. Even so I stuck to the *garum*-free rabbit stew, of which there was plenty, and the salmon wrapped in chard over which fierce battles were fought. Mark contributed a few bottles of wine and also sent a couple to the poor diggers. They had been excluded from the feast to keep the numbers down and would soon be queuing at the catering van for more conventional suppers as another session of the dig came to a close.

When the feast broke up the Romans, of whom only Brian had been invited to partake, began to pack up their camp in order to return to the twenty-first century. Annis went back to her mural while I took a stroll around Tarmford Hall in the evening light. When I came to the place where the urn had crashed to the ground I saw that the extreme left door of the coach house stood open. I stuck my head around the door jamb. Then I stuck the rest of me around it as well. Immediately in front of me were the wooden stairs that led up to the floor above where the technicians had set up their computers. Down here the coach house was now a six-bay garage, four bays of which were occupied. As I had expected from an old-school rock star, there was a Rolls Royce; it was a blue 1980s model dripping with chrome. Next to it stood a racing-green Morgan, a two-seater convertible that had seen a lot of use and was covered in mud. The next car up was a Ford van – Sam the gardener's, I decided – and the one closest to me was the tiniest Mercedes imaginable, which was probably what Carla the housekeeper used to get around.

I was just about to leave when from upstairs came a sound that made me stop in my tracks. It was the noise I had recently heard inside the helicopter, now played through a tinny loud-speaker. Then Guy's voice as he started effing and blinding. 'Look what the bastards did. Down there. There, you dickhead! There! In five-foot bloody letters! You can hardly miss it, can you? Pilot, go back, fly back, get us down there this instant!'

The recording stopped and there was laughter. 'What a shame it won't be broadcast, it's my favourite bit,' said one voice.

'Whoever did that got his money's worth, it was inspired,' said another. I recognized the voices as belonging to the technicians who walked around joined at the hip.

'Do you think they'll ever catch whoever fired the bolt?' said the first voice.

'I doubt it, unless they left fingerprints on the apparatus. My money is still on Cy; why else would he have asked us to say he was chatting to us when the screaming started?'

'Because he was wandering around by himself and would have been an obvious suspect? Everyone knows he hates Guy. And it's obvious the bolt was meant for him. Want to watch it again?'

'Go on, then.'

The recording played for a second time. 'There, you dickhead! There . . .!' More laughter.

I slipped out of the garage and sauntered back to the house. Two suspects eliminated and one incriminated; it always pays to be nosey. Satisfied with my day's work so far I climbed up to the attic room, which now had all of Annis's luggage in it, climbed over her bags and flopped on the bed for a post-prandial doze which would help me to be awake and sober by the time darkness fell. I was still hoping Guy might relent and ask me to follow him to the landing stage when he paid his blackmailer later tonight but it wouldn't matter if he didn't.

Because I would follow him anyway.

I must have drifted off soon afterwards because I woke with a start when Annis fell into the room. She looked dreadful and sounded worse.

'Make room on the bed,' she croaked, 'I want to die.'

I shot off the bed to make space for the invalid. 'What happened? You look bad.'

'Food poisoning,' she groaned. 'I threw up in the pool house, the downstairs toilet and would have thrown up again in the bathroom up here but someone was already chucking up in it.'

'What did you do?'

'Threw up out of the window.'

'Inspired.'

'I heard a lot of retching on the way up, I think half the house is sick. Must be the Roman feast.'

'I feel fine.'

'I'm so happy for you,' she groaned.

'Anything I can do?'

'Go kill that woman who cooked the stuff.' Beads of perspiration had gathered on her forehead. I left her with a glass of water and a promise to return soon. As I stepped into the corridor Carla appeared from the bathroom, ashen-faced, steadying herself against the wall as she went.

'You can use it if you must but be quick, I might need it again in a hurry,' she said weakly.

'I don't seem to be affected,' I said, feeling almost guilty. 'Which dishes did you eat?'

'A bit of everything.'

'Is everyone ill?'

'Some or all, I don't care. My insides are on fire and . . . and . . . excuse me.' She groped her way back to the bathroom.

On the first-floor gallery where the production team had their rooms everything seemed quiet at first. The door at the end opened and Mark Stoneking appeared. He looked fine.

'How is Annis?' he asked.

'Wanting to die.'

'Don't say that. I've called my doctor, he should

be here soon. I feel fine but most people who had the Roman food are feeling pretty awful. You're all right too?'

'So far. What did you eat?'

'Same as you. I'm not one for offal and all that and I didn't want to fight the girls over the custard.'

'It must have been the fish sauce, it went into everything apart from the dishes you and I ate.'

'My doctor suggested I make a vat of peppermint tea for the invalids, keep everyone hydrated. I'm off to the kitchen.' He clattered down the stairs.

I rapped on Guy's door. There was an indistinct sound I chose to interpret as an invitation to enter. Guy was on his knees in front of the toilet bowl, looking wretched. 'It's you,' he said in an accusing tone. 'Go and fetch me a doctor.'

'Doctor is on his way,' I assured him.

'I'm dying,' he wailed. 'I've been poisoned.' Pearls of sweat ran down his face.

'You and the rest of the crew. Everyone who ate the Roman food.'

'Then why aren't you ill?' he asked. 'I saw you eat it.'

'I had already swallowed the antidote.'

'Oh, *God*,' he groaned. 'I want to throw up but can't. I'm empty. So why do I feel so bad?'

I helped him to his bed where he flopped on to the pillow, wild-haired and sweaty. Through the open window came the sound of distant retching and the flushing of toilets. Outside it was getting dark.

Guy noticed it too. 'Oh God, what time is it?

199

I have to hand over the money. I don't think I can make it.'

'Surely he'll understand? And for all we know he might be feeling the way you do.'

'I can't risk it. At the very least he'll demand even more money next time.'

'I'll do it.'

'You can't, he'll be expecting me.'

'Exactly. I'll borrow your hat and jacket. It'll be dark. He'll be expecting you and in the dark that's what he'll think he is seeing.'

Guy probably felt too weak to argue because he showed me where the money was, a considerable wad of notes in a Manila envelope. I slipped into his jacket and took his hat. 'I'll look in on you when I get back.'

'Just send in the bloody doctor you promised. And don't lose that money.'

On my way back up to our attic room I passed a window from where I could see that the bloody doctor was getting out of his car. When I reached our floor Annis was just returning from her latest trip to the bathroom. She let herself fall back on the bed. I thought her pallor looked slightly less worrying.

'Threw up again?' I asked unnecessarily.

'I threw up everything I ate at the feast. I threw up today's breakfast and yesterday's supper. I threw up green stuff I've not seen before. I threw up stuff I probably still need.'

'The doctor has arrived; he'll be making his rounds. I've got an errand to run for Guy.'

'At this time of night? What time is it?'

'Nearly eleven,' I said, using a rubber band to

pull my hair into a ratty little ponytail. 'Back soon.' Just then there was a knock at the door. I answered it.

'Mint-flavoured rehydration for the inflicted mural painter.' Stoneking came in balancing an enormous brown teapot and some cups on a tray.

I grabbed Guy's hat and hurried downstairs, let myself out of the front door and rammed the hat on my head. The sliver of a waxing moon had risen above the woods, making the night brighter than I would have wished. It was very still in the grounds. No Britons, no legionnaires' camp, and the catering van long locked and shuttered. It was going to be a sticky night. There was a single cricket in the grass somewhere, rasping hope-lessly, making the silence feel even larger. I hurried across the lawn, keeping an eye out for unscheduled holes and tools left lying about. The scale of the gardens and the absurd statuary dotted about here and there made me feel like I was walking through a James Bond set; in this light any one of the sculptures could have been a person standing very still, waiting to attack with improbable weapons. I patted the envelope bulging the jacket pocket, dived through the gateway in one, then another hedge and came to the edge of the lake. There was the narrow wooden landing stage, pointing like a scrawny finger at the black silhouette of the wooded island. The old rowing boat was again nowhere to be seen. There had been no instruction as to where Guy should leave the money, just to be on the landing stage by eleven. I checked my watch: it was eleven now. Slowly I made my way across the dry, creaking planks to the very end. I took the envelope out so it could be seen and patted the palm of my hand with it. Two thousand pounds. Was this about greed for the money or was it simply a way of hurting Middleton? Very distantly I could hear the odd snatch of talk or laughter from the digger camp in the woods; no retching there, of course, since they had all eaten Delia's food from the van. I checked my watch again. Five minutes past. Were blackmailers usually on time or was making the victim wait yet another power play blackmailers enjoyed? There was the odd croak and quack in the reeds and a fish rising sent tiny ripples across the moonlit surface of the lake. I kept my head bowed a little to shade my face under the broad-brimmed hat. Was it too flimsy a disguise? Had I failed to pass myself off as the *Time Lines* presenter? The thin moon sickle moved into a cloud, plunging the entire scene into darkness. With no visual reference points I was beginning to feel uncomfortable out there with water all around me.

I heard quiet footfall behind me and turned. Then there was a light, too, the beam from a powerful torch, dancing along as its owner moved through the trees. The beam swept towards the landing stage, picked me out and stopped, resting on my face and blinding me. I shielded my eyes but said nothing. If I had to speak I would groan as though feeling sick from food poisoning. The beam left my face, the unseen person moved on a few paces, then the beam picked me out again for a second look. After that it went out completely, leaving me squinting into the dark and listening out for the footsteps. They continued behind a hedge now, quietly moving in the direction of the glasshouse.

I waited. The moon reappeared from its hiding place and I could see my surroundings more clearly again. There was no one near. Had I been rumbled? I had not really expected the black-mailer to turn up in person; I had thought I would find another note or sign at the end of the jetty, some kind of hollow-tree scenario. I waited. Perhaps the blackmailer was himself wrapped around a toilet bowl back at the hall? Sixteen minutes past. I would give it another four, then go back and check on Annis. A distant splash but no ripples showed on the lake. Three. Then it occurred to me. If the blackmailer didn't show because he was feeling as bad as his victim did, it would mean he had been at the Roman feast, which would narrow the field a bit. Two more minutes. Unless he was double-bluffing, and had *not* been at the feast but was pretending to have been to make Guy think he belonged to the circle of VIPs. One minute. Then again if he did show up he could have been at the feast and not been affected, like Stoneking and yours truly. Another brilliantly useless bit of reasoning from Aqua Investigation's top operative.

Right, sorry, blackmailer, your time is up. Then I heard it. A soft, whirring kind of sound, out on the lake. The moon played hide and seek in the clouds and for a moment all was dark again, too dark to make out what was producing the noise. I concentrated on it, noticing variations in pitch. It was changing directions, moving across, coming closer, now directly towards me. Then it stopped. There followed a long, agonizing minute of standing very still in the dark on a narrow, rickety landing stage until at last the moon reappeared and I saw what it was, sleek and grey, pointing a gun up at me.

Twelve

A Royal Navy frigate. Very slowly and quietly it glided nearer to the landing stage now, turning to starboard. The engine cut and it came to an elegant stop at the edge of the landing stage, port side towards me. The grey Second World War frigate was about 24 inches long and probably 'faithfully reproduced in every detail'. Had this been a Bond movie then the guns would of course have fired deadly miniature shells; as it was the little boat just sat there. There were no instructions but as a method of collecting money with menaces it was perfect. I got to my knees and wedged the envelope between some deck fittings behind the front turret and the bridge and stepped back. The boat listed a little to port now. The motor whirred and the miniature warship glided away in a playful arc towards the island until it was lost in the dark; then the sound too faded and the money was gone. Whoever was operating the remote control of the model frigate could obviously see me, but try as I might I could not spot him out there. The knowledge that I was being watched by unseen malicious eyes made me uncomfortable enough to move quickly away from the lake. For a moment I considered trying to hunt for the blackmailer around the lake but he would definitely have had the edge on me. I'd get him some other way, I decided, when the odds were in my favour.

Back at the house the doctor was still making the rounds. All the patients seemed to be stabilizing into a post-puke stupor. 'Food poisoning is the most likely cause,' the doctor told me when I managed to grab him between rooms on the first-floor gallery. 'It would be difficult to tell what it was now, unless there are samples left, but even so it would take chemical analysis.' I told him about my fish sauce suspicions. 'Yes, home-made fish sauce could do it, if it wasn't produced properly. But then again if it hadn't been it would probably stink to high heaven. We might never know what caused this outbreak. None of the patients are elderly or very young, which is a bonus. I'm not too worried; they are all feeling less sick already. My guess is they'll be up and about again soon and fine in a few days' time. But in future, please, no more food labelled "best before 100 AD".'

'Should we contact the woman who cooked the food?'

'Yes, the TV director gave me her number. I'm going to check on her too once I'm through here, as she might not be feeling too clever herself.'

'Let me have the number, I'll do it now.' I was feeling guilty for having had nothing but murderous feelings for the woman, never thinking that she might herself have been poisoned. It was a Bristol number. I called from the desk in the cluttered gunroom on the ground floor by the light of a green-shaded banker's lamp. At the other end the phone rang and rang for a long time before it was answered.

'This better be good,' a voice croaked.

'Hilda? It's Chris. Chris Honeysett.' Silence. 'Rabbits? Tarmford Hall?'

'Yes, yes, sorry, I'm not feeling too good; got some kind of food poisoning.'

'How bad is it?'

'Well, I stopped puking and my heart rate seems to be going back to normal, so I expect I'll live.'

'Most people who were at the Roman feast went down with it.'

'I was afraid you might say that. I was too scared to call, to be honest. I've been wracking my brain over what could have caused it; all the ingredients were so simple, so safe.'

'I have a theory about that. I think it was the fish sauce, the *garum*.'

'No, absolutely not.'

'Both Mr Stoneking and I are fine and we had nothing with *garum* in it.'

'The fish sauce is not to blame,' Hilda insisted.

'How can you be so sure?'

'Because I didn't make it. It was Thai fish sauce and I bought it at the supermarket and poured it into a fancy bottle. I can't be arsed to ferment fish guts for months. It stinks so bad even the Romans didn't allow *garum* to be made inside their towns.'

'Then that theory's out of the window.'

'I suppose everyone thinks *that stupid cow Hilda Carson poisoned us with her Roman muck*?'

'I think you can take them off your dinner party list.'

I would never get used to these stairs; I didn't know how Carla did it all day long. The house was quiet now, as the constant flushing of toilets had stopped and hopefully all the invalids were on their way to recovery. Annis stirred under the sheets as I entered our moonlit room. I undressed and slid into bed beside her.

'How are you feeling?'

'Exhausted. But I no longer feel the urge to turn inside out. How did your errand go?'

I told her of the blackmail and the novel way the money was collected.

That Guy had attracted a blackmailer didn't surprise her. The way the money was collected did. 'How can you be sure it was the blackmailer? Could have just been someone playing around with model boats. Two grand.' She yawned and turned over. 'I hope you got a receipt, hon.'

I lay awake for a long time, watching the moon shadows creep across the wall.

Despite worrying for what seemed like hours over whether I had given away the blackmail payment to a lucky remote-control model enthusiast by mistake I woke early, feeling refreshed. It was much cooler this morning than it had been and a fresh north wind was blowing. Stoneking was the only one at the breakfast table.

'Reduced service this morning; Carla was feeling too ill to make breakfast,' he said. 'There's eggs and bacon, that's all I can manage in the kitchen, I'm afraid. Emms was here a moment ago, looking ghostly. She poured herself some black tea and went upstairs again. No filming today and no digging, she said. Everyone feels too iffy or too tired. How's Annis?'

'I left her asleep.'

'Why didn't you tell me she was your girlfriend?'

'Didn't I?' I hadn't at the time, not wanting him to think I was recommending her purely because of it.

'You never mentioned it and I nearly made a fool of myself.'

'Sorry, I thought I had.'

'Never mind.' He poured himself more coffee. 'Lucky bastard.' He walked to the window and looked out over the lawns. 'I don't suppose she'll want to do any painting today and they'll not do any digging either. What am I supposed to do all day?'

'Whatever you used to do before the circus came to visit,' I said and dropped an avalanche of crispy bacon across my scrambled eggs.

'Mm,' Stoneking scoffed. 'Not a lot, then. I suppose I could mow the lawn with the sit-on mower. Needs doing, with all those people trampling it down.'

'Get some sheep. That's what we do. We borrow them from a neighbour.'

'Ha! Sam would go ape if he thought I was going to replace him with livestock.' He was smiling now. 'I'll think about it.'

'You'll need a small flock of them for this place.'

After breakfast I took my mug of coffee for a walk through the grounds. Some diggers were queuing for breakfast at Delia's van. News of the unscheduled holiday had reached them and I thought I detected more than a pinch of *schadenfreude* in the enjoyment of those who had been excluded from the feast. Delia told everyone she had seen it coming. 'She might be a good historian,' she said, 'but I knew the minute I looked at her setup that food safety wasn't high on her list of ingredients.'

Julie and the goateed Adam were there, drinking tea and wolfing bacon butties, Julie with one eye on her paperback, Adam with both eyes on her. Neither of them had much sympathy for the suffering VIPs. 'I'm glad you and Mark Stoneking escaped,' Julie said, squinting up at me against the sun. 'But for the rest I like to think of it as karmic revenge for treating us as second-class citizens and always keeping all the perks to themselves.' She lifted her egg-and-bacon roll up high and waved it towards the house. 'I hope they can smell this!'

'I prefer brown sauce to fish sauce any time,' Adam added.

'That's because you're an inverted middle-class snob who likes to pretend he has working-class tastes,' Julie said in a matter-of-fact tone. She put down her paperback and turned to me. 'The nighthawks were back last night. There's two holes dug in the woods and two more on the lawn as well. We'll need to organize a night watch.'

'I'll give it some thought,' I promised.

'They're very strange nighthawks,' Julie said. She reached into a breast pocket on her jacket and pulled out a small plastic bag. As she held it up for my inspection I could see it contained a coin and what looked like a bent piece of wire. 'I found that in the spoil from the holes they dug. A third-century coin and the bronze pin from a brooch. I don't know if they found something and left this behind or never even saw it, but it seems rather odd.'

'I'll give that some thought too,' I said and moved on. As I did, Adam took up what sounded like a well-rehearsed argument between the two.

'Inverted middle-class snob? I think what you meant to say was . . .'

I left them to it and walked on, right around the Hall, stopping from time to time to sip my coffee and admire. I wondered how long it would take me to get bored of a huge house, ninety acres of land, swimming pool, sports car and Rolls Royce, as Mark Stoneking so obviously was. Just deciding on which bit of your football-pitch-sized lawn to laze around would surely kill some time.

The roof repair team had arrived. They were a specialist outfit that had expertise in the repair of manor house and cathedral roofs and charged specialist prices, Stoneking had told me over breakfast. I could see them now, chatting to each other on walkie-talkies, workers on the roof, boss on the ground, Stoneking standing next to him. My mobile rang. It was Giles Haarbottle from Griffins insurance. 'How are you progressing with Mike Dealey?' he asked.

'I'm sticking to him like glue,' I said. 'I'm watching his front door at the moment, been here for an hour already. Nothing's moving but I don't think he has spotted me watching his house.'

'Well, he would find that rather difficult since you appear to be standing in front of Tarmford Hall drinking tea from a blue and white mug and chatting to me on the phone. I'm the chap sitting in his grey VW waving at you.'

'Ah.' I looked up. Sure enough Haarbottle was there, parked on the gravel next to my Citroën. I put my mobile away and walked over, frantic-ally trying to think of a plausible explanation. I failed. This was one lie I couldn't explain away. His window slid down and I leant jovially on his car roof for a chat. 'What are you doing here?' I asked.

'This pile of tottering masonry is insured with us. I've never been here, so I grabbed the chance to meet the famous man and have a look around. I had no idea *Time Lines* were digging the place up. Now explain why you are hanging around out here instead of watching Mike Dealey's every move?'

'I'm looking after Guy Middleton while they're filming the dig here.'

'How long?' he asked menacingly.

'End of the week. Then I'm back, full-time, shadowing Dealey.'

Haarbottle grunted doubtfully. 'What's Guy Middleton like, then?'

'Bit of a pain.'

'Celebrities can be, I suppose. Mind you, Mr Stoneking seems very nice, but then we are

211

handling his claim for the roof. Honeysett, have you ever actually been to Mike Dealey's place?'

'Oh, absolutely. And there's nothing to do here today so I'll go over in a minute and have another shot at him.'

'You do that.' He started the engine. 'And for pity's sake keep in touch, Honeysett. Do call, even if it's only to lie to me.'

'I promise.' I put on my most sincere face and watched him drive away with my empty coffee mug on the roof of his car.

I was true to my word. I told Annis I'd be away for a while and set off towards Bath with good intentions. These were soon somewhat diluted by the realization that I had no thermos of coffee to keep me company and also needed to stock up on munchable items to keep the hunger at bay and to keep my teeth from getting bored, which they frequently did when staring at houses out of the car window. I swung by the Thoughtful Bread Company in Green Park Station, got side-tracked into browsing for pickles while buying French butter and milk in town, dropped into Goodies deli in Larkhall for Parma ham and some goat's cheese and by the time I fell through the door at Mill House with my shopping it was time for lunch anyway.

Annis had been right, there was nothing but pinto beans left in the cupboards. My fat pay cheque from *Time Lines* would soon take care of the larder and an equally good-looking cheque from Griffins Insurance – always assuming I found Dealey was faking it – should make sure that it remained well-stocked for a while. In the meantime there were now four mouth-watering sheep standing in the meadow and I wondered if I should make the farmer an offer for them when I got paid.

I rescued some of the herbs they hadn't eaten, added them to some sweated onions, poured in three beaten eggs, dropped in a few pinto beans and crumbled goat's cheese over the top. I left it on top of the stove until it was beginning to set then shoved it under a hot grill for a couple of minutes. Simple stuff really, this cooking lark. While I lunched on my frittata I called Tim at work.

'How is your rock 'n' roll lifestyle?' Tim asked.

'Not all it's cracked up to be,' I said with my mouth full.

'What are you eating?' he demanded to know. I told him. 'Sounds nice. It's anaemic ham and cheese sandwiches here,' he complained, 'and there were no ketchup sachets left. I had to use tartare sauce to disguise the taste and half of it ran into my keyboard and now I have a bit of gherkin between D and F that doesn't want to come out.'

'Another tough day at the office.'

'Is this just a courtesy call?'

'No. There's trouble up at the big house. Death threats, drugged whisky, poisoned food, black-mail and assorted night prowlers. Annis has been laid low with food poisoning but is recovering. It would be nice if we could see what went on in the dark up there.'

'That can certainly be arranged. We have

213

enough night-vision cameras to keep tabs on your prowlers. What are they on the prowl for?'

'All sorts, I shouldn't wonder. Among other things they are digging unauthorized holes in the ground. I fell into one.'

'Big holes. What are they digging for?'

'Anything worth flogging, one assumes; it's now a known archaeological site. But there may be more to it than that, I just don't know what yet.'

'Why don't I meet you after work? I could drop the gear off at Mill House or you could come round to my place.'

'I'm not sure yet, I'll be spending the day watching Mike Dealey's house since there's no filming today; everyone's feeling too ill with a stomach bug. And anyway, you know I'm useless with electronic stuff, and Annis is feeling crap, so you will have to set the things up for us.'

'Does that mean I'll get to see Stoneking's stately pile?'

'Of course. Are you into Karmic Fire too?'

'I loathe them with a passion. What an incoherent racket.'

'I think Stoneking would agree with you but if you meet him don't tell him I said so. Can I give you a few names?' I rattled off a list of names I had copied from an insurance form left lying about by Cy. It included Andrea Clementi, the head archaeologist, Julie Rhymer and Adam Horspool, the two diggers, as well as some names from the production team. 'See what you can find on them when you get a moment or two. I'll call you after work.'

The day remained cool and cloudy, perfect surveillance weather. The last thing you want is a bright sunny day where you get baked sitting in your car while your subject is lying in a deck-chair out the back slurping iced drinks and going nowhere. I managed to find a space right at the top of Dealey's road from where I could just see half his bungalow and his Honda parked outside. PC Whatsisname had been persuaded to furnish me with Mike Dealey's ex-directory number. He answered with 'Hello' on the second ring.

'Hi, is Tamzin there?' I gushed in my best teenage voice. 'It's Keenan.'

'Tamzin? There's no Tamzin here, mate.'

'Sorry, wrong number.' At least I knew he was in, or rather I knew *someone* was in, if I wanted to be scientific about it.

Three hours later and I had eaten the sandwiches, finished the flask of coffee, snaffled the bag of cough sweets the last owner had left in the glove box and was now contemplating the nutritional value of my bubble pack of antacid tablets, my last edible option inside the car. I had jumped radio stations *ad nauseam*, fiddled with my phone and rearranged my card wallet. I was bored bored bored bored bored and I wasn't even getting paid for this. If Dealey was genuine then I was simply wasting my time here. But just as I was getting the urge to bump my forehead against the steering wheel to see if the pain might alleviate the boredom there was movement.

A silver Astra arrived and squeezed itself behind Dealey's Honda on to the drive. A man got out. I took a picture, and a couple more as he rapped the door knocker on Dealey's front door, then immediately let himself into the house with a key. Carer? Family, judging by his build. I zoomed into the picture on my SLR's screen. Brother, I decided. Same hair, similar features but unencumbered by walrus moustache. I made a note of the car registration just in case.

Well, that was positively exciting compared with the last three hours. Gloom descended once more as I imagined the conversation inside the house. *Dealey: 'Hi bro, fancy watching this entire box set of Downton Abbey?' Bro: 'I sure do, Mikey. Let's just order in beer and pizzas and not move from the couch for days . . .'*

Twenty minutes of frustrated sighs and groans later the door opened and out came the Dealey brothers, Mike in his wheelchair. I started the engine and sank low in my seat as they got into their respective cars. Mike in his red Honda was leading the way, his brother followed and once they had passed my car I did a hasty three-point turn and tagged along. Hoping this would not be a five-hundred-mile run I kept a respectful distance from the silver Astra since even when sprayed a sensible black, a forty-year-old Citroën would make an unusual sight in their rear-view mirrors. But I needn't have worried; we weren't going far at all. A few turns left and right and finally left again and the convoy halted at the Cross Keys pub on the corner of Southstoke and Midford Roads. Mike parked his Honda on the forecourt, his brother found a space on the road opposite. I slid into a parking space on the quiet

Southstoke Road and walked up to the front door just as the pair was negotiating the two stone steps. Close up I would have put money on the two being brothers. I watched the routine indignity suffered by the paraplegic as Mike was being bumped backwards up the steps in his wheelchair, then turned around in the tiny vestibule, after which he moved himself into the lounge on the right. I followed them inside. The place was quite busy for a midweek early evening. Mike's brother moved a chair out of the way for him as they chose the second table along and I heard Mike say 'Cheers, Tom'. Tom fetched two menus from the bar. I took one myself. Unfortunately the nearest unoccupied table to theirs was a few steps down into a further dining room from where I would have trouble overhearing their conversation but at least I could watch their table from there. Since it looked like they would be here for a while I called Tim; he had just got home.

'Find me at the Cross Keys on the Midford Road,' I told him.

'I'll bring the night-vision stuff with me.'

The Dealey brothers became engrossed in the menu; I followed their example. The Cross Keys menu was as flowery as you could ask for. Here almost everything was 'infused' with one thing or another. It featured delights like half roasted lemon & herb chicken, which I hoped referred to the portion, not the cooking time; mysterious items like 'prepared folded flat bread' and 'hand beer-battered onion rings' as well as reassuringly 1970s nonsense like gammon topped with egg and pineapple.

When Tom went to the bar to order food and drinks I went up too. They had both chosen the mega mixed grill (lamb chops, steak, gammon, chicken breast, sausage, black pudding, topped with two fried eggs, mushrooms, tomato, chips, peas and coleslaw as well as the famous hand beer-battered onion rings) while I chose the less dizzying pumpkin ravioli. I let Tom get ahead to join his brother and carried my beer slowly past their table. Mike was taking a good gulp of lager, then said temptingly: 'There's tons of ready meals in the freezer, too.'

Tom sipped from his Guinness, licked the foam from his lips and said dismissively: 'Yeah, all of it Indian, of course.'

'No, no, not *all* of it,' I heard Mike protest, then I was past them and out of earshot. I fished my mobile from my jacket and took a couple of stealthy shots of them, to later send to Haarbottle as proof that I was working hard on Griffins' behalf, then settled back. It felt good to be away from the hotbed of resentment and strangeness that was Tarmford Hall. Even from this short distance away it looked like a theatre where an absurd play was being performed, or perhaps more than one play, running parallel across the same stage, intersecting here and there, towards an uncertain ending. Was there more than one playwright at work, more than one director? What was certain was that, perhaps with the exception of Carla, everyone thought they were the leading character. Or was I wrong about Carla? She seemed devoted to Mark Stoneking and had obviously been at Tarmford Hall for a while.

Stoneking himself thought she was indispensible; did she think the same of herself? How much did Carla resent the intrusion of the *Time Lines* crew? Surely if it pleased Stoneking she would put up with it for a week without sabotaging it. Stoneking himself was torn between loving and hating the programme makers. It was the archaeology he liked and the TV circus he loathed. Olive Cunningham seemed to resent everything and everybody, and despite her age did swing a good stick. But was she mad enough to climb on to the roof of the Hall in a thunderstorm and put her shoulder to a stone urn weighing at least 150 pounds? Had some dishes at the Roman feast been deliberately poisoned? It was of course a cliché that poison was a female weapon but I couldn't rule out a man's hand in that either. Yet all my suspects had been taken ill . . .

Tim's arrival interrupted these pleasant musings. He acknowledged me with a nod of his woolly head, bought drinks at the bar and joined me at my table, putting a fresh pint in front of me.

'Perfect timing,' I said and drained my first pint, then started on the next.

'You can never tell just from looking at them, can you?' Tim said with a tiny nod in the direction of the brothers.

'Quite. If someone unequivocally said to you that those two were up to no good you'd soon find things that looked suspicious, yet if someone said, "Those are the Dealey brothers, really nice guys", then you'd see the opposite. My problem is that I *want* him to be guilty. Because there's money in it.'

219

'How much?'

'Seven and a half.'

'Not bad money for sitting in the pub,' Tim acknowledged.

'Yeah, well, it has its moments.' This was one of them, since just then the waitress arrived with two enormous oval platters for the Dealey brothers. The barbecue aroma of their grill carried all the way to our table. A minute later the waitress reappeared and brought my own colourful plate of food.

'What is *that*?' Tim said doubtfully.

'Pumpkin ravioli and salad,' I said defensively.

Tim groaned. 'You're incorrigible. Why couldn't you have ordered something real like those two?'

'Because you'd have pinched half of it?'

'Well, you have certainly nothing to fear from me with your rabbit food.'

'I had rabbit food yesterday, too. You would have liked it; it had a rabbit in it. Did you have time to find out anything about the menagerie at Tarmford Hall?'

'Some.' He pulled out a crumpled piece of paper from his jeans and smoothed it out on the table where it absorbed some beer spillage. 'Right, Cy Shovlin, your producer. He seems totally unremarkable. Started in children's telly like they all do, did local telly, then a couple of pilots for history documentaries that sank without a trace. *Time Lines* is his big break but his ambition is limitless, apparently.'

'Yes, I believe that.'

'Those two production workers I could find nothing on apart from various credits for TV work, all nuts-and-bolts stuff; both have been on the programme from the start. Mags Morrison, your director, has also been there from day one. She worked her way up through cookery shows and some docu drama – you won't have heard of them since you don't have a telly. The archaeologist, Andrea Clementi, she's quite a big cheese at Cambridge when she's not doing this, specializing in something or other, I didn't write it down, it had too many letters. She gets some flak in the press for being on a populist show.'

'Are there any suspicions that things on the show might be rigged?'

'Like what?' Tim said, squinting at his piece of paper where his felt-tip writing was fast dissolving in beer stains.

'Like artefacts being brought in from elsewhere so they can be found on camera?'

'Not that I saw. I don't think her integrity is in question in that way. It's probably envy of the telly money that prompts the criticism anyway.'

'Anyone else?'

'Julie Somebody, my ink is running . . .'

'Rhymer,' I supplied, spearing a pillow of ravioli.

'Field archaeologist, studied in Bristol, got her degree two years ago, volunteered on the programme during her degree, got a paid job last year. The chap, Adam Horspool, is fresh from Cambridge, must have studied with the Clementi woman. Perhaps she got him the job.'

'I'm sure half her students would give their right arm to get on telly with her; must be quite a queue.'

'And that's your lot, I think,' he said and crumpled up the paper. Tim's filing system is worse than mine. 'Did it help?'

'Not yet. I don't feel I'm learning much either by watching those two put away half a farm-yard. They must have digestive systems made of steel.'

Both brothers managed to get through their enormous platters in the same time it took me to eat my rabbit food under Tim's disapproving eye.

'Hey,' said Tim, 'I think they're leaving.'

'Damn, I meant to get outside before they did.' But it was a false alarm; they were taking a toilet break. Their pints were still half full, I noticed. I knew the toilets in this pub and didn't envy Mike the task. 'When they look like they're about to leave we'll go outside before they do. We'll follow in your car.' Tim was going cross-eyed with boredom. 'Just to see what happens next. If they both go back to Mike's bungalow we shan't bother watching; you can't see in.'

'There's gear we can use, you know,' Tim suggested suggestively.

'Yes, I know. But getting caught installing it in his house could cost more than the job is paying,' I reminded him.

'Yeah, yeah. OK, how about a honey trap, then? We'll get a woman to make advances towards him. See if he suddenly gets the use of his undercarriage back.'

'What if his injury is real and he genuinely falls for her? That would be cruel. And when you say "a woman", just which woman exactly did you have in mind?'

222

'All right, it was just a thought,' Tim said defensively.

When the brothers came back from the toilets, Tom did not sit down – our cue, I thought. 'Let's go.'

I had been right. Mike finished his Guinness, Tom drained his lager and just as we squeezed past them he mumbled: 'Please no one mention food for at least a week.'

'We'll follow them in your car,' I told Tim, 'in case they remember my DS.' We watched from inside Tim's new Audi TT, another black little number, as the brothers left the pub. Tom stood by the side of Mike's Honda, helping him in and stowing his wheelchair for him. 'This looks like a farewell,' I said. 'Tell you what, I'm sick of Mike's bungalow; let's see how the walking brother lives. He drives that Astra over there, follow him. If Mikey is faking it then Tom must be in on it, surely.'

'I thought we were going to Mark Stoneking's manor?' Tim complained.

'Yeah, we will,' I said soothingly. 'Just follow him home for now. Not if he lives in Drumnadrochit, obviously.'

Tom Dealey did not live on the shores of Loch Ness but in Paulton, an ex-mining village southwest of Bath. He drove fast, often overtook cars, which at some stage made me think he had noticed us following, but he slowed down once he reached the village and we followed him without problem into a fairly prosperous estate of modern detached houses. He stopped in front of a bland house with a well-kept bit of lawn and a single garage. Tom Dealey parked his car on the road, which elicited groans from us – since it meant he might just be visiting someone – and when he got out he didn't give us a second glance as we drove past. Tim drove around the corner and stopped. 'Now what?'

I was already out of the car. 'Just wait here,' I said and legged it back to the corner, hurrying to catch him before he disappeared, but I needn't have worried. The garage door was open and when I walked past as though I had business further down the road I saw why Tom Dealey had parked his Astra on the road: in the centre of the garage, its lines unmistakable, stood a wine-red Hayabusa GSX1300R motorcycle. He was just admiring it for a moment, then he closed the garage door and let himself into the house. I legged it round the block and fell back into the passenger seat next to Tim who sat, hands folded on top of the steering wheel, resting his head on his hands.

I put on my seatbelt. 'Right, let's go.'

Tim started the engine and drove off. 'And what did we learn from this exercise?' he asked.

'That the family are bike nutters. Mike Dealey is in a wheelchair after his bike accident but brother Tom still rides a Hayabusa.'

'And what's that when it's at home?'

'It's a thirteen-hundred cc Suzuki. It does nought to sixty in less time than it takes you to say it. If he rides the bike the way he drives his Astra he might come a cropper without the aid of a white-van man talking on his mobile. Perhaps I'll get PC Whatsisname to check him out, see if there's a family history besides biking.'

224

Back at the Cross Keys I hopped into the DS and Tim followed me down the country lanes. Chatting on the hands-free mobile (21st-century Honeysett!) on the way to Tarmford I filled Tim in with what had been happening at Tarmford Hall. From the kind of questions he asked I suspected he was more of a Karmic fan than he cared to admit. But the picture I painted of life at the Hall must have been less than glamorous, because Tim said: 'Perhaps you really can have too much money.' As we crossed the Tarm at the ford the signal began to break up. It was just before sunset when we arrived at the gate, which soon groaned menacingly open.

Tim stuck his head out of the window. 'Holy Moly, it looks like a holiday camp run by the Addams Family.' He followed me very slowly, weaving along the drive to dodge the countless potholes that had not been improved by the recent traffic, and which were now filled with rainwater. We parked on the lawn. 'Okay, I'm impressed,' Tim admitted as he took it all in. 'It's amazing what a dozen LPs of incoherent noise can buy.'

'Wait until you see the back of the place.' We walked around the south side of the Hall where the view opened up across the lawns towards the lake and woods.

'Wow. Capability Brown?'

'Not quite. Sam Gower, Stoneking's jailbird gardener. He'll not like what's been happening here.'

'I'm not surprised. Still, it's only grass.'

Though *Time Lines* was still observing a day of rest the devastation of the lawn was becoming

225

ever more obvious. Not only the excavation – three trenches so far, one of them ever-widening – but also the spoil heaps, holes dug by the nighthawks, yellow patches where the camps had stood and black patches where camp fires had been lit. The digger had not been kind to the grass either and a path trampled by the crew between excavation and catering van had also become quite pronounced.

'He didn't design it, of course, just keeps it all going.'

'Nice job.'

'Depends what your employer is like.'

Some of the intestinally unchallenged diggers and geophysics experts enjoyed the sunset on the terrace, drinking, chatting or reading dog-eared novels. Of the rest of the team there was no sign.

'So where do you want to stick the cameras?' Tim asked.

I pulled him out of earshot. 'Not so loud; half of our suspects are sitting on that terrace.' We ambled over to the large trench.

Tim stood and admired the mosaic. 'That's some mosaic. I wouldn't mind a floor like that in my bathroom. What are they going to do with it once they have finished?'

'Fill it back in.'

'Seriously? But why? It's a waste, isn't it?'

'Best way to protect it for the future, apparently.'

'What for? Why's the future more important than the present?'

'It isn't. But you're not supposed to steal from it.'

'Wouldn't it be more like stealing from the past?'

'Both. Which makes it worse.'

'Okay, Socrates, let's go to work.' Tim looked about. 'So, we have blackmailers, saboteurs, potheads and nighthawks all crawling about this place. Now I'd be inclined, if this was my place, to dig a hole, about twelve-foot deep, lightly cover it with Astroturf and see who drops in.'

'You forgot the sharpened stakes at the bottom.'

'They're optional. All right, since we're supposed to be kind to our fellow blaggers we'll give them their five minutes of fame on the telly instead. We have three cameras we can use for this, two with fairly good night vision. Is there any illumination here at night?'

'None at all.'

'Sky is clouding over. Is there a moon at the moment?' I nodded. 'In that case we may get to see something or we may not. They're really designed to work in ambient light in cities. But we have one infrared. Nothing escapes infrared, night or day, rain or shine. As long as your night prowlers are flesh and blood, we'll see them. I'd say we get one camera looking up towards the house, one looking across the lawns towards the lake. What about the infrared?'

'We'll have to take pot luck; there's no telling who will go where and do what to whom around here. Stick it in one of those sweet chestnuts and point it at the lower end of the lawn. The night-hawks aren't yet bold enough to dig holes right by the house.'

In order to make sure that the cameras remained

227

a secret at least for one night we were going to install them in the dark. In the meantime I took Tim to see the invalided Annis only to find that she had recovered enough to return to the pool house. And she was painting at last. According to her, the purging of the food poisoning had inspired her. I was glad to see it had not inspired her choice of colours.

Stoneking was there on the opposite side of the pool, sipping a long drink and looking happily across the waters, though was less enthusiastic at seeing yet another new face approaching when I brought Tim to meet him.

'Tim works for me sometimes,' I explained. 'He's good with the electronic side of things. He'll help me set up some cameras outside to see if we can work out who is creeping around your gardens.'

'Much obliged,' Stoneking said. 'If you see anyone give me a shout and I'll give them a blast with my special anti-intruder cartridges.' Here he winked at me. 'I'm just about sick of the whole palaver. I never thought it would get this hectic. But watching your girlfriend at work is quite the antidote, I could watch her for hours.'

'So could we,' Tim said, 'but it's getting dark. Let's get out there.'

The equipment came in an aluminium briefcase, complete with the rugged laptop they would be wirelessly sending their images to. I took Tim around the north side of the house, away from the terrace where a couple of people were still sitting and talking. The glowing tips of two cigarettes could be seen at the furthest end. We slipped past the shuttered catering van and the nests of gas bottles and vegetable crates it had spawned, then walked along the paved path that hugged the hedge which screened the greenhouse area. No one appeared to be near as I took Tim under the trees at the bottom. 'I disturbed someone near here the other night. Perhaps this place is a good candidate for the infrared camera. Point it that-a-way.' I waved towards the dig.

'As good a place as any. It's clouding over now; I can't see any stars. If we're unlucky we'll see bugger all.'

'Shame they're not all infrared then.'

'They all have their pros and cons. You might be able to clearly see the heat signature of a person but you might have trouble distinguishing between one person and another, except by shape. Especially with our camera, which is of course crap.'

'Is it?' I asked, surprised. 'Why did we buy a crap camera?'

'Because it was all you could afford.'

'Another mystery solved.'

There was no great mystery to the installation of any of the cameras either; they were so small that they were easily stuck into the crook of tree branches with a bit of putty. Getting them sited so they actually pointed in the right direction took a while longer. Tim was right about the night-vision cameras: when we tested them they showed mainly nothing. Anyone wearing dark clothing would be practically invisible. Where to site the laptop was the next question. It would be pointless sitting in the attic bedroom watching the screen, as it would take too long to get down into the grounds if I did see something. 'How about some room on the ground floor?' Tim asked.

'It could easily give the game away if someone from the house saw me. People do ghost about at night.'

The first raindrops were falling. 'Looks like you'll be up a tree under a brollie then, doesn't it?'

'I don't think so somehow.' I shut the laptop and made off with it towards the house.

The engine of the DS 21 is wonderfully quiet. I drove slowly across the grass without headlights to the extreme south side of the lawn and stopped near the mini digger. The car being black, it was virtually invisible from twenty paces away. Tim had no intention of spending the night in the car and went back to keep Annis company while I sprawled on the rear seats with the laptop open, staring at the feed on a split-screen display. If anything moved in any of them I could go to full screen for a better look. I had of course chosen the worst possible night for my vigil. It was pitch dark out there and was now raining in a half-hearted sort of way. If I were up to no good, would I choose to go out on a night like this? Which brought me to another question: never mind the weather, why do it now at all? Nighthawks went scavenging on archaeological sites because they wanted to get at valuables before the archaeologists did. But this *Time Lines* dig was very limited in scale and would be over in a few days. It would be much safer to wait until the hordes of people had left and sneak into the grounds then. Why the rush? What also intrigued me was the sloppiness of the night-hawks. They appeared to dig holes and then leave valuable coins behind, which would be difficult to miss with a metal detector in your hand.

Pitch black. Lazy rain. Blank screen. The occasional hum from the laptop fan. Stomach growl. Jaw-splitting yawn. Midnight. I had no flask of coffee to keep me company – bad planning on my part – and should have insisted that either Tim or Annis took turns at this. A whole night of staring at that laptop would render me completely useless the next day. More yawns. I was bored again and this time I knew for certain there were only antacid tablets to keep me amused.

Another few minutes and my brain was screaming for me to do something, anything, to keep it from turning to jelly. Surely a brain like mine could amuse itself? After all, it was full of stuff. Decades of stuff, all kinds of stuff. Things I knew, things I had seen, people I had known, memories of where I had been, memorable journeys, memorable meals . . . My stomach growled again; it was as bored as my brain. I gave in. I set the programme to record. If something happened during the short time I was inside that was just tough, at least I might have it recorded on the computer. I dashed through the rain to the hall and let myself in.

The house lay silent. I climbed up the stairs. Tim's car was still here so perhaps I could bribe him to do a stint at the laptop and if Annis was well enough to paint she could jolly well do an hour of watching the laptop screen. It seemed like a perfectly reasonable request. Only I never got to make it. Up in the attic I opened the bedroom door. The room was dark. Through the open door the light from the corridor fell across their sleeping forms. The sheets were a tangled mass near the bottom of the bed. Annis's red hair sprawled over Tim's broad chest, one of her hands resting on his shoulder. Sweat still beaded down her narrow back. The room smelled darkly of sex and wine. Tim stirred, disturbed by the light. I gently closed the door again on Tim and his half of the girl.

Okay . . . coffee, then, I supposed. In the yawn-ingly empty kitchen I shoved the kettle on the stove, furtled about for coffee and found a large jar of it. Beans, naturally; Annis would have approved. Even though here in the north tower I was far from the posh living quarters, the sound of the grinder made me cringe as it seemed to tear the silence apart. I caught the kettle before it started whistling and splashed water into the cafetière. Then on a whim, while I waited for the coffee to settle, I opened the little door next to the pantry. There was that narrow stone staircase, leading up, leading down. I imagined a well-stocked wine cellar below but couldn't quite imagine what I would find if I went the other way. A faint draught came up or down the steps, hard to tell which, and a smell reminiscent of empty churches. Then, far away and from upstairs came footsteps, slow at first, then speeding up. Quickly I closed the door. Now what? I grabbed the cafetière, ran to the light switch, flicked it off, skidded back past the little door and dived into the pantry and shut myself in. Didn't spill a drop. Almost immediately I heard the door to the staircase open and close. Holding my breath I quietly lifted the latch on the pantry door and opened it a crack. All I could see was the distorted shadow of a person moving towards the light coming from the corridor, then it was gone. Back in the kitchen I poured myself a mug from the cafetière, then opened the little door again. All was quiet now. On the third step up lay a light bulb and next to it stood a little rubberized torch that hadn't been there a minute ago; tied to the handle with a red ribbon was a two-foot length of garden cane. Idly I picked up the torch and flicked it on. It bathed the stairs in a filigree web of diffused green light. Eerie green glow, indeed.

I sighed. There was no time to run up and down spiral staircases now if I wanted to catch whoever was haunting the grounds at night. I topped up my mug and made my way through the rain to the car. Nothing showed on any of the three cameras; only the infrared images gave even a hint that it was raining. I reduced the size of the screens and stopped the recording, then played back the last twenty minutes at high speed. Nothing . . . nothing . . . there! Something had flickered through the infrared screen. This was more like it. I stopped, rewound and there it was, a badger waddling ghostly through the corner of the view. I let the recording run to the end but saw no more. Once more I concentrated on the three live screens. It was difficult, since there was only blackness to see and my mind kept drifting. The moon was out now as the rain lessened and the clouds broke up in the east but even so I could see precisely nothing on the screen. Then a movement made me look up. For a moment I thought I could see something through the car windscreen, a person moving across the lawn. I bent forwards for a better look and poured half a mug of coffee into the laptop. I panicked. Wasn't that one of the things you were not supposed to do to laptops? I turned it upside down so it could drain on to the spotless interior of my DS while I scrabbled around for something to mop up coffee with. Finding only one crumpled paper napkin that had come with a jam doughnut I started mopping, dabbing sugar crystals from the napkin on to the wet keyboard. 'Would you like cream with that, Chris?' I asked myself.

The dabbing had the effect of launching half a dozen programs and dialogue boxes all over the screen. By the time I had restored a sticky kind of order to things and my three screens were back, the figure I had seen through the windscreen had disappeared. And then like magic it reappeared, there on the extreme left of the infrared screen. Was it the same figure or a different one? At the moment it was standing still. It appeared to be wearing a wide-brimmed hat à la Guy Middleton. The next moment two things happened: the figure that had been standing quite still made a sudden movement, then something dark interposed itself between camera and the person with the hat and a second later the figure was sprawled on the ground, not moving.

Another second and I was out of the car and running across the lawn into what felt like a pot of ink. I stopped, fumbled my Maglite from my pocket, then ran on by its dancing light past the spoil heap, the mosaic trench, the smaller trench and on towards the sweet chestnut trees. Then I found him. He was lying face down on the grass, not moving. In the light from my little torch it looked much worse than it had on the screen. Bright blood from his head wound mingled with the rainwater. His hat was lying nearby. I picked it up. It was Guy's, I should know; I had been wearing it the night before. I knelt down. My hand trembled as I felt around for a pulse at his bloodied neck. I felt here and there – where were you supposed to find it? And then I did.

Paul was still alive.

Thirteen

Once I knew ambulance and police were on their way I was nevertheless left with a dilemma. I needed to alert the house so that the gate might be opened but I also could not leave Paul lying injured in the rain. Whoever attacked him might come back and finish him off properly. Should I move him into the recovery position? Should you move people with head injuries at all? And what exactly did the recovery position look like? I covered him with my jacket to keep him warm.

I realized that I didn't have a single phone

number to alert the *Time Lines* team or the house. I called Annis on her mobile. 'I found the cameraman badly injured and unconscious in the grounds. I've called for an ambulance. I need you to raise Carla so she can open the gates to let them in. I could also do with blankets and umbrellas and some lights would probably help as well.'

'We're on our way.'

In my mind's eye I could see Annis, freckled and naked, next to Tim's hairy and athletic body, as they got dressed. It was the 'we' in her response that, even in this crisis and after all these years of our strange little triangle of a relationship, managed to send a small sting of jealousy through me. I didn't have long to ponder it; lights came on all over the house, then Tim and Annis, soon followed by Stoneking, came running to where I stood waving my Maglite. They brought blankets and umbrellas and Stoneking carried a large yellow torch. We made Paul as dry and protected as was possible by putting an umbrella by his head and laying blankets over him. He hadn't stirred once or made a sound, which worried me.

'I saw it happen on the infrared screen, looked like someone clouted him from behind,' I said.

'Did you see what they looked like?' Stoneking asked.

'No, it was right at the edge of the screen.'

'Pity.' He swept the torch beam up and down the ground. 'Can't see any kind of implement lying about.'

'Don't go looking for it,' I warned him. 'The police are going to be unhappy enough with all of us trampling the ground around here. Whatever it was, it's probably in the lake now anyway.' Now more figures appeared silhouetted against the light in the French windows. 'Probably best if not everyone comes down here now.' I could see one cagouled figure coming towards us already.

Stoneking handed me the torch. 'I'll shoo them back into the house. Nothing I can do here anyway.'

It was not long afterwards that the ambulance drove on to the lawn with blue flashing beacons, bathing us all in light from its headlamps. The paramedics briefly asked who he was and what had happened while they got oxygen to Paul and a drip into his arm, but otherwise they focussed on the victim. By the time they were ready to move him into the ambulance two uniformed police officers with torches were walking towards us and behind them, inevitably, strolled Superintendent Michael Needham. He was wearing a black raincoat over his suit but no hat. When he stepped into the beam of the ambulance headlights I could see he was not a happy man, but apparently his unhappiness had deeper roots than not enjoying getting wet at three in the morning.

'Honeysett, I would have put money on you standing next to the victim. And now you have brought the rest of the gang with you,' he growled. 'It was inevitable, I suppose.' He exchanged a few words with the paramedic men who had now lifted Paul into the back of the ambulance, then, as they drove off in a wide circle across the lawn, turned his attention back to us. 'Let me begin by thanking you for trampling all over the crime scene and thereby making our work so much harder. Can we all walk away from here in the direction the ambulance took?' We followed him some twenty yards towards the house, then he started on us. 'Okay, who found the body?' I put my hand up to that, knowing that in the police handbook called *Three Easy Steps to Solve a Murder* whoever reported the finding of a body shot right to the top of the suspect list. 'Anyone with you?' he asked, looking at Tim and Annis.

'No, those two were . . . asleep at the time,' I said.

'Right, start explaining what you were doing out here in the middle of the night, in the rain, on your own . . .'

I explained. I explained the nighthawks, the nightly comings and goings. I left out the greenhouse full of cannabis and how it attracted visits from the diggers and also failed to mention Guy being blackmailed – I could claim client confidentiality as an excuse there – but I did explain the cameras in the trees. I also mentioned that the hat Paul had been wearing was in fact Guy Middleton's. 'In the dark it would have been easy to assume that one was clobbering Middleton when in fact one was braining someone else wearing his trademark hat.' Even by torchlight I could tell that Annis was giving me a meaningful look. I didn't mention but I hadn't forgotten that only last night it was me masquerading as Guy Middleton under that hat.

'Then why the hell was . . .' Needham searched

for the name and found it '. . . Mr Fosse wearing it tonight?'

'I saw the hat lying in the drawing room earlier,' I lied. 'For some reason Paul decided to borrow it.' In truth I had left Guy's hat and jacket in the drawing room on my return to the Hall the night before. Guy had remained groaning and moaning in bed all day so there the hat had probably stayed until Paul decided to put it on.

More police arrived, a lot more police, both plain-clothed and uniformed. Generators and arc lights were being set up; a forensics van drove on to the lawn. Watching the ghostly army of white-suited scene-of-crime officers from the downstairs windows of the Hall were the entire VIP crew. A growing group of diggers and geo-physics technicians were gathering on the lower edge of the lawn, held back by a police constable in a yellow high-vis jacket. I was made to point out the location of the cameras and after a forensics technician had taken a good look at the laptop in my car he promptly confiscated it.

'Over here, Super,' a SOCO called to Needham from beside the hedge along the greenhouse.

Needham, himself wearing crime-scene gear now, strode across. Soon he was back. 'Looks like we have a good candidate for the weapon. A spade, chucked into the hedge. It has fresh blood and hair on it. I've no doubt it will match. Okay, you and I,' he pointed a latex-gloved fore-finger at my nose, 'will have a private little chat. Do they serve coffee in this dump?'

A short while later Needham and I sat down with a cafetière of coffee and some biscuits courtesy of Carla. I made an inviting arm gesture. 'There you are, Mike, it's Mr Honeysett in the library with a candlestick.'

Needham sniffed as he looked the place over, wrinkling his nose at the stuffed alligator and Indian statuary. 'Not what I expected to see in a rock star's mansion.'

'All courtesy of the previous owners. What *did* you expect?'

'Not sure, come to think of it.' Then his eyes fell on the musket hanging on the wall above the fireplace. 'He'd better have a licence for that thing,' he growled.

'He's got a couple of fine shotguns in his gun locker.'

'Yeah, I know.'

Of course he did; what had I been thinking? At the first sign of trouble at Tarmford Hall the computer would have spat out the information about firearms licensed to the homeowner. Needham was merely looking for an opportunity on which to vent his displeasure. And I was it.

'This whole thing stinks,' he said emphatically. 'That's the second attack now. I have a mind to scoop up the lot of you and put an end to this palaver. The last victim, the re-enactor that got himself shot with the bolt, is recovering, though still in hospital, but this one looks bad. I spoke to the paramedics. Now I'm aware he was wearing the TV chappie's hat and that Middleton wasn't universally popular, but did Paul Fosse have any enemies himself?'

'Not that I know of. He's the main camera operator, he seemed okay. Mind you, he wasn't

240

a great fan of Guy Middleton's, so pinching his hat was probably just sticking two fingers up to him. Apart from the fact that it was still raining.'

'Why would he wander about the place in the middle of the night?'

'Couldn't sleep? Visiting one of the diggers in her tent? Perhaps he was looking for nighthawks and found them – that's what my money is on. There is one other thing. Did you know the mechanical digger was sabotaged?'

'No one mentioned it.'

'It was. Someone poured water in the tank. Now if you wanted to sabotage this dig then bashing Guy Middleton's head in would probably work. But then so would laying low the cameraman, although I've no doubt the producer has already screamed down the phone for a replacement.'

Needham slowly nodded his head, digesting it, then sighed. 'This coffee is pretty good. That's the one thing I can say for you, Chris, wherever you are a good cup of coffee is never far away. How do you manage it? Wherever I am there's usually brown water in a polystyrene beaker.' He poured himself another cup and proceeded to shovel sugar into it. 'The figure you saw coming from the house. Was it Paul Fosse?'

'Couldn't say.'

'Think!' he barked. 'Hat? Did you see the hat? It's pretty distinctive.'

'I didn't see them clearly at all.'

'You're useless, Honeysett. Call yourself a detective.'

'I was miles away in my car and it was dark

and raining and I had just poured a mug of coffee into my laptop.'

'Really? You're not supposed to do that, I'm told.'

'I'm aware of it. But it's still working and one of your chaps has confiscated it.'

'Good.'

'Is it?'

There was a knock on the door, immediately followed by a plain-clothed officer I had not seen before. He was a tall and eager-looking man in his mid-thirties with tightly curled brown hair; he wore a brown leather jacket and reminded me of an Airedale terrier.

'What is it, Reid?' Needham asked. DI Reid, who as it turned out was the superintendent's new sidekick, stayed by the door and beckoned Needham who went to have a murmured exchange. The officer left and Needham turned to me. 'We have just made an arrest.'

'Really? That was quick. Who?'

'We arrested Mark Stoneking.'

'Really? You think he clobbered Paul Fosse?'

'No. But his greenhouse is full of cannabis.'

'Oh, that.'

Needham had lifted his coffee cup but set it down again hard. '*Oh, that*?' he boomed. 'Are you telling me you knew about it but didn't think it worth mentioning?'

I tried to look innocent. 'Erm, well, I wasn't *completely* sure they were cannabis plants. I mean how would I know?'

'Don't give me that. I wasn't born yesterday and neither were you.'

'Well, I happen to be of the opinion that an Englishman ought to be able to grow what he likes in his greenhouse as long as it doesn't hurt anyone.'

'You can opine all you want; it's illegal and I'm going to throw the book at Stoneking. Just because you're rich and surrounded by acres of land doesn't mean you're above the law.'

'I don't think Stoneking knows about those plants.'

'That's just what he said, apparently. What makes you think he didn't know?'

'Because he's not a pothead and it didn't look like a professional cannabis factory. I think that's his gardener growing himself a year's supply of the stuff.'

'Right, I'll have him. Where is he?'

'You already have him. He's Sam Gower and he's doing time.'

'Sam Gower rings a bell.' Then he remembered. 'The Bristol Bullion robbery, he was the driver.'

'He's now Stoneking's rehabilitated gardener.'

'Rehabilitated? I beg to differ.'

'He's inside for some ancient burglary you lot fingered him for.'

'DNA, don't you just love it?'

'Due to be released this week.'

Needham smiled grimly. 'Into my open arms.'

It was the arms of Morpheus I wanted to sink into but when after another hour of bickering I eventually opened the door to my room Annis and Tim were once more asleep. Our rickety triangle had never included any hint of three-in-a-bedness so I grumbled downstairs again and made myself uncomfortable on a sofa in the drawing room, just as the first finger of dawn touched the sky above Tarmford Hall. A few short hours later I woke with creaking joints and a back that refused to properly straighten up. Feeling ancient and hard done by, I followed the smell of coffee to the dining room. With the exception of Paul, Annis and Tim, everyone who stayed at the house was here; there was a new face sitting next to the sad-eyed soundman who I presumed must be the new camera operator. Apart from the newcomer everyone looked as tired as I felt, having all been forced to stay up and give statements. I had tried to subdue my hair on the way to breakfast but had obviously failed because Stoneking, who had been reluctantly released on bail by Needham, looked up from attacking a sausage on his plate and said: 'Not another one who had bad dreams. Did you see eerie green lights too and hear whisperings in your dreams?'

'Not me. Who did?'

'I did,' Middleton said through clenched teeth. 'And I wish people would stop trying to make fun of it. I was not *dreaming*. I woke up and there was a strange green light in my room and someone was whispering.'

'That's interesting,' I said and meant it. 'What were they whispering?'

'I couldn't make out any words but it was menacing and when I tried to switch on the bedside lamp it didn't work.'

'What did you do?'

'Well, I . . . er . . . I . . . er . . . hid under the

sheets.' Giggles rippled round the room. 'I know, I know, you all think it's pathetic but I would like to see you wake up and find a strange presence in your room!'

'So what happened?'

'It disappeared. Eventually I put the central light on and there was nothing. I had put the chair against the door; no one could have come in that way.'

'Told you the place is haunted,' Stoneking said.

'You didn't see the ghost of a girl, did you?' Emms said, suppressing a laugh. 'Perhaps she wanted her drawing of a horse's head back.'

Middleton kicked his chair back impatiently. 'You're not funny, Emms.' I thought he would storm out but all he did was get himself some scrambled egg which he slapped angrily on to his plate. 'Last night someone hit Paul over the head while he was wearing my hat. What if someone thought that was me? What if it was me they were after?'

'No one expected you to be out there,' I said reasonably. 'No one waited out there for you with a shovel on the off-chance you might turn up in the middle of the night. Paul probably went looking for nighthawks and when he ran into them they laid him out.'

'Then maybe it serves him right for wearing my hat without asking,' he said prissily.

Perhaps it was wise to change the subject. 'Is there any news of Paul?'

'Yes, he was briefly conscious,' said Emms. 'I called the hospital a few minutes ago. They think it's a good sign but he's out cold again.'

'Did he say who hit him?'

'He didn't say much apparently. His skull isn't broken but he has a slight swelling on his brain. His chances are good, though.'

I looked surreptitiously round the table, looking for any out-of-place reactions but everyone just got on with their breakfast, giving nothing away. The new camera operator, whose name was Keith, looked benevolently from one speaker to the other, probably wondering if taking over from Paul had been such a wise move. In his shoes I would have too.

Emms reached for another croissant from the basket on the table. 'Now I know everyone's tired and it's a bit of a shock of course about Paul, but we have to crack on.'

'Too right,' Cy said. 'We can't afford any more delays.'

Andrea Clementi shrugged. 'We'll be fine. The diggers probably got as much sleep as they get on any other night. It's us oldies who are going to feel a bit second-hand come this afternoon.'

As if by way of demonstration we could all see Adam come jogging up the lawn towards the house. He ran up to the window, shielding his eyes with one hand against the glass and tapping excitedly against it with the other. Stoneking opened the window.

'There are three more holes dug by the night-hawks,' said Adam breathlessly. 'At two of them they left coins behind again. But the third one you'd better have a look yourselves.'

Andrea lifted her dark eyebrows. 'We're having

our breakfast, Adam. Don't be mysterious; just tell us what it is.'

'Human remains.'

Keith the cameraman was the first out of the starting blocks, closely followed by the sad-eyed soundman. Andrea seemed delighted, telling Adam she'd be there as soon as she had finished her grapefruit, but Emms looked less excited. She turned to Stoneking and me, the only outsiders, and explained. 'It's a distraction. Archaeologically it's interesting but in terms of the programme it'll throw our schedule even further off course. It's bound to have nothing to do with the Roman villa. And it'll mean higher post-production costs. Everything we find has to be logged and analysed and endlessly written up, long after the filming is finished. Mind you, the kids will love a skeleton.'

'Kids?' asked Guy.

'We have a busload of kids from a school in Bath turning up tomorrow; they'll get a tour of the place in exchange for an afternoon of washing the finds. Educational remit and all that.'

I saw Stoneking rolling his eyes theatrically as if about to faint from the shock of the news. A minute later, when everyone but me had left, he grinned. 'Ghostly whisperings and now a real skellington. Tarmford Hall really does deliver, don't you think?'

'Not to mention people getting shot and having their heads staved in with shovels.'

'That was the damn nighthawks, nothing to do with us.'

'Paul's shovel-over-the-head, maybe. I don't think the *ballista* dart was shot by a nighthawk.'

Stoneking shrugged. 'Maybe not.'

'Wait a second, this skeleton, it couldn't be one of Olive's relatives, could it?'

'No, there's only the mad grandmother under the fig tree and some other ancestor of Olive's but he's on the other side of the house and he has a slab of granite on top of him.'

'To make sure he stays down.'

'I just hope this doesn't mean the archaeologists need to hang around even longer. Honestly, I can hardly wait for them all to go away again. I have had enough entertainment to last me. To top it all, yesterday I got arrested by a chap half my age because of a few marijuana plants in the greenhouse. He treated me like I'm an international drug dealer or something. I'm here, in my own house, *on bail*, would you believe?'

'Did you know about the cannabis plants?'

'I knew Sam smoked the odd joint and as long as he didn't do it in the house why should I care? But I didn't know he grew his own. But surely it must be better than giving money to drug dealers? Growing your own, I mean. What harm can it do?'

'I've been reliably informed that the prevailing view is: if it's against the law then it's against the law, and that's the end of the story.'

'Bah humbug. Let's go and look at human remains.'

The police had returned, or were still there, it was hard to tell. They were taking photographs of everything and walked about with sticks, poking hedges and shrubs, looking for anything out of the ordinary that might be connected to the attack on Paul, and were scratching their heads at the half a million boot prints left all over the area. The consensus was that any intruders had probably come in across the fields below the lake.

Two of the fresh holes the nighthawks had dug were located close to the area where Paul had been attacked, but the one the archaeologists clustered about was more than thirty yards further on, closer to the lake near a solitary pollarded oak tree. Everyone was there: even Olive stood nearby, dressed in black, leaning on her stick and glowering. When we got closer I noticed that it was different from the other holes, larger and much deeper. We stood at a respectful distance until Keith changed camera angles and Emms gave us the nod. Mark and I peered down into the hole which was at least three feet deep. Visible at the bottom was the unmistakable eye socket and nose cavity of a human skull. Julie, Adam and Andrea were all on their knees, working frantically with their trowels.

'This is going to take ages,' Guy complained. 'Why don't you use the digger or at least a shovel?'

'Because we're not here to lay sewage pipes, Guy,' Andrea said without looking up.

Dan, the digger driver, turned up with a large, state-of-the-art metal detector and swept the area with it. It gave a loud, annoying yowl when he came close to the burial site. 'That's a meaty signal; that's why they kept digging so deep, I guess,' he said.

'That makes sense, then,' Julie said.

'Yeah, and when they came down on a human skull they got the heebie-jeebies,' Adam agreed.

'Not cut out to be tomb raiders,' Andrea said. 'Just run-of-the-mill petty thieves.'

'But vicious enough to hit Paul over the head,' I reminded them.

Andrea straightened up and stopped her scraping. 'That's what puzzles me. It isn't as though this place is known to have yielded treasure or anything.'

I had thought about that too. 'As far as you know,' I said. 'What if they did find something very valuable in one of the first holes they dug and are now looking for more of the same?'

She flicked at a bit of soil with her trowel, thinking. 'You know, that's a possibility. And every time they do dig a hole they seem to leave things like coins or brooch pins behind as though it was beneath them. They're not *that* valuable but it's the best a realistic metal detectorist would expect to find. I mean they'd think finding a coin is a good reward for a weekend's sweeping. Mostly it's buttons and bits of barbed wire, you know.'

'With a signal this strong there could be interesting grave goods down there,' Emms said.

'I'm glad this is a one-week special, otherwise we'd have already been and gone,' said Andrea.

'How long will it take you to get down to the level of the bones?' I asked.

'If you let us get on with it, about an hour,' Andrea said.

Mark and I took the hint and walked back to the Hall while the sun made an appearance again after the night of rain. Annis was also just making an appearance on the terrace, coffee cup in one hand, a slim book in the other. She waved it at us. 'Look what I found,' she beamed.

I took it from her. It was an old paperback, so old the price was marked on the front page as 1/6d. Two ghostly black and white figures on the cover held a dagger and a gun, respectively. '*Peril at End House*. By Agatha Christie,' I read. 'Crime club, one and six. What's so good about it? I hate Agatha Christie. *You* hate Agatha Christie.'

'Everyone hates Agatha Christie. No one reads this stuff; it's utter piffle. But the twist in *Peril at End House* is interesting.'

'How do you know if you don't read Agatha Christie?' Mark asked reasonably.

'I had to sit through a telly version of it at my mum's a couple of Christmases back. In this one a woman gets threatening letters and several attempts are made on her life. Then she lends someone a distinctive cardie of hers who promptly gets murdered and everyone thinks the murderer mistook her for the woman who had been threatened. Turns out she staged the attempts on herself so she could kill the woman in the cardie. Follow me?'

'Are you saying Guy Middleton wrote himself threatening letters and poisoned his own whisky so he could bash the cameraman's brains in, first making him wear his hat?'

She shrugged. 'I told you Agatha Christie was piffle,' she said and walked off, no doubt to find more coffee.

'Interesting theory though,' Mark said, taking the book from me.

'Seen that before?' I asked.

Mark pulled a face. 'Told you, if it's from before the Sixties it ain't mine.' He opened it at random, squinted at the print and rolled his eyes. 'Did people really talk like that?'

'No, never.'

He let the book fall shut. 'But why would Middleton want to kill the cameraman?'

'Don't know. Let's find out. Have the police searched Paul's room?'

'Last night and again this morning.'

'Did they take anything away?'

'Not that I noticed.'

'Then let's go.' Mark led the way up the stairs from the central gallery. 'Does anyone ever use the grand staircase at the front?' I asked.

'No, not really. I think it was just there to impress your guests and make sure they walk past the portraits of your ancestors and paintings of your horses, you know, so they understood how important you were.'

'Does anyone ever use the little stone staircase in the north tower?'

The flicker of a smile. 'How did you find that? No one uses that, and for good reason. There's no light and nothing to hold on to. If you fall you'll go arse-over-tit all the way down. There we are; that's Paul's room.'

It was the third door on the long corridor that had Mark's master bedroom at the very end of it. 'No police tape, so I suppose we're free to enter,' I said.

The room was quite messy, but whether as a result of two police searches or because Paul liked to drop his stuff all over the place was hard to tell. There were a few magazines, clipboards with schedules, lists and stills of the dig printed out on cheap paper. There was a lightweight travel printer on top of a chest of drawers; on the bed stood a camera bag with an SLR and long lens. I switched on the camera; the display told me 'No SD'. 'They took the SD card out, I suppose. Also there's no sign of his laptop. He had a snazzy one, too, so they probably took that.'

Mark looked unenthusiastic. 'What can we find that they haven't?'

'Don't know,' I admitted. 'But they're looking for things and find what they're looking for. We're just looking, so we might see things. Unlooked-for things, as it were.'

'Very deep, I'm sure.'

'Zen and the Art of Rummaging.' I picked up an aluminium briefcase. It was empty apart from sheets of paper relating to his work, an empty crisp packet, a mint humbug covered in fluff and a model boat magazine called . . . wait for it . . . *Model Boat*. I held it up. 'Getting there.'

'I don't follow.'

'Never mind. Can't tell you what it's about yet.'

'In that case I'll leave you to it and go and watch Annis paint. Much more fun.' He left, allowing me to step up my search a bit. I looked under the bed, under the mattress, inside the pillows, opened all the drawers and chucked everything on the floor, then heaved it back in.

Then I took the camera out again and unscrewed the lens – nothing inside. I dropped the camera on the bed and felt the foam rubber lining of the camera bag. There was a lump, a tiny hard-edged bump, barely noticeable; the bump I had been looking for yet I did not know it. The lining came out without putting up much of a struggle and the unlooked-for thing dropped on to the bed sheet. A tiny black micro SD card. Anyone could feel like 007 these days. Anything worth hiding was surely worth finding, as long as it hadn't just slipped under the lining by accident. All I needed now was somewhere to stick it. I took out my mobile phone, opened the back, fiddled the SD card out and inserted Paul's.

From the moment I had found the model boat magazine I was pretty sure that it was Paul who had used a toy boat to collect the money he extorted from Guy. When I found the SD card I was pretty sure what I would find on that, too, and I was not disappointed. The pictures were large in size and good quality. These had not been taken on a mobile but on a very nice SLR with a long lens, the one now lying on the bed in front of me. They were, as Middleton had indicated, pornographic enough to prove without doubt that he had more than just held hands with an underage schoolgirl. I looked at Middleton and his little ponytail, I looked at the girl, who was attractive and fresh-faced, and wondered what made her roll around in the grass with a guy three times her age. The power of television and the pull of celebrity, I supposed.

I turned my mobile off and pocketed it. On the

way downstairs I contemplated my dilemma. I now had pretty good evidence that Paul was blackmailing Guy Middleton, which was a serious crime, while the photographs and the place where I had found them were pretty good circumstantial evidence. Unfortunately I had not found the money. More unfortunate still was the fact that I had also promised Guy to keep the fact that he was being blackmailed secret. Rash words. Then again I didn't like Guy much and he was not, strictly speaking, my client. It was the production company that had hired me. And I liked them even less.

Back on the ground floor I stood irresolute in the open French doors to the terrace. I could see a lot of people crowded around the burial site, which probably meant they had managed to reach the level of the skeleton.

What if I did hand the pictures over to the police? Even Superintendent Needham would surely jump to conclusions. And he would jump a bit like this: Paul blackmails Guy. Guy finds out it's him and decides it's time to get rid of him. Guy groans in bed all day pretending he still feels rubbish after the food poisoning. He somehow gets Paul to meet him outside in the middle of the night and hits him over the head. Case closed. Before you could say *News at Six* Guy Middleton would find himself in a police cell, arrested on suspicion of having had sex with a minor as well as attempted murder. I could see Guy from here, standing by the excavation, minus his hat since the police had taken it away – not the fashion police but the forensics people – and wondered whether it was my job to arrange that particular nightmare for him or whether I should leave Needham to figure it out for himself. And I came to a Honeysett kind of conclusion: I decided to do nothing and let things take their course. Everyone can make a mistake.

Oh, OK, everyone can make two. I sauntered across the lawn towards the dig. The new camera operator was busy pointing his camera and everyone else was taking pictures on their mobiles, so it was probably worth having a look, though generally I'm not desperately keen on dead people, fresh or dried. When I got there I could not get near the trench; everyone was talking at once, Cy was talking on his mobile, Emms was having some sort of argument with Andrea while Julie was rattling on about something to Guy from which I only caught the words 'spanner in the works'. Stoneking was there, enjoying himself.

'Everyone seems very excited,' I said.

'Yes, it's the grave goods that got them all worked up,' he said.

That was more like it. 'What kind of grave goods?'

'A tin of Huntley & Palmers biscuit assortment.'

I opened my mouth and closed it and opened it again. When my goldfish impression was done the implications had sunk in. I fought my way to the edge of the trench. The skeleton was now partially exposed, lying on its back. The body had been arranged with hands on its chest, as in a Christian burial. By its left side lay a round, six-inch mud-encrusted rusty biscuit tin on which the brand name Huntley & Palmer was still faintly visible in faded pink. A heated discussion was under way.

'We can't open it,' Andrea said firmly. 'We can't even lift it out of position. Not until the police have looked at it.'

'Are you mad?' Cy nearly shouted. 'It'll be the best take of the entire shoot! At last a bit of mystery! Looking for a Roman villa where you think there's a Roman villa and then finding a Roman villa is utterly boring, but this is Tales of the Unexpected. Right, if you won't do it, I will.' He turned to the new camera operator. 'And you make sure to get a close-up of the reveal. Don't mess this up.'

I looked around for the police officers who had earlier been in evidence, poking around in bushes. Never one around when you need one. I dialled Needham's mobile number. Blackmail was one thing; actual dead bodies, even only vaguely contemporary ones, were quite another. I could already feel the roasting I'd get if I stood idly by while Cy messed about with the finds. As soon as Needham answered I launched into my explanation. 'The diggers have uncovered contemporary human remains and the producer is about to mess around with them.'

The camera was rolling. Cy knelt down and reached for the tin. Without comment Andrea stabbed his hand with the point of her trowel. Cy jerked it back and drew it across his mouth. 'Ow! Are you mad, woman? Look at my hand. I don't believe it, you actually drew blood! I could get blood poisoning. I'll probably get tetanus! I'll . . .'

'Phone for you,' I said and handed him my mobile.

I couldn't distinguish the actual words but I could tell they were delivered into Cy Shovlin's ear with something like storm force eight. He never said a word in return, just handed the phone back to me as he stood up. 'Just . . . make sure no one touches anything until the police give their permission,' he said quietly and walked away towards the house. Even from behind I could tell he was talking to himself, throwing up his head and waving his arms about. When I turned back towards the deposition site of the body and the hubbub of people, all speculating as to the nature of their surprise find, my eyes travelled beyond them and to the still figure of Olive Cunningham, standing twenty yards away under a chestnut tree. She was leaning on her stick as though she really needed it today. I pulled out my mobile and took a picture of the skeleton and tin. When I looked up again Olive Cunningham was gone. Neither on the lawn towards the house nor on the path beside the greenhouse was there any sign of her. After nearly a week at this place I would not have put it past her to have a secret tunnel with a concealed entrance through which she could pop whenever she felt like weirding me out. The truth was more prosaic. When I dived through the gap in the overgrown hedge below the trench I could see her walking away slowly beside the lake, her back bent, her head bowed.

Once more the gate to the grounds opened wide to let in first a trickle, then a flood of police vehicles. This time Needham was the first to arrive at the graveside. 'You did well,' he said, looking down at the partially exposed remains. 'Huntley & Palmer biscuits, I remember those from when I was a kid. This body is probably pretty ancient.'

'Perhaps in your terms,' Andrea said. 'To us it's modern.'

'Are those boots, at the bottom?' he asked.

'Could be, looks like decayed leather. And there are a few fibres left, probably of clothes. The soil here close to the lake is quite damp and it's acidic, so that's why there is very little clothing left.'

'You'd make a pretty good forensic investigator,' Needham said.

'Ha!' Andrea gave an ironic laugh. 'Most of what they know they learned from us, Inspector.'

'Superintendent. Want to hazard a guess as to the age of it?'

'What, the deceased? Yeah, I might.'

'Actually, I meant the burial, but go on.'

'Well, it's a male and I'd say he was in his twenties. As for the burial, I'd say fifty, sixty years ago.'

'Please make that sixty, then I don't have to investigate it.'

'Are we sure it's murder yet?' I objected.

'No, not certain,' Needham said. 'But it's the wrong depth for an official burial and there's no coffin. That says to me "shovels at midnight".'

Andrea agreed.

'Amazing that a biscuit tin lasts that long,' I mused.

259

'Not that much oxygen down there,' she said. 'If you left it above ground it would all but disappear after twenty years or so.'

Soon the forensics people turned up and shooed us all away. 'Do you mean to say,' I needled Needham, 'that if forensics say he was murdered but that it was sixty years ago, you won't look into it?'

'Absolutely. Brilliant, isn't it? If he's sixty years dead I get to go home since the killer is likely to be dead as well. Work it out. If your killer was thirty then he'd be ninety today. No point. Let the Almighty have a go.'

'So if you do kill someone then it really is worth digging a deep enough hole.'

'Oh, definitely,' Needham agreed. 'That's where a lot of murderers go wrong. They go to all that trouble of killing someone and then they can't be arsed to dig a decent hole. Of course, if you bury someone in your own back garden there's always a chance that someone'll come along and dig him up. Laying a pipe, digging a drainage ditch or hunting for treasure. We will have to have a word with Mrs Cunningham in a minute, since it obviously happened while she was living here, and I'll need some convincing that she had nothing to do with it.'

'It's a big place. It doesn't necessarily follow that she knew about it.' But even while I was saying it Olive Cunningham's vehement opposition to the *Time Lines* dig seemed to take on a more sinister motive.

One of the SOCO team stood up and waved. 'Superintendent?' Needham went across, had a five-minute conversation with the officers, then came back.

'Definitely murder. Shot through the head, in one end, out the other.'

'Any clues in the tin?'

'None at all. They lifted it and the bottom had rusted away and the content eaten by mice or whatever, though they think it may have contained papers, letters, perhaps.'

'Superintendent?' The SOCO called Needham back once more. He jogged over, looked into the grave, nodded and came back.

'They found a weapon as well, a World War Two Webley .38. I seem to remember you keeping one. *Illegally.*'

'Told you, it dropped into the sea in Cornwall.'

'I wouldn't believe that if I'd heard the splash. Now where do you think we might find Mrs Cunningham?'

I led the way along the right shore of the reed-fringed lake where I had last seen Olive Cunningham walk away pensively into the less-explored corners of the Stone King's realm, a realm that for most of her life of course had been her own. I imagined the life she would have led, growing up here during the war, playing pirates perhaps on the little island, and still here today, powerless to stop the place being invaded, surveyed, changed or dug up. It was a pleasant walk along the lake, with trees on the right, the water on our left where reed beds alternated with grassy banks and rocky outcrops that looked too picturesque to be real.

We found Olive at the western end of the lake,

looking across the water, sitting on a large willow trunk placed near the water's edge for just that purpose. Both her hands rested on top of her walking stick, the other end forming an equilateral triangle with her feet, firmly planted on the ground in their sensible black shoes. We sat down either side of her and for a while no one spoke, until Olive said: 'Why couldn't they just leave things alone?'

'I can imagine you would rather the body had not been found,' Needham said.

'All of it! I mean all of it. The Roman villa, what difference does it make? This is the twenty-first century, what does it matter? The beastly Romans with their hideous square houses, their war machine, their right angles and their fussy food.'

I felt I should try and defend the Romans at least a little. 'They had a tremendous influence on British culture, for instance . . .'

'Poppycock. As soon as they left we went back to our own ways. We dismantled their houses and used them to repair our sheds. We didn't even make pots for a few hundred years. We didn't start cooking like the Romans again for another twelve hundred years and half of us still don't have central heating. They were only here for the tin, gold and silver and if they could have done they'd have taken everything they brought here with them when they left. And if they had, then people wouldn't go and dig up hundred-year-old lawns to gawp at their old bathroom tiles.'

Needham was getting impatient with this chat.

'I've not really come to discuss the Roman legacy in Britain, Mrs Cunningham.'

'No, you've come to talk about Bertie.'

'You are referring to the remains found today?'

'That's Bertie. I knew he was around there somewhere, but the hedges have changed and the statuary got moved about and I forgot. And grass is marvellous of course but it does all look the same. Did you know that each blade of grass is a separate plant?'

'Can't say I've given it much thought. Who was Bertie?'

'Herbert Brush. He was a farm worker on the estate. We were lovers, for a very, very short time.' Olive spoke without great emotion. Her voice was saying: *it was a very short time and it was a very long time ago, so why are you bothering me with it?*

'What happened?'

'It was the summer of 1957. My husband was away on business in New York, my idiot brother Charles was in the house, to keep me company. Chaperoning me, I imagine. Didn't do too good a job. He surprised Bertie one night as he was leaving after making love to me, thought he was a burglar and fired at him with Daddy's army revolver. He said he never meant to actually hit him but it was quite dark. He was quite dead by the time I came down into the drawing room.'

'And you didn't report it?' Needham said incredulously.

'Of course not – what would have been the point in that? Even then shooting people through the head because you happened to find them in your sister's drawing room wasn't considered the done thing. It would all have come out about me having an affair, my husband would have divorced me, I would have lost the house, I couldn't have kept it up without him, and I might have seen my brother go to prison.'

'And your brother played along with it.'

'Didn't need much persuading. There was only one domestic here at the time who witnessed the aftermath. My brother bought him off.'

'Did no one miss your dead lover?' I asked. 'Didn't people wonder what had happened to him?'

'No. As it happened some money had gone missing on the farm. People assumed he had taken it and run away. That's what the police and the papers assumed then.'

'And you buried him in the garden.'

'My brother did. Did I mention he was an idiot? I expected him to bury Bertie in the woods but the wheelbarrows were locked away. He had to carry him and when his arms gave out he buried him where he had dropped him. He did quite a good job in the end. When my husband came back three months later you couldn't tell.'

'What was in the tin?' I asked.

'Just a few notes and the few letters we had exchanged. Sentimental things. Nothing of earth-shattering importance.'

'Is your brother Charles alive?'

'Died in 1980.'

'Your husband?'

'Died in '86.'

'The domestic?'

'No idea, Inspector; he would be in his nineties now.'

'It's Superintendent, actually.'

There was a long pause while we were all busy thinking it through.

'Well?' she finally asked. 'Are you going to arrest me now?'

'I'd certainly like you to come down to Manvers Street police station and make a statement.'

'Isn't that what I have just done?'

'A proper statement; we'll record it and get you to sign it afterwards.'

She stood up. 'Very well, then.'

'It was quite understandable, then,' I said as we walked slowly back, 'that you weren't happy about the excavation going on around here.'

'I just knew they would dig Bertie up. For a while it looked as though he might be safe but then those treasure hunters started digging holes all over the place. It was only a matter of time.'

'And you began sabotaging the dig.'

'Just a little bit,' she said, wrinkling her nose with pleasure.

'The digger?'

'I remembered my husband telling me about putting sugar in the German's petrol tanks. Ruined their engines. I didn't want to ruin them. So I used water. Quite spectacular, all that smoke, I never expected that.'

'The urn that nearly flattened Mr Middleton?'

'What do you take me for, young man? Can you see me climbing around on the roof in a thunderstorm? Mr Middleton is a revolting specimen by all accounts but I wouldn't risk catching cold just to break his head.'

'By all accounts? Whose accounts?' Needham said sharply.

'There's no casual chatting with you, Inspector, is there? Every female who has had the misfortune of having been left alone with him, I should think.'

'Any more sabotage attempts? The *ballista*?'

'Didn't go near it.'

'Hitting the cameraman over the head?'

'No, that's not where I would have hit him.'

'The food poisoning?'

'Not my style. Try the boy who helps his aunt in the catering van. I saw him picking herbs that day along the stream near the tents and not all of them make good eating.'

'The drawing with the horse's head?'

'Guilty. I was hoping that if I could scare the presenter away that might make them give up.'

'Eerie green torch light on a stick?'

'You found that?'

'I was hiding in the pantry.'

She sighed. 'We used to have such fun in this house. You can get into Mr Middleton's room from the servant's stairs and through the back of his wardrobe. My grandparents were great practical jokers. They liked to pretend there was a ghost. I carry on the tradition.'

Needham looked unimpressed but didn't say anything until we were once more on the lawns below the hall. 'If you would like to get your things, Mrs Cunningham, I'll drive you to the station. I'll be waiting by my car.'

'What things, Inspector?'

'I don't know, jacket, keys, handbag, those kind of things. It might take some time. We'll arrange for transport back.'

'You're a confounded nuisance,' she said and crossed the verandah towards her end of the house.

'You do realize,' I told Needham when she had gone, 'that if she doesn't show up in the car park it could take you days to find her in that house if she doesn't want to be found?'

Needham shrugged and walked off. 'I'm not even sure I'd want to.'

Fourteen

I stepped through the French windows and could hear that there was a lively discussion in progress in the dining room next door. I went to join it. Nearly the entire crew was sitting around the table, minus camera operator and sound man, who were outside, filming every move the police made from the top of the cherry picker. The assembly barely gave me a glance as I entered. Stoneking sat at the top of the table, looking like he was once more enjoying himself. The crew were discussing dates, delays, insurance, as well as airing their grievances. Cy's hand now sported a theatrical bandage where I was sure a sticking plaster might have sufficed. Middleton sat quietly and morosely, staring at something in his hand.

He looked dishevelled, as though he had given up looking after himself. He also looked drunk. 'It's the ghost,' he whined when there was a lull in the discussion. He held up a little glass phial, the ghost bottle from the library. Middleton had checked on the imprisoned ghost and had found it gone. 'Look.' He sought my eyes and held up the bottle in evidence. 'It really was a ghost in my room. Look, someone let it out.'

'Put it in the recycling box, Guy,' I told him. 'There's no ghost. The old lady did all that to spook you.' I then told the rest of the room what I had learned from Olive Cunningham.

Cy was delighted. 'It makes a fabulous story, a real *Time Lines* special; we must interview the police, the old woman, people in the village. And there is still all that mystery about who shot Morgan with the *ballista* and who hit Paul over the head. It could end up a two-parter, with a cliff-hanger at the end of part one.' There were groans around the table and Andrea was resting her head in her hands in a gesture of despair.

When I left the room to find Annis and share the news, Stoneking came with me. 'I must admit I was getting bored with archaeology but maybe I'll take up an interest in forensics. But seriously,' he said, looking worried, 'do you think they'll charge Olive with anything?'

'Don't know. "Preventing the rightful burial of a body" springs to mind. I'm sure they could make her life difficult but I doubt the Crown Prosecution Service will see much chance of a conviction.'

'They won't put her in jail, or anything?'

'I doubt it. Not if she's been telling the truth.'

I was about to open the door to the pool house when it was opened from the other side. It was Annis in her multicoloured, be-spattered painting gear. 'Oh, there you are. I was just coming to find you.' She held up the local newspaper, the *Bath Chronicle*. 'Mark here gave me a few papers to wipe my brushes on. Look at this article.'

MOTORCYCLIST CRITICAL AFTER TRACK DAY CRASH was the headline. I read it out for Mark's benefit. 'A motorcyclist who crashed his superbike on the way home from a track day is in intensive care at the Royal United Hospital. Thomas Dealey, 36, is in a critical condition after crashing his Hayabusa motor-cycle, the fastest production bike for sale in the UK, after having attended a public track day at Castle Combe race track. No other vehicle is thought to have been involved.'

Annis tapped the picture. 'That's your wheel-chair man's brother, isn't it? It was the make of the bike under the picture that caught my eye.'

'Yes, the family are bike nuts,' I agreed. Stoneking looked mystified so I quickly explained who the Dealeys were. 'I watched him drive a car and thought afterwards that if he rode his bike like that then he'd come a cropper.' There was a picture of the mangled Hayabusa; it was unrecognizable. 'Nothing fake about this chap's injuries, I expect. His brother will want to be at his bedside.'

'Might be a good opportunity to get close to him,' Annis said.

'Yes, I think I can feel a hospital visit coming

on.' I left Stoneking to tell Annis all about Olive's dead lover and made for the car.

The RUH car parking charges looked challenging, to say the least. I did quite enjoy the 'up to twenty minutes FREE' challenge to visitors and wondered if anyone had yet managed to get to a loved one's hospital bed and back to the car in that time. I didn't really want to visit Tom Dealey in intensive care and listen to his life support bleep. I doubted they would let me, and what would be the point? But I had spotted his brother's red Honda in a 'disabled' space, so I hung around near the exit for a while. I was good at hanging around, half a lifetime of watching paint dry had prepared me well for it, though my boredom threshold had begun to crumble a little with age. Wasn't there something more meaningful I might do with my life than stand behind a concrete pillar and wait for Mike Dealey to show up and do something even remotely interesting?

Apparently not. It took him forty minutes to make an appearance. I had to sprint to my car since his was parked close to the exit and he was well-practised in getting into it from his wheelchair. I caught up with him just as he turned right out of the car park into the main road. I hung back a little but never let the red car get out of my sight. One problem with hanging back a little is that traffic lights can throw a serious spanner in the works and lose you your target for good if you're unlucky. But my luck held as I squeezed behind Dealey across a junction just as the light changed and he drove his car west out of town.

It soon became clear that he was driving to his brother's house in Paulton, perhaps to check that nothing needed doing or securing at the house. Since I was pretty sure where we were going I could let a couple of cars get between us and relax. By the time we got to Paulton and near his brother's house the other cars had peeled off so when Dealey turned into his brother's street I carried on out of sight and parked, then walked back. But I had left it too late – by the time I had sight of the house the front door was just closing behind him. I carried on nevertheless and strolled past, holding my mobile against my ear as though engaged in a phone call and thus obscuring part of my face, until I got to the next corner. Then I looked back at the house and seriously regretted having given Dealey all that breathing space. In front of his brother's front door sat a big fat doorstep, at least eight inches high. Who had helped him up across that with his wheelchair? I *had* seen the front door close, though only just. Was someone else in the house who had helped him up that doorstep? Maybe. Was I going to stand here all day and wait until he came out? Unlikely. I had a good squint at the step and decided that he would probably be able to come down it unaided; it was just how he had gone up it that was the mystery. Next time; I would catch him next time. I took a picture of the house and car on my mobile and sent it to Haarbottle, which might brighten his gloomy life. On my way back to the car I called PC Whatsisname and left a message for him: *Could he give me any information on Tom Dealey who had just crashed his Hayabusa?* Then I drove back to Tarmford Hall.

Annis was making progress with her mural, a vast eruption of painterly energy across the expanse of the pool house wall. She was excited by just how different working on a large scale was. She needed litres of oil paint, much larger brushes and much longer arms. Brushstrokes that before would have been the result of a sweep of the arm now had to be executed at a run. Several times a day Annis ended up in the pool, surveying the progress from a watery distance. Stoneking was no longer bored; he was now torn between watching Annis at (and in) the pool and following the progress of police and archaeologists outside. I found him beside the pool and Annis in it. While she tread water I told her how I had just missed Dealey's miraculous ascent.

'I hope that won't turn out to be the moment when seven grand slipped through your fingers. Why don't you come in? The water is lovely . . .'

'I might at that. My shorts are still in the changing room.'

I was still climbing out of my street clothes when rapid footsteps approached down the corridor and the door to the changing room was flung wide. Guy Middleton. He was flushed and breathless. His earlier depressed state had now given way to agitation.

'Bloody hell, there you are. I've been all over this damn pile looking for you. Where have you been? And what do you think you're doing? You're supposed to protect me, not swan about elsewhere. Your car wasn't even here so presumably you weren't even in the grounds when you should have been right here keeping an eye on me; it's what you're getting paid for. They're going to kill me, Chris, they've decided to finally do it. It wasn't Paul they were after; everyone knows it was really me. And here.' He whisked a piece of notepaper from his jacket and held it out to me. In its centre I read the laconic statement:

We will finish it here.

I read it and thought I shared the sentiment. I stepped into the shower cubicle and turned on the water.

'What the hell do you think you're doing?' he asked querulously.

I snapped. 'I am going for a swim in yonder pool, Guy. Stand next to it if you want to be protected or lock yourself in the loo until I'm done. Alternatively do what normal people would do, go to the police and tell them everything. The nasty notes, the blackmail, the pranks and why you think everyone wants to kill you. Excuse me.' I dripped past him out of the changing room and marched righteously down the corridor towards the lovely blue wetness shimmering at the end of it.

'Mr Honeysett!' A different voice this time but I didn't care, I marched right on into the pool house. 'Chris Honeysett!' Just as I reached the edge of the pool the place suddenly got crowded. Not just Middleton but Needham's Airedale terrier, DI Reid, a huge uniformed PC wearing a

273

stab vest and Carla were all bearing down on me. 'Chris Honeysett,' DI Reid said again. He added: 'I'm arresting you on suspicion of attempted murder; you do not have to say anything . . .'

The rest of the caution was lost in a spray of water as I bombed into the pool. 'You what?' I asked when I surfaced. A satisfying amount of water had landed on the DI's trouser legs, though he didn't look well-pleased. He started rattling off the caution again so I dived. *Suspicion of murder?* Had everyone gone mad? From under water I watched Annis swim across. I surfaced next to her.

'Who did you try and kill, hon?' she asked, unconcerned, while above us by the edge of the pool the Airedale terrier had another go at arresting me, starting the whole litany again with 'Chris Honeysett . . .'. Of course, until he had completely read me my rights I wouldn't legally be under arrest, so I waggled my fingers at him in a friendly goodbye and dived. I can hold my breath for quite a while but even so this couldn't go on for much longer, yet at the moment it seemed like fun. I was wondering what he would do next. Would he go and get his cozzie? I found out when I surfaced again. 'Constable, get in there and haul him out!' he said with precisely the voice a Bond villain uses when he says: 'Release the sharks.' Now Stoneking was standing up there too. He began to berate the DI for the intrusion but was cut short. 'Shut up!' Reid bellowed. 'You're out on bail, Mr Stoneking, best to remember that.' He turned to the constable. 'Well? What are you waiting for?'

The constable looked reluctant. 'Couldn't we, I don't know, drain the pool?'

'Don't be daft, that'll take forever. Get in there.'

The constable pulled a doubtful face but started unlacing his boots. Suddenly Carla spoke up. '*Nobody* is going into that pool without first having a shower! The changing room, *Constable*, is over there!' She pointed and glared menacingly at the officers.

DI Reid took a deep breath but I got there first. 'Shut up, Reid, I'm coming out.' I swam to the side and heaved myself up. 'Stand back,' I growled at Reid, 'or I'll shake myself like a dog.'

This time he rattled the whole caution off and finished with '. . . may be given in evidence. Do you understand?'

'Only too well. Mind if I dry myself?'

Chlorine was actually quite a nice smell, I decided as I sat in the back of the police car and sniffed a strand of my damp hair for something to do while we drove down to Manvers Street police station. Easily recognizable, it was without doubt the ugliest building in Bath, no matter how often they changed the entrance lobby. Inside too they kept trying to tart it up with public money that would have been better spent on a few sticks of dynamite.

And on some decent teabags, I contemplated as I tasted the beige water I had been offered after much pleading. The afternoon had passed unpleasantly. Everything in police stations takes a very long time. I had been processed, fingerprinted, despite my dabs being on file, had my phone and other stuff taken from me, all but the fluff in my pockets. It was getting late, I had been fed triangles of sandwich and was now sitting in Interview Room No.1 with a PC at the door and DI Reid across the table from me, and that poly-styrene beaker of rapidly cooling tea was my only resource. I had been told the tragic news that Kate Grimshaw, my solicitor, was at present kayaking in Canada and I had declined the offer to choose a replacement from the offices of Norfolk & Chance, solicitors. DI Reid had brought a DS along, a fussy-looking chap in a polyester suit who never said a word, which is probably why I can't remember his name. Reid and I had been through an hour of the 'Did!', 'Didn't!', 'Did, too!' bit and now he was trying a new tack.

'On the night in question you were watching the lawns remotely from your car. You had in fact earlier secretly set up surveillance cameras all over the grounds.'

'Neither secretly nor all over the grounds. At least Mark knew about it.'

'That would be Mr Stoneking? Sorry, I'm not on first-name terms with the stars like you so obviously are, Mr Honeysett. You are aware that Mr Stoneking is himself on bail pending charges relating to illegal substances discovered on his premises?'

'Tell me: why do police officers talk like that? *Relating to illegal substances discovered on his premises?* What's wrong with cannabis plants found in the greenhouse? And yes, I am aware of it, but I think it's his gardener who grew the stuff for his own enjoyment.'

'My governor re-arrested him the moment he was released earlier today. Very keen to liaise with local cannabis growers, is the Super.' The DI's silent sidekick smiled unpleasantly. Reid folded his hands comfortably. 'So you hung around out there, keeping the place under surveillance until the victim showed up on your infrared camera. Then you went across in the dark and hit him over the head with a spade.'

'Nope.'

'This spade.' He reached under the table and produced the spade that had been found with Paul's blood and hair on it, wrapped in clear plastic. 'I am showing Mr Honeysett exhibit B. This is the spade you used in your attempt to kill your victim.'

'Nope.'

'Then how do you explain that it had your fingerprints all over it?'

'Not sure I can.'

'And *only* your fingerprints,' Reid said happily.

'Oh, hang on, I *can* explain it.'

'Thought of something, have you?'

'A few nights ago I couldn't sleep and heard noises. I went down to have a look around and found the spade lying on the lawn. I picked it up and put it out of the way against a tree.'

'How convenient. And there are no other fingerprints on it because . . .?'

'We had nighthawks at Tarmford Hall. They probably wore gloves. Look. What possible motive could I have for hitting the *Time Lines* cameraman over the head?'

'You tell me. There's always the possibility of

277

course that you thought it was Mr Middleton you were hitting.'

'And what would my motives be for that?' I was about to say when someone at the door called the DI away. 'Interview suspended, DI Reid leaving the room,' he said for the tape, though why they still do that when the whole thing's on video anyway is beyond me. In case they get a blind jury, perhaps. Okay, so maybe 'It must be the spade I touched a few days earlier' wasn't the most convincing explanation but it would have sufficed for Needham because Needham would *know* I didn't do it. He'd still go through the whole due process, of course, but he wouldn't need convincing. Then why did he leave me in the clutches of his Airedale terrier? I never thought I would miss the Superintendent.

Reid stayed away for what seemed an age, which gave me plenty of time to think the events through. Would nighthawks, in the grounds to dig up bits of metal their machines detected, wear gloves? In summer? Perhaps they didn't want to get their hands dirty. But no fingerprints at all still seemed odd. I had found that the tool shed had been broken into; could the spade have come from there, and if it had, should there not be Sam the gardener's prints on them? Had the spade been deliberately put in my path so I would leave prints on it? But how could anyone have foreseen me being there in the middle of the night?

When Reid did return he was carrying a manila envelope and looked smug. He told the tape he was back, then sat opposite me with a smile that was meant to be unnerving.

'So,' he said happily, tapping the envelope on the table. 'Now it's all beginning to make sense.'

'I doubt it.'

'Oh, don't you worry,' he said, reaching inside and pulling out a sheaf of colour prints. 'It'll make sense to the jury.' He spread the photographs out on the table. 'Bit of a peeping Tom, aren't you, Honeysett?'

The photographs looked horribly familiar but even more pornographic blown up large by the police lab: the pictures I had found on a mini SD in Paul's room and had left in my phone. Where the police had found them, jumping to the obvious conclusion.

'Now we know. Middleton was a naughty boy by the looks of it. You photographed him doing it and no doubt blackmailed him. Middleton refused, perhaps? You wanted to teach him a lesson? Only who you thought was Middleton turned out to be Paul Fosse, wearing Middleton's hat. Something like that, was it?'

'I didn't take those pictures. Paul took them.'

'You were in this together? Had a quarrel? You hit him with a shovel.'

'No, we were not in it together. I found the pictures on an SD card in Paul's room after he had been attacked.'

'That room was thoroughly searched and all things like USB memory sticks and SD cards taken away.'

'Apart from this one.'

'I'm sure Middleton would have been quite willing to pay blackmailers since the girl was very young indeed. We know because we also know who she was and the data tells us when the pictures were taken. So that girl was fifteen at the time he was . . . doing that to her.' He tapped one of the pictures.

'You know who the girl is?'

'Was, sadly. Yes, the sergeant in IT who examined your phone recognized her. She remembered seeing her picture from when she went missing. The girl killed herself by jumping into the River Wye with her pockets full of stones. Her name was April Rhymer. In due course we will have a serious chat to Mr Middleton about it.'

'Hang on, April Rhymer? There's a Julie Rhymer working on the dig. They could be sisters.'

'Fascinating. These photographs, where did you take them and how did you manage to get close to Middleton? Just tell us the whole story. From the beginning.'

'I already have. Look, all the things that have been happening to Middleton, they could well be connected with . . .'

'What things? He was alive and kicking when we arrested you. Nothing's happened to Mr Middleton as far as I'm aware.'

'Your awareness doesn't stretch very far then. DI Reid, you know how the condemned man is allowed one phone call?'

'Well?'

'I'll make mine now.'

'After this interview has concluded.'

'It has. I'll not say another word until I've had my phone call.'

Yet Reid managed to drag it out for another hour before he was willing to escort me to an office where I would be allowed to use a landline. I demanded to have my mobile back since the number was on there. I was told they would get it for me so I could look up the number but would not be allowed to use my mobile. This too seemed to take an age. Outside it was beginning to get dark. Finally a PC came in with my phone.

Naturally you're not allowed to call just anyone, in case you tell them to dispose of evidence or tell them to do a runner. He wouldn't even let me dial, the suspicious so-and-so. 'Who is it you wish to call?' Reid asked.

'Mike.'

'Mike who?'

'Mike Needham. Your boss. Sorry if you're not on first-name terms with the Super.'

'How did you get his mobile number?'

'The usual way. He gave it to me.'

Reid looked doubtful but dialled. I held my breath until at last he got an answer. 'DI Reid here, Super. Mr Honeysett would like a word . . . yes . . . no . . . ah-huh . . . okay.' Eyebrows raised, he handed over the receiver. 'He'll speak to you now. Keep a civil tongue, mind.'

I was glad now that my last phone call to Needham had met with such approval. 'Mike? It's Chris. Guy Middleton has been shagging an underage girl called April Rhymer who later killed herself. A Julie Rhymer has been working on the dig. Middleton has been getting threatening notes. The last one said 'we'll finish it here' or something in that tone. He got it earlier today. The dig is practically over. I have the ominous feeling—'

'I'll be down in a minute,' was all I heard Needham say before he hung up. I handed the receiver back to Reid. He looked like he was getting ominous feelings too.

Five minutes later I had been released into DSI Needham's custody and we were off in his big grey Ford. 'Do you know that they are sisters or is it just speculation?' he asked.

'I don't know anything but it's too much of a coincidence.'

'Soon find out.' Mike made a call on his airwave while zooming the big car out of town. It didn't take long to get confirmation. Julie was April's older sister. 'You knew about this child abuse thing?' Needham asked sharply.

'He told me he was being blackmailed by someone. Looks like it was Paul Fosse. I found photos of Middleton and the girl in Paul's room. Middleton has been paying him at every dig.'

'Did he smash Fosse's head in?'

'Hard to say. I didn't see whoever did it, just saw him being hit.'

'And you think the sister blames him and wants to revenge herself on him?'

'I think she tried at least once before to kill him. The *ballista* dart was surely meant for him, but hit the re-enactor chap instead.'

Needham heaved a grim sigh, grabbed the blue beacon and stuck it on his roof. When we left the main road he turned his siren on too. 'Problem is we have nothing on her sister, not a fingerprint, nothing.'

'Talking of fingerprints, mine are on the shovel that did for the cameraman. I was looking for nighthawks in the dark when I stumbled over it. They must have dropped it. Probably wore gloves.'

'I'm sure they did. Because they weren't night-hawks and weren't after Roman stuff.'

'Oh?'

'I've just had a long chat with Stoneking's gardener. He's been shooting his mouth off to cellmates that he has a big nest egg of bullion from the Bristol robbery buried somewhere at Stoneking's. Word got out and some ex-cons have obviously been digging up the place looking for it. Only what they dug up was Olive's long-lost lover. It's all nonsense of course, the gold thing, there is no nest egg. All the gold was recovered; he was just trying to show off. He was hopping mad when I told him the lawns were full of holes as a result of his own bragging.'

I was holding on tightly now as Needham splashed the car through the ford across the Tarm and then heaved it left into the narrow lane along the boundary wall of the Stone King's realm. Mike stopped the car in front of the gate and I jumped out and rang the bell on the intercom. There was no answer. I waited a long minute. I paced impatiently along the length of the gate. From the furthest corner I could see flickering lights where I could glimpse the house through the trees. I went back to the car. 'It looks like there's a fire of some kind, could be a bonfire but I doubt it. And there's no answer.' Needham reached for his radio and I gave the gate a push, then lent on the bell again. Then I decided I'd had enough and started climbing the wrought-iron gate.

'Where do you think you're going?' said Mike, getting out of the car.

'You said yourself it's like a climbing frame. See you on the other side.'

'Remember you're still under arrest and in my custody. Don't do anything stupid like breaking your neck.'

It really was just like a climbing frame. I resisted the temptation to jump down the other side and climbed impatiently to the bottom. For a few moments I tried to somehow open the gate but there was no release mechanism that I could see. 'Sorry, Mike. Have to wait until I get to the house.' I left him standing there holding his radio and jogged off towards the hall. It didn't take me long to discover what the flickering lights were. The fire was in the car park in front of the house. Guy Middleton's Range Rover was completely ablaze. There were people standing around watching and some were running around. Stoneking was there with a fire extinguisher, one of the technicians was holding one too, but the petrol fire was so fierce neither could get near enough to even attempt to put it out. Next to the Range Rover stood a white van whose paint was blistering. I found Emms standing there, arms folded across her chest, her face shining in the glow from the fire.

'What happened?' I asked her.

'Don't really know. Carla suddenly called for Middleton and told us that the car was on fire. We all came out here but it suddenly went whoosh! Not much left now. I hope it won't spread to that van . . .'

The one person missing from the ring of spectators was the car's owner. 'Where's Middleton?'

'Don't know, Carla couldn't find him.'

'Tell Carla to open the gate. The police are out there.'

I jogged on past the strange spectacle of people solemnly observing the burning of a 4×4. It had something ominously ritualistic about it and I hoped they wouldn't start chanting. Through the hall, the central gallery and the drawing room, out on to the verandah. It was quite dark now on this side of the hall, which was not illuminated by the car fire, and the gardens lay silent and empty. I walked out on to the lawn, making do with the feeble light of a moon obscured by high cloud. A feeling that Guy was in trouble had been growing into conviction the moment I had seen his burning car. Would calling for him be any use or make things worse? With ninety acres out there what else was I going to do?

'Guy Middleton!' I hollered. 'It's Honeysett! Where are you?' I walked rather than jogged now, but I walked fast. The large trench was once more covered in the khaki tent against more rain, a darker presence in the darkness. I found the entrance and stuck my head inside. It was utterly dark within. I had been relieved of my little Maglite at the police station but even without it I could sense that no one was breathing in there. I walked on cautiously past suddenly-looming test pits, roughly filled-in holes dug by treasure hunters and the long hump of the spoil heap. 'Middleton, you out there?' Nothing. The first of the hedges loomed like a black brushstroke inked across the dark landscape. Sensing more than seeing the overgrown opening in it, I dived through. On the other side the still figure of a garden sculpture made an eerie shape in the space between the hedges. From memory I found the next opening to the left. I stopped in front of it and held my breath, listening. There were distant sounds behind me now, back at the Hall. I tried to tune them out and instead listened ahead. A tiny noise. It could have been anything, a bird, a rabbit. Then it occurred to me that if Middleton was in trouble then I had been shouting the wrong name. 'Julie! Julie Rhymer!' I called. I stepped through the opening in the hedge.

There were three dark shapes on the other side. One I knew to be a four-foot terracotta griffin. The other two were breathing. 'Julie? Guy?' There was a simpering sound from the shape to the left. Then torchlight blinded me.

'Don't move. Go away. No, stay where you are. I have a gun.' It was unmistakably Julie's voice but it was shaking, not with fear but with suppressed emotion.

'Do something, Honeysett,' came Guy's querulous voice. The beam of light left me and moved to Middleton who was standing with hands raised head high, as if to ward off a blow. 'She's got one of Stoneking's shotguns; she says she's going to kill me.'

I could see now that Julie was indeed holding one of Stoneking's expensive guns, with a long torch taped to the barrels. Julie swung the barrels and pointed the gun at me. 'You'll do nothing at all, Chris. I'd hate to shoot you but I swear I will

286

if you get in my way.' The torch beam swung back to Middleton who had been inching towards me, his protector.

'Stop moving, you arsehole,' Julie hissed.

'And you're going to kill him because naturally that's what April would have wanted?' I said flatly.

At the mention of her sister's name she stiffened. 'What would you know about it?'

'Very little.'

'Exactly, so keep out of it. This piece of scum here is responsible for her death. The stupid girl had a schoolgirl crush on him from watching him on telly, with his tomb raider outfit and his stupid ponytail. And he took advantage. He screwed her and what's more he got her pregnant. And when my dim-witted sister told him he got scared. He sweet-talked her into getting rid of her baby, saying it was the wrong time for them and a child would get in the way or some such lie, then as soon as she'd had the abortion he broke off all contact.'

'It was just a schoolgirl crush,' Middleton said.

'Shut up!'

'A child would have been a millstone round her neck.'

'Yours, more like. God, how I wish I had a millstone now so I could hang it round your neck and drown you in the lake. I wanted to drown you. I often thought about it, the bubbles, especially your last bubbles. But this will do, a shotgun will do. They use shotguns on vermin, don't they?'

'What about your parents?' I said. I was

standing just beyond the opening in the hedge and could hear quiet footsteps behind me. I wasn't sure Julie had heard them. I was trying to slow Julie down and at the same time make sure that whoever was approaching knew what he was walking into. 'If you shoot Middleton now they will effectively lose both their daughters.'

'Since my sister's death my mother has spoken only when spoken to first. It destroyed her.'

'Sounds like she needs you.'

'What about what I need?' she asked angrily, pointing the gun at me, then turning it back on Middleton as he took a couple of quick paces towards me. 'Don't move a muscle, Middleton,' she bellowed. He was only about twelve feet away from me now. Any closer and Julie could no longer be certain that a blast from her gun wouldn't also fell me. I felt a presence close behind me, then a hand in the small of my back. 'Move aside,' murmured Needham.

I took a step towards Middleton on my left.

'Not that way, you moron,' said Needham loudly.

'Stop there!' Julie shouted, waving her gun from side to side.

'Do something!' Middleton screeched.

Needham stepped through the opening and turned on a strong flashlight, illuminating the scene. He was careful not to blind any of us, keeping it pointed in the centre of the space between us. 'Stay calm, everyone,' said Needham in his most sonorous baritone. 'Deep breaths, everyone. I'm Mike Needham. I'm a police officer, Julie. You've met me before, the night you missed Guy Middleton and shot Morgan with the *ballista*.'

'Yeah, well, I didn't get to practise with that thing, did I?'

Ten feet of self-interest made me ask: 'And have you had much practice with shotguns?'

The gun was pointing straight at Middleton now; she was making sure of her quarry. 'No, but any moron can use a gun. The safety is off, in case you all wondered, and it was conveniently loaded when I found it in Stoneking's office.'

'Nevertheless,' Needham said in his most reasonable voice. 'I'd like you to lower it for the moment so we can talk.'

'What's to talk about? You're trying to keep me talking until you get armed police here so they can put a bullet through my head.'

'No, but I do want some answers. Not about him; we know about Middleton and your sister. We saw the pictures Paul Fosse took of them together.'

'You saw them? So did I. Paul was blackmailing him. I caught him collecting the money from under a stone once and eventually we talked. I thought he was on my side. But when I told him I was going to exterminate the bastard he said he couldn't allow it.'

'So you hit him over the head with a shovel?' I asked.

'No one gets in the way of this; let that be a warning.'

Needham made a small move towards her. 'Middleton will get what he deserves if you leave him to us, Julie. He won't get off lightly, I promise. We'll throw the book at him.'

'I have a better idea,' Julie said, swinging the gun round to him. 'You take Chris here and piss off or I'll do some shotgun practice on you. Move! Now!' She was extremely agitated now, perhaps sensing that time was running out.

There was a pause, then Needham had made his decision. 'Walk to me, Honeysett,' he said quietly. Julie responded by turning her gun back on Middleton.

'Don't leave me here, Honeysett!' Guy begged. 'You're supposed to protect me. Protect me!'

'I'm not obliged to stop bullets for you, Guy,' I said and slowly moved away from him, feeling more like a coward with every step.

'Get behind me, Honeysett,' Needham said, pushing me along without taking his eyes off the gun. 'Now please, Julie,' he said as he moved slowly, bravely forward, 'think of your parents. Middleton isn't worth it, none of it. And I promise you, I'll make sure he'll go to prison.'

'I'll make sure he goes to hell!' Julie stiffened and pulled the trigger. Guy's scream was cut short as the blast knocked him clean off his feet. Julie stepped closer and fired the second barrel into the writhing figure on the ground.

Seconds after the blasts had rung out Needham had taken the gun from Julie, dropped it on the grass and handcuffed her in the eerie light from the two torches where they had dropped to the ground. I picked up Mike's torch and rushed over to Middleton where for the first time I could see at close quarters what devastating effect a double-barrelled shotgun blast of two portions of pudding rice can have on the human form. Middleton was gasping for breath and groaning. The impact of countless rice grains had broken his skin all over his hands and face. He was holding his midriff where the second blast had hit him like a sledgehammer. His jacket was in tatters.

Soon the space between the hedges was flooded with police, followed immediately by an ambulance crew. Needham was as surprised as Julie that Middleton was alive, only he didn't spit in his direction like Julie did when she was led away by two officers. I explained to Needham.

'Pudding rice,' he mused as we walked back to the house. 'Quite effective. Perhaps we should arm officers with it. Did you know it was loaded with that?'

'No.'

'Do you think she knew?'

'I doubt it.'

'Shame. Real shame,' he said shiftily. 'It makes a difference to the charge. To coin a phrase.' He gave me a sideways glance. 'Didn't do too badly back there.'

'Didn't stop her from shooting him.'

'But we were there to stop her from using the blunt end to finish him off.'

'That's a good thing, is it?'

Needham didn't answer that.

The house was ablaze with lights from every door and window. Arc lights and generators were being set up in the grounds. Mark Stoneking stood on his verandah, watching with fascinated horror as police and ambulance swarmed over the gardens once more. Behind him stood Carla, watching him watching us. Keeping an eye on everything from a window in the north tower was the figure of Olive Cunningham. Mark Stoneking looked very much like he had finally had enough excitement to get him through his old age.

Epilogue

By the middle of the next morning things at Tarmford Hall had quietened down considerably. The filming had been abandoned and the production team of *Time Lines* had shaken Stoneking's hand, crossed his palm with silver and driven away. The cherry picker was taken away but the digger remained; it would be needed eventually to fill in the large trenches. What remained were the archaeologists. Ungraciously the production team had pulled out the catering van but Carla had volunteered to feed Andrea and her tented gang of diggers. The atmosphere around the table at lunchtime was quite different now. The diggers all appeared to get on with each other and showed quite a different kind of enthusiasm from the TV crew. To them, television had just been a distraction.

The expected rain had not materialized and the weather was once more fine and warm. When I suggested we walk off our lunch in the gardens, Annis shook her head.

'No thanks, the gardens give me the creeps. Why don't we check out the village instead?'

We walked. The wrought-iron gate to Tarmford Hall stood wide, almost as though it had been left open to give the whole place a good airing. The village of Tarmford was picturesque but felt under-populated. We stood by the green and the pond for some time and saw just one elderly lady walk up to the village shop and disappear inside.

'Don't know about you but after that excitement I think we deserve a drink,' I said and made for the Druid's Arms. I tried one of the local beers while Annis was playing it safe with a pint of lager which shone golden in a patch of sunshine on our window table. It was while we were mulling over the events of the last week that the message alert on my newly returned mobile chimed. It was a text from PC Whatsisname.

Tom Dealey, Paulton, electrician, single. Crashed Hayabusa uninsured, no tax / MOT. Idiot family. That do ya?

It did. It made me think. 'What is it?' Annis asked, noticing my brain working. I pushed my mobile across so she could read the text and continued to picture the Dealeys in my mind. One brother had recently cashed in on three-quarters of a million pounds compensation after a crippling bike crash, the other was an electrician, living in a detached house on a prosperous village estate. This brother drove a car but in his garage kept an expensive superbike. Which was uninsured, untaxed and had no valid MOT.

'Why do people usually drive around uninsured?' I asked.

'Because they can't afford the premiums?'

'And if they can afford them?'

'Because they don't qualify.'

'And they don't qualify because they don't have a driver's licence.' I know, it was slow, but I was getting there.

'Hon, that's my lager you're drinking,' Annis complained.

'Exactly. It should have been Guinness,' I said and got up.

'Are you feeling all right, hon?' Annis asked.

'Never better. I suddenly feel quite well-off, too.'

It took me several hours to track Dealey down. I had called Mike Dealey's bungalow and got no answer. I had let it ring and ring at Tom Dealey's Paulton house. I had driven to both properties and leant on their doorbells. It was once more at the Royal United Hospital that I spotted Mike Dealey's red Honda in the disabled car park. Just in case I missed him inside I blocked his car in by parking an inch away across his rear bumper. It might land me a hefty parking fine but I could put that on expenses.

I eventually found Dealey in the observation ward where his brother had been moved to. He was sitting in his wheelchair by the side of the bed, staring at the unconscious form of his brother who was connected to oxygen and feeding tubes. Monitors bleeped quietly. Dealey looked up, unsurprised and without moving a facial muscle, as though he had expected me. Perhaps he had. I found a slightly creased business card in my jacket, blew the fluff off it and handed it to him. He took it, glanced at it, then dropped it on the bed.

'What's the prognosis?' I asked.

'He won't wake up,' he said hoarsely. 'He might never wake up.'

'You can't stay in that wheelchair forever, you know,' I said quietly. 'Helping your brother fake his wheelchair-bound life is one thing. But taking over from him just because he had another bike crash is something else. What if he stays like this? What if he died? Would you sit in that chair forever? Would you wear that silly moustache for the rest of your life?'

'I wasn't that convincing then?' he asked.

'I followed you to the Cross Keys. You finished each other's drinks after you had swapped chair and moustache in the toilets. You reached for the Guinness.'

Tom Dealey pulled the walrus moustache off his face with obvious relief and dropped it on the bed next to my business card. Then he got up out of the wheelchair, pushed it away from him and massaged his behind. 'It doesn't half make your bum hurt sitting in that thing all day. Sorry, bro,' he added more quietly. 'But I do hate drinking lager.'